"The nighttime was associated with the Host, its appearances generally occurring as distortions in the visual field triggered by light . . ."

Tyler closed the book about murder trials. There was no need, never as long as memory lasted, for him to look at the photos or read the words surrounding them. The medications he took were as much to keep the past at bay as to keep the drug's symptoms—the bitter taste in his mouth, the blue light edging objects in the night, the excitement ticking the blood faster in his veins—from seeping back . . .

And the final symptom, the sight that would mean that he had been pulled into that other world. The Host.

Triggered by the absence of light . . . the Dark Seeker

Also by K. W. Jeter in Pan Horror:

SOUL EATER
THE NIGHT MAN

K. W. Jeter

DARK
SEEKER

PAN BOOKS
London, Sydney and Auckland

First published in America 1987 by Tom Doherty Associates, Inc
First published in Great Britain 1991 by Pan Books Ltd,
Cavaye Place, London SW10 9PG
1 3 5 7 9 8 6 4 2
© K. W. Jeter 1987

ISBN 0 330 31680 X

Printed in England by Clays Ltd, St Ives plc

To Claude Bessy and Philomena Winstanley

ONE

Midnight, and he was late. Tyler twisted his hand on the steering wheel's curve so he could see the dial of his watch. Blue light swung in and out of the car as it slid under the freeway's overhead lamps. Twelve-fifteen, later than he'd thought. An invisible needle pricked at the skin of his arms.

He swung the car onto the Melrose Avenue offramp, out of the stream of headlights that pulsed through Los Angeles at night. The watch hands crawled through another thin segment of time. There was still the grid of surface streets to work his way through, before he'd be inside his apartment and twisting the caps off the orange plastic prescription bottles. The pills and capsules would rattle like tiny dried insect shells as he shook his delayed ten P.M. dose into his palm . . .

The light at the bottom of the offramp flicked to red, too far away for him to go on through. He braked to a stop. *You're a tame rat now*, he thought in grim amusement. *You could be going straight out of your mind, but you still can't run a light.*

Darker off the freeway—the only light that which spilled over the concrete rim above, and the luminous white ice of a twenty-four-hour gas station a few blocks away. The car radio, no longer masked by the traffic roar and the Chevy's engine clattering to keep

9

up with it, murmured distant music. Tyler switched it off, letting silence fill the car along with the darkness. He tasted, or imagined he could, an acrid chemical tang seeping into the saliva under his tongue. Every second that passed was a small knife that sliced away a bit more of the medication's dulling haze.

The light changed to green. He turned left onto Melrose. Santa Monica Boulevard would have been the straighter shot back to the apartment, but he didn't want to get caught in the traffic that crawled along that street even at this hour, the cars slowing to look over the hollow-eyed boys slouched against the light posts. Better, and faster, to go out of his way, where there were only a few cars on the road. The dark part of town.

He drove on, shifting gears and braking, catching two lights green, then another red. The warm desert wind breathing through the car's rolled-down window tightened his skin, drawing sharper the pinpricks beneath.

None of this—the hurried drive, the tiny first symptoms of medication's receding—would have been necessary, Tyler knew, if he had the little foil-wrapped cluster of pills and capsules that he usually carried in his pocket. He could've stopped at any gas station or liquor store along the way, bought a can of Coke, and swilled them clicking against his teeth and down. Down to where the pills could relock all the little doors at the base of his spine, secure against the night. But the packet was sitting on the kitchen table where he'd left it. *Because you thought you had so much time*, he told himself, foot on the brake, waiting for the signal.

The ancient movie theatre he managed down at the

other end of Wilshire had finally had something decent booked into it. Welles' *Macbeth* and Polanski's version of the same. He'd come out of the office behind the cashier's window and sat through both films, at the back behind the sparse Thursday night cinema-nut crowd. Nobody stayed for the second showing of the Welles, so he had gone up to the projectionist's booth and told him to pack up and go home.

He had been dawdling over greasy chicken and limp coleslaw at the nearest coffee shop. And when the magic hour arrived, eleven P.M. and the far edge of the safety margin he gave himself, he'd reached into his pocket, found it empty—and smiled at the little conspiracy between his subconscious and his body against him. *Maybe not even subconscious at all*, he thought.

Across the intersection, a line of hookers maintained a careful spacing down the unlit sidewalk. The ones nearest the corner were silhouetted by the dim light filtering from somewhere inside a drugstore's plate-glass window.

Tyler watched them waiting as he waited for the light. No other cars passed between.

When he first got out and came to live in these parts of L.A., he'd seen these women on this corner and wondered why they didn't ply their trade up on Hollywood or Sunset along with the other working girls. They all had the same belted leotard and high-heeled uniform, tiny purses slung from their shoulders. But a couple times driving past them, late at night, was enough for him to have seen that these were the ones whom time and the business had aged too harshly to face the main cruising drag's bright neon. They had worked their way, block by block as their faces had tightened and hardened, down here to meet another kind of customer.

The girl on the corner swung her gaze across the street and through Tyler's windshield. A death's-head face under a straight nylon wig the color of unraveled sutures. A hipbone that would lay a crease in the palm of one's hand like the hard edge of a dissecting table. Cold radar locked on to his face for a second, then continued the flat arc of its scan across the earth's empty surface, looking for trade.

He could see, as though his own vision magnified her, the two colored glass eyes in the snake head dangling from the scaly metallic belt slung around the short skirt.

The chemical taste was stronger in his mouth now, curling his tongue. A blue light traced the edges of the shop buildings down the street. He wondered how precisely the girl would've calculated her price if she'd been able to recognize him, a face out of newspapers yellowed by five years. Or if she would've thought there was any greater risk than with her usual clientele.

He wondered what they bargained with, what words were printed on the black money, and what the men paid to be done to them.

That's crazy thinking. A little more of the medication had ebbed out of his bloodstream. Part of the old familiar symptoms, the bitter taste seeping under his tongue, the edge of electric blue around dark objects. *Knock it off*, he told himself, and focused his gaze hard upon the signal. He shifted his sweating hands upon the steering wheel.

Just before the light changed, a Mercedes eased around the corner ahead. Slick and clean, the driver obviously able to afford anything desired. Tyler watched as it slowed and stopped. The corner hooker leaned into the Mercedes' window as it slid down.

She got in as Tyler eased on the gas and crossed the intersection. The Mercedes pulled away from him and made a quick right, heading back toward the Hollywood Hills.

Then the road was all straight and dark ahead of him, the backlit plastic signs of restaurants and theatres just squares of color pinned on black. He could reach out and peel them away if he wanted. The pulse at his wrists and temples ticked away, deepening the night. He drove, letting it and the impulse to go on driving into it wash black across his arms and chest.

The thin edge of the telephone's ringing worked its way into her ear. It pressed deeper until the black shell of sleep split open. She rolled her head on the pillow, tasting her own hair tangled against her dry mouth.

Her eyes pulled open as the telephone again drilled its idiot clatter from the floor by the bed. The room's familiar outlines—door, closet, chest of drawers—ebbed into the darkness as she pushed herself up on one elbow. The luminous green hands on the alarm clock by the telephone were angled close to one A.M. Another ring was cut in half when she reached down and fumbled the handset out of the cradle. She hoped it hadn't been ringing long enough to wake her son in the other bedroom.

"Hello?" Still half asleep, tongue thick against her teeth, she sank back onto the pillow, the phone across her cheek.

Nothing on the other end—seconds ticked past

with no reply. She was about to speak again when the voice came to her ear.

"Hello, Linda." A man's voice, the words with a sharp edge, as if he were smiling as he said them.

She stiffened, raising her head into the room's close silence. The last wisps of sleep drained from behind her eyes. Nobody had called her that, her right name, for five years. Nobody knew.

Still a chance that it was a coincidence, some drunk who had dialed the wrong number, trying to get hold of somebody else named Linda. Her pulse tapped faster in her throat as she wrapped both hands around the phone and brought it close to her mouth. "I'm sorry, but—"

"Knock off the shit, Linda." The smile was gone from the voice. "I know who you are." It returned, thin enough to cut. "And you know who I am."

Even through the years between now and the last time she'd heard the voice, she recognized it. The connection to the past linked and grew taut, a current of fear tingling under her skin. "Slide," she whispered.

"*That's* right," the voice crooned. "Nobody should ever forget their friends, should they?"

She could see him, the night's shapes projected on the blank screen inside her. Somewhere outside the little house, his narrow face was leaning into another telephone, its coiled wire snaking through the interchanges buried below L.A. to her ear. She pulled the blanket closer across her breasts, the warm Santa Ana winds now chill on her skin. "What do you want?" she said.

"Ah, it's not what I want. It's what *you* want, Linda. What do you want, Linda?"

"Please. Slide—I don't know what you . . . Don't—"

"What do you want, Linda?" The voice kept on tapping at her ear. "Do you want your little boy? Do you want your little boy, Linda?"

"Slide—" The chill sank through her flesh.

"Where's your little boy, Linda? Where's your little boy?"

The blanket fell away as she scrambled out of the bed. The phone thumped against the floor, the voice, tinny and distant, following as she ran out into the hall. "Where is he, Linda? Where's your little boy?"

Light snapped against the walls of her son's bedroom. She stood frozen in the doorway, her hand on the switch, looking at the empty bed, the blankets rumpled and wadded at the foot. A row of toys on top of the dresser, little blue gnomes out of a Saturday morning cartoon show, smiled across the vacant space at her. An airplane on a string rotated in the soft breath of air from the open window, gouge marks from something like a screwdriver showing through the sill's layers of paint to the raw wood beneath.

"Oh, Jesus." She shook her head, a slow twisting on the pulsing knot that had clamped in her throat. "No . . ." She stepped backward, unable to lock away from the empty room.

Then she was running down the hall again, her shoulder slamming against the wall in darkness.

She knelt by the side of her bed, pressing the phone against her mouth. "Where is he? Where's Bryan?"

Five years ago, she and the others in the group had called it *the hammer*—finding the right, the cruelest question, and repeating it over and over. Until the person broke. "Where's your little boy, Linda?" The smile could break into laughter any second now.

"Slide . . . please—"

"Where's your little boy, Linda?"

She sank under the blows, curling into a ball as she knelt on the floor, the telephone clutched at her center. The line was a hollow tube into the darkness where the voice came from.

"Where's your little boy?"

"Please . . ." Her whisper broke through the sobbing that burst in her throat. The taste of wet salt trailed into the corner of her mouth. "Where is he?"

The hammer stopped, its work done. "That's a stupid question, Linda. I've got him, of course. Don't worry. I'll take real good care of him. Real good."

"No—" Her hair fell across her face, the ends sweeping along the floor. "Don't . . . Whatever you want—I can pay you . . ."

The voice at her ear twisted with mock kindness. "But you don't have anything I want, Linda. Not now."

"Please, Slide—"

"You shouldn't have run away, Linda." Hardening again. "It took me a long time to find you. But I did. And now you're on the outside, Linda. All the way out. And you won't be coming in again."

Then the voice was gone, the telephone a dead thing of plastic and wires in her hands. A dull buzz clicked on out of its silence. "No," she moaned, dropping it. The phone hit her knee and slid to the floor, the insect noise humming from the cluster of tiny black holes.

She gripped her legs and squeezed, digging her nails into the flesh, the pain drawing her thoughts tight. Her gasping breath burned cold through her teeth. She stood up and brushed the tangled hair free from her damp face.

Other people, other women whose children were stolen, could call the police; she couldn't. She stared down at the telephone at her bare feet. Even if the police could find Slide—and they hadn't in five years—and get her child, they wouldn't give Bryan back to her. Not in the kind of place where they'd put her. She'd lose her child either way.

She lowered herself to the edge of the bed, then reached down for the telephone and set it on her lap. The silence wrapped around her when she pressed the button to cut off the phone's humming. She knew her ex-husband's number by heart, though she had never dialed it before; she'd found it, the name that used to be part hers, in the book and had let it etch into memory. Now she slowly started to dial.

Before the first two digits rattled past her fingers, she heard the voices at the front door. She froze, listening. Then the noise of the thin wood around the locks splintering. The voices were loud inside now.

She dropped the phone, ran to the hallway, and saw, as the lights blazed on, the police uniforms standing in the front room. The faces above looked back at her. "Linda Tyler?" said the nearest one.

The kitchen doorway was blocked off by another officer coming in from the back. He leaned against the doorframe, filling the space as he watched her with folded arms. She turned around again to the front room, then nodded wordlessly. Slide had told them where she was—she knew that.

As they put the handcuffs on her, then draped over her shoulders the robe they found hanging inside the bedroom door, she recognized the face of the oldest one in the room. He wasn't wearing a dark blue police uniform, but the same shabby brown suit she remembered from five years ago. All the pieces

of the past were coming out of memory and forming
a solid unbreakable wall around her.

"Hello, Linda," he said. "Long time." The face
was creased deeper, but still broad and unsmiling.

The name came back as well. "Kinross," she
said. She leaned toward him, her hands trussed behind her, the short chain between the cuffs held
easily by one of the officers. "He took my baby.
Slide took him."

He gazed back at her for a moment, then turned
and brushed past the others, through the door. The
tears broke and coursed again as they pushed her,
gently as possible, into the darkness outside.

With the sound of a woman's fright still echoing in
his ear, he smiled and hung the pay phone back into
its chrome hook. That had been fun, he decided.
Unnecessary, but fun. He pulled open the booth's
glass door and stepped out into the warm night air.

The child in the car watched him as he walked
across the couple of yards of deserted gas station
asphalt. He slid behind the wheel and the smile grew
wider as he reached across to stroke the boy's hair.

"I want to go home." The boy shrank away from
the hand, his eyes round and locked on the man's
face.

"Sure," he said, brushing the soft strands at the
child's brow. Kids' eyes always looked so big, with
lashes like tiny soft brushes. He slid the key into the
ignition and turned it. "I'll take you someplace nice.
Someplace you'll be nice and safe. Okay?"

The boy said nothing, only went on watching him
as he swung the car out of the dark lot and into the
street.

*   *   *

One A.M. by the time Tyler reached home. He
found a space big enough to wedge the Chevy into
halfway down the block. With the key slipped into
his pocket he walked toward the apartment building
at the corner.

Beyond Fountain he could see all the way to the
bright lights and slow traffic of Sunset. A few blocks
behind him the gay-bar scene on Santa Monica continued to work its way to the two o'clock closing
hour, the heart-battering, bass-heavy music leaking
out to the sidewalk whenever the thick padded doors
opened and closed. In the narrow zone of old apartments between the two neon streets everything stayed
dark and quiet. The dry fronds of spindly trees rustled in the wind off the desert.

He looked up and saw the luminous blue outline
around the buildings. The chemical taste was stronger
and more acrid in his mouth; he could walk farther
into the darkness if he wanted, and it would never
come to an end. The dark streets would keep unfold-
ing, one into the next, the hollow-eyed women guard-
ing each corner he would pass.

He could ignore the night now. The worst danger,
the temptation, had passed while he was in the car—
the lure of turning the wheel and following the night
wherever it led, beyond darker corners and hookers
and their customers moving even farther away from
the light than the ones he'd seen.

He stepped off the sidewalk onto a path winding
between overgrown banks of ivy. Something small
with red-dot eyes scuttled away in the courtyard's
dead foliage.

Stephanie was waiting upstairs in the apartment for
him. He could see the living room light spill into the
hallway as he closed and locked the door. Her wait-

ress apron lay on the coffee table, its deep pockets heavy with the quarters and dollar bills of her tips. Her feet were propped on the edge of the table, the thick anatomy text from one of her classes on her lap. A red miniature Corvette, which he'd put together for her four-year-old Eddie, had rolled to a stop at the edge of the couch. "Hi," she said. "I got worried about you."

He walked past her. "I know. I left it on the table."

She stood in the kitchen doorway and watched him as he ran a glass of water, then unfolded the little aluminum foil square that held the pills and capsules. A sort of joke: "Time for your medicine, Mike," she said, smiling. Perhaps only from relief.

"No, baby." Between thumb and forefinger he held one of the capsules, blue at one end, white at the other. "This ain't medicine. Medicine makes you well." He laid the capsule on his tongue and felt its skin start to dissolve. Steff watched him swallow it, then the others in a single handful.

Sprawled across the bed, he felt the drugs' slow seepage into his bloodstream, the night fading to ordinary darkness. Silhouetted in the bedroom doorway, Steff worked the buttons of her blouse loose. A chemical overlay blurred his fatigue. He turned his head on the pillow, closing his eyes, waiting until the absence of light became the absence of dreams.

TWO

The sound of the morning rush-hour traffic over his head, a big steely wind vibrating down the concrete pillars into the loose earth of his nest, woke him from tightly curled sleep. Bad dreams: the rumble of the cars and trucks had slowly built through the hours before light, like artillery shells walking closer through tracer-lit fields.

He opened one eye and saw over his hunched shoulder the sun's edge sliding through the underpass, the light red enough to startle him fully awake. The back of his jacket scraped the rough underside of the concrete above him as he scrambled onto his hands and knees, staring at the glare burning from the windshields lined up and crawling along a distant onramp. For a moment his breath wouldn't come, then he remembered where he was. He rolled onto his back, grateful for the shallow hole he'd scraped out at the top of the dirt bank sloping under the freeway overpass; grateful for the nest of rags that smelled of his own sweat; grateful for his little home, no wider than the reach of his arms, near the city's heart.

With one finger he reached up and traced the straggling white letters of the name scrawled on the concrete ceiling. JIMMY. He'd written it there him-

self, lying on his back with a dusty lump of survey-
or's chalk he'd found outside the gate of the maintenance yard under the freeway. Through his finger-
tip, stopped at the bottom of the Y, he could feel the
vibrating weight of the traffic surge through the surface world's slanting daylight. A distance of concrete
laced with steel between him and the hurtling metal
shapes—he was safer here under the cars' wheels
than he would be shuffling through the trash at the
sides of the roads, looking for aluminum cans to
crush flat and add to his paper sack.

He could have stayed in the cozy safe hole except
for the advancing pang of hunger under his ribs.
"Ooh, right, Jimmy," he murmured to himself, eyes
closed in anticipation. He'd scored big yesterday,
hiking all the way out to the Safeway in Hollywood
and getting there just when the gone-soft and with-
ered produce was dumped out into the bins behind
the store. He'd climbed right into the big green
dumpster, careful where he stepped for fear of smash-
ing some precious edible. Rooting through the flattened cardboard boxes and crumpled wet paper, he'd
come up with almost a dozen tomatoes, the skin just
starting to wrinkle and tear, plus two cantaloupes
dark on only one side. The corn he found still in its
husks was useless—you had to cook that to eat it.
And limp heads of lettuce he left behind—might
as well eat fuckin' paper, for all he cared for it.

He'd had to take off his denim jacket to wrap and
carry all the treasures in, the tomatoes' wetness seeping through the oil-stained fabric.

When he'd climbed out of the supermarket's trash
bin, he found a tiny old lady with frizzy gray hair
and rheumy eyes warped behind thick glasses watching him. One hand, all brown-spotted bones, clutched

the handle of a two-wheeled wire cart, the kind all the old ladies went to the store with. As he'd hunched over his bundle and hurried away, he'd looked back and seen her futilely stretching to look over the bin's edge.

The pang in his stomach sharpened, moistened by his swallowed saliva. He lay on his back playing with it, the way one rubs a thumb over the edge of a knife. Hunger was fine, the most pleasurable sensation in his life, when he knew he had something to eat tucked away. He'd hidden his stash away from the nest; sometimes, if others found you while you were sleeping, they'd use a razor to get at any food you had with you, or just crack your head open and roll you down the dirt slope. Better, he knew, to sleep in one place and keep your stuff in another, even if you couldn't keep an eye on it. There were some really wacked-out people under the freeways these days.

He rolled onto his stomach and peered over the shallow nest's rim to see if anyone had come wandering below the overpass. No one in either direction. The loose dirt tumbled away from his feet as he climbed down the slope, leaning back on one hand to keep his balance.

The alarm clock always gave a little pause in its thin, distant-sounding electric hum, just before it started ringing, as though drawing breath for its shrill metallic shout. That little gap in the night's weave—wind and traffic outside, Mike's slow breathing beside her—was what brought Steff awake.

Usually she could get one hand from under the covers in time to push the button at the back, cutting off the alarm before it began. This morning she let it ring, gazing up at the bedroom ceiling as the clatter stitched through the dim light seeping around the window shades. She turned her head on the pillow and looked at Mike. The alarm hadn't woken him, never did. He slept on, mouth slightly parted to whisper his shallow breath. Sometimes when she watched him sleep, it seemed as if he'd stopped breathing completely, the medication at last having drained the blood from his heart, his gaze a waxy death mask. Now, if she woke in the middle of the night, she no longer turned on the lamp beside the bed, preferring instead to see just his profile beside her in the dark.

The alarm went on ringing. She pushed herself up, sitting against the headboard, reached and shut off the clock. Her breathing and—faintly—his, in what passed for silence in Los Angeles, the sound of distant traffic. Five minutes had slid by on the clock's face since the time she should have been up and in the shower, getting ready for her first class. *Screw it*, she thought, pulling the blanket up over her breasts. Outside, the cars would already be crowding Fountain and Santa Monica, working through the signals toward the office towers of Century City in one direction, the freeway onramps and downtown in the other. She could use another couple hours' sleep before facing the drive to the university with the Toyota's fading clutch and tissue-thin brake pads.

In her mouth the brackish aftertaste of the two pots of coffee she'd gone through last night while studying reminded her: quiz today. Not in the first class, but the eleven o'clock physiology. *Thank God for that*, she thought, squeezing her eyes shut under her forearm—she could sit out her tenner in the library going over her notes. But first she had to get there, and her kid to the day-care center. Though she'd rather have curled up against Mike's warmth, matching her breath in time with his, she swung her bare legs out the side of the bed, kicking aside last night's clothes piled on the floor.

"Up." In Eddie's bedroom she jiggled the shoulder of the small figure under the blanket. "Up, up, up." He burrowed his face into the pillow, so she knew he had heard her.

In the shower she turned her face up into the stream, letting the stiff needles of water sluice the night's fatigue from under her closed eyelids.

Toweling her hair, the straight brown fall between her shoulder blades dampened to almost black, she could see Mike's face in the corner of the dresser mirror. Still in the same position, pale against the white pillowcase. The sound of running water hadn't woken him, or the sound of the hair dryer as she switched it on.

He looked older when he was asleep. She went on watching him as the dryer wound her hair around her fingers. Much older than the gap of years between them; the one time he'd come over to the university to pick her up, the Toyota's battery having gone dead, somebody had asked her later if she was dating one of her instructors. And he was only thirty-something—a ten-year difference. *Next time I'll tell anyone who asks that he's my father.*

"There you go." She poured milk on top of the cornflakes in front of Eddie and put the carton back in the refrigerator. While she watched him eat, his gaze fixed raptly on the toy Corvette on the table, she pinned her hair in a coil at the back of her head. That would save time—she'd have to go straight from class to her job. It would save even more time if right now she put on the waitress getup—short black skirt, white apron, cloddy air-pillow nurse shoes that almost kept the ache from traveling up her legs by the end of her shift—and walked into the classroom that way. *That'd fry 'em*, she thought. Some of those daddy's-money coeds would probably want to know where she bought the cute outfit, though.

"Mike up?" asked Eddie hopefully.

"No. And don't go in there. We gotta take off." She tucked her blouse into her jeans, then gathered up the waitress gear from the floor beside the bed and stuffed it into her canvas carryall—she could change in the restaurant ladies' room.

Books and notes piled on top of the white apron, she walked back into the bedroom. No reaction from Mike when she bent down to kiss him. Whatever dreams he walked through, ran through, were locked under his sleeping face, the slurry of pills in his blood sinking him deeper under the waves of his pulse.

So make it into med school, she told herself, gazing down at him. *Make it all the way through, go into research, get the hugest grant ever handed out, find the cure for him*. The pill to end all pills; the cure for the past. That should be good enough to take her from balancing hot plates along her arm, all the way to a Nobel Prize. *At least*.

"Shit," she said out loud, catching sight of the clock. Eddie looked up at her, his fingers in a stubborn wrestle with one of the snaps on his jacket. More than a half hour had slipped by—she'd have to fly now. Pushing her son in front of her, she headed for the hallway, picking up her bag in mid-stride.

The morning paper was outside the door. She scooped it up and tossed it inside. "Come on," she said, getting out her car keys. "We're running late."

* * *

Tyler knew he was awake before he opened his eyes. That toxic sleep had drained from his blood, the shapes outside the apartment filled out, made solid and real by the bright L.A. sun; he knew that. He kept his eyes closed, tasting his own saliva soured from breathing open-mouthed. The fold of sheet across his chest rose and tightened with each slow inhale.

This isn't cutting it, he told himself after several minutes, measured by his breathing. *Get your butt out of bed, get dressed, get something to eat*—that was what he should do, if he could lift himself out of the deadening inertia settled on his arms. He wondered what time it was—he only had to open his eyes and turn his head on the pillow to find out. And that would mean giving consent to being awake. As bad as it was—and it had been filled with formless dreams of suffocation, the result of the drugs' damping of his respiratory center—he preferred sleep to waking.

And night to sleep. That other night—stop it. The unbidden thoughts snapped off. *Don't even start that.*

He rolled on his side and picked up the clock from the bed table, holding it close in his blurred vision. The hands read almost noon. A small knot of hunger loosened in his stomach. He'd feed himself lunch. Plus there was the other reason for getting up, getting back into clock time with its sectored hours and slow mechanical progress through them—the row of orange plastic prescription bottles lined up in the kitchen cupboard. After last night's slipup—*oh, an accident? Really? Shut up, shut up*—he'd have to be more careful, get back on the track with the carefully measured medication stops every four hours. Walking that narrow tightrope that kept the proper level of chemicals percolating in his blood, and the luminous night safely throttled down below his vision.

Another face had looked at him from behind the prostitute's. One that he remembered from years ago. One that he had only seen at night.

He threw aside the sweaty covers. In the bathroom he splashed cold water in his face—the apartment building was old enough, the pipes buried deep enough, that the water ran cold no matter how hot the day got—until the skin stung and he gasped for breath. Leaning on the sink, as water drops trickled through the coarse black beard stubble, he watched the corner of one eyelid tremble, a familiar tic pulsing in the fine muscle. The face in the glass was fully awake. *More's the pity*, he thought.

As it was, his time sense, the little biological clocks ticking inside him, was all thrown off. He'd woken, gasping for breath when the first trace of morning light had been filtering into the bedroom— that must have been before six. Steff had still been asleep beside him, curled up with her cheek on her forearm. He'd raised himself on one elbow and looked at her. The sleeping profile and fringe of black eye- lash had been outlined in a trace of another light, a thin crack of the electric blue he'd seen around the buildings as he'd driven home. As if his blood had burned up his usual dose of medication and had let the night vision begin to seep in. He'd padded out to the kitchen in the dark, snapped one of the small phenobarbs in two, and swallowed half. That had been enough to sink him back under for a few more hours, the dull grogginess building in him as he'd lain listening to Steff's breathing until he couldn't hear it anymore.

In the kitchen again, the water on his bare chest

drying in the window's sunlight, he dumped the stale grounds out of the coffeepot and reassembled it with a fresh paper filter. While he waited for the stove's gas flame to bring the kettle to boiling, he began setting out his noon dosage, lining the pills and caps on the counter edge.

There's a good boy. Humorless sarcasm. *Take your medicine.* The phone rang as he twisted the last plastic lid shut again.

"Hello?" Tyler lifted the phone from the wall by the kitchen doorway. The kettle was making its preliminary murmur.

"Mike—how you doing?" A familiar voice came out of the handset. "This is Bedell."

He might have expected it. It had been a couple of weeks since the last call, something to do with some German reprint royalties that had come in, and Tyler's share of them. Bedell liked to keep in touch, whether there was any actual reason to call or not. As if there were long-standing friendship between them, and not just the book.

"Hello, Bedell," said Tyler. He hunched his shoulder up to hold the phone. The kettle's murmur had changed to the whistle of steam.

"Hey, Mike, what I'm calling about—" His voice was full of its usual busy cheer, a terrier on a low hit of speed. "What I want to know is, uh, have you seen today's paper?" Bedell's tone arched in a hint of intrigue.

The grounds darkened as he poured in the hissing water. "What paper?"

"Hey, any paper, man. The *Times*. You take the *Times*?"

"Yeah, I get it." Steff had made him take a subscription after she'd quizzed him on things like the

Vice President's name and he'd flunked. Now he was careful to always open the paper and jumble it around on the coffee table, whether he read it or not.

"The morning edition? You looked at it?"

"I just got up."

"Hmmm . . ."

Don't buzz at me, asshole, thought Tyler. *You aren't my parole officer, or my shrink, or anything else. So just back off.* He watched the thin drizzle of coffee splatter the bottom of the glass pot, and waited.

"Well, anyway," Bedell went on, "check out this morning's *Times.* Page, uh—" The sound of paper rustling came over the line. "Page three. Metro section."

"Why?"

"I think you'll find it interesting." Happy mystery-hunting. "I'll call you back when you've had a chance to read it."

Christ, thought Tyler as he hung up the phone. Kneading his forehead with one hand, as though the remnants of sleep were a dead skin that could be rubbed away, he walked through the front room. He found the paper on the hallway floor. Steff must have thrown it there before she left.

He opened the paper on the kitchen table, careful not to hit the line of medications or the cup of coffee he'd poured himself. A tremor in his hand when he lifted the cup scalded his lip and dribbled brown spots on the front page.

The local L.A. news was in the paper's second section. He pulled it out and folded it open to page three. For a few seconds all he saw was the Broadway department store ad filling most of the page. Then the headline of the article at the top: WYLE GROUP MEMBER ARRESTED. Below that, *Cult Murder*

Figure Eluded Authorities for Five Years. The black and gray dots of the photo coalesced into his ex-wife's face.

I'll be damned, he thought. He leaned back in the chair and took a long swallow from his cup, unmindful of the coffee's heat. The name in the headline, familiar to him as his own, and the face looking up at him from the newsprint overrode the random misfirings in his nerves, and steadied his hand. *They got her. They actually got her*.

He bent over the paper, spreading the crease flat with his hands. The picture of Linda was an old one, probably dug out of the *Times* files; Bedell had used it in the photo section of his book. Even in the newsprint's fuzzy dots it showed her eyes glancing cold and hard over her shoulder at the photographer's flash that had caught her at the first arraignment hearing five years ago—her hair, a curve of solid black ink, swept across the high ridge of her cheekbone. *You were right to take off,* he told his ex-wife's flat image. It was the kind of picture that sang murder to a jury; one look at that alone and they'd have put her on ice.

Maybe we could have got adjoining rooms in the mental ward. The grim humor pulled at the corner of his mouth. *We could be there now, crazier than shit. If I wasn't nuts when I went in, I soon would be*.

He realized he had been staring at the newspaper photo for several minutes when the phone rang again. Carrying the folded page to the phone, he scanned quickly down through the article.

Linda Tyler, a key figure in the "Wyle Group" cult murders of the mid-'70s, was taken into custody early Tuesday morning, a Los Angeles

County Sheriff's Department spokesman reported. Tyler, 35, was arrested in East Hollywood at one of a series of houses she had rented in the Los Angeles area since—

The phone's ring broke off as he picked it up. "Yeah, Bedell," he said, still reading. He knew that was who it would be.

"What'd you think of it? Told you it'd be interesting."

Tyler let a moment of silence translate as a shrug. "So they got her. They were bound to, eventually."

Bedell's voice dropped, crafty. "Puts the Wyle Group back in the news. Makes a good hook."

He suspected what was coming. Lowering the paper, he gazed across the living room to the bright square of sunlight held in the window. "Hook for what?"

"I don't know—whatever you'd be interested in." Casual. "A magazine piece, maybe something for *California*. Christ, *The New Yorker*. Maybe even another book. Have to bounce a proposal off a couple editors. See what kind of advance we can line up."

"Book?" Tyler closed his eyes, wearily shaking his head. "About the Wyle Group—haven't you beaten that to death yet? One's enough, for God's sake."

He could almost see the other's face grow red with argument. "About what's happened to the group," said Bedell. "You and some of the others. And Linda, now that she's been caught. Should be a lot of public interest."

Tyler looked back down at the newspaper. "Fine," he said. *Held without bail.* "Have a good time. See you on the best-seller list." *Booked on charges of.*

Bedell's voice lowered, serious. "I thought you might want to get in on it. Like last time."

He felt tired now, as though the coiled phone cord had penetrated his heart, bleeding away the ticking energy. "Hey . . . just fuck off, Bedell. I don't need any more money from you. And people don't need to know where I am, what I'm doing, anything. I'm just fading away, man. Right into the sunset. All right? So just write your little book without me."

"It's not you, Tyler. Nobody really wants to know about you, anyway. I need your help for something else."

He knew it, had been able to see it coming, since the newspaper had drawn the line between the first phone call and this one. "You want me to get in touch with Linda. Talk with her. Pump her for you."

"You were married to her once, man," came Bedell's voice. "You got the inside track."

"Screw you." Tyler threw the paper into the angle of the couch. "You know what your problem is— you write this stuff, but you don't believe any of it's true. It's just good stuff for a book. The hell with you. You'll have to do your grave-robbing on your own."

"Hey . . . Tyler—"

He hung the phone in its hook, squeezing the rigid white plastic until the pulse at the side of his throat stepped down a notch, slowing with his breath.

In the kitchen, glass of water in his hand, Tyler picked the medications off the table one by one. *East Hollywood*, he thought as the capsules slid down his throat. *She was out here all the time. Hiding right under everybody's nose*. He admired the cunning, the little sharp-toothed animal that could be seen in the eyes of the picture in the newspaper. It hadn't been there when he and Linda had gotten married; it had grown until it took over, peering out from its burrow behind her eye sockets. Wyle had done that; one of his many accomplishments.

Swirling the last quarter inch of water in the glass, he sat down on the couch, smoothed out the paper, and read the rest of the article. Another name out of the past caught his eye. *So old Kinross was there, too.* The paper listed him as retired but acting as special adviser to the county sheriff's office. *The past can't let go of you, either,* he thought, smiling thinly. *Or can you?*

The desert air, the first Santa Ana of the season, seeped through the apartment walls, drawing his sweat along his ribs. He leaned his head back against the couch and closed his eyes, feeling the small capsules unlock underneath his heart.

"Hey, Jimmy. What's going on, Jimbo?"

He looked up at the black dude who had come walking along the street. Sitting on the concrete edge of the curb surrounding a parking lot near the freeway, he'd been able to hide from the noon sun in the small circle of shade cast by a palm tree's shaggy head, and keep an eye on the underpass where his little sleeping nest was tucked. He could also watch the dusty T-shirts and hard hats of a construction crew gathering around the roach coach as it announced lunch break with the sharp bleat of its two-note horn. The driver of the catering truck came out with his change-maker hooked to his belt and swung open the shiny aluminum panel to reveal the ranks of wrapped sandwiches and fruit inside.

"Listen up—don't you space out on me, man. I *said*, what's going *on*."

The black's hands were tucked inside the pockets of his denim jacket, balled into rocklike fists. *I could take him on*, thought Jimmy; the black wasn't any bigger than he was. But he had a knife. Jimmy had seen the skinny flash of the blade, blue in a corner of a streetlamp sliding under the freeway, when the black had been terrorizing some little runaway, all acne and dirty-blond hair down to the shoulders, the black hissing that if the kid's little pink butt was good enough to peddle to those rich fuckers up in Hollywood then it was good enough for him, too. So now Jimmy kept a careful eye on the black dude's hands, or what he could see of them. The jacket was no longer blue, but gray with the embedded fine grit of the underpass slopes.

"Nothing," said Jimmy easily, peeling the cellophane away from a green cardboard tray of tomatoes. There were six of them in the tray; that plus the tail end of a loaf of bread was all that was left from yesterday's foraging. When he'd gotten his stash out from where he'd hidden it, he'd been unable to stop eating until his gut was stuffed. This would be the end of it for today, though—every supermarket dumpster in L.A. was probably picked clean by now. "Nothing at all," he said. The clear film clung wetly to where the tomatoes' wrinkly skin had split open to reveal the pulp beneath. "Same old shit."

The black didn't seem to care what was said, as long as some kind of answer, any words at all, had been made. He jerked his face away from Jimmy and glared, eyes little slits, down the empty street at the freeway. Even when the small industrial zone's parking lots had been filled with cars, there had hardly ever been any traffic on the roads except for a freight truck shuttling around the warehouses. Now, in the silence of the brown weeds lacing up through the padlocked gates, the knot jumping at the hinge of the black's jaw could almost be heard, a drum under the skin.

"Man, I'm *done* with that sleeping in the rough. Fuck that shit. Fuckin' bugs and rats running over your face. I'm going downtown to the mission, sleep in a goddamn *room*, with a door on it." The black swung his fierce gaze back around to his audience sitting on the low concrete wall. "And a hot meal spooned up by some nice Salvation Army bitch. That'd be fine, huh? Wouldn't it? Just fine."

Jimmy said nothing, but went on mopping up the sour juice and seeds in the bottom of the tray with the loaf's heel. If this dude wanted to sleep sitting up in a hard folding chair, breathing in a bunch of drunks' gassy belches and farts all night long, with all that slobbering snoring of white-stubbled old men while you shifted from one bone in your butt to another, trying to keep the chair's edge out of the blood-numb flesh for even a second—*Welcome to it, man.* Jimmy would be glad to see him leave the underpasses, anyway. He suspected the big black had been busting into the maintenance yard and prowling around the bulldozers and trucks at night, looking for tools he could take and hock. Which wasn't cool— there was a lot of folks nice and comfortable in their burrows tucked up under the rumbling concrete, who didn't need being rousted by the LAPD looking for whoever was ripping off the city's Public Works Department. Maybe it was pity for people caught in hard times, or just reluctance to go crawling around in the cramped dirt and trash, but so far the cops had ignored the freeway campers. *People gotta sleep somewhere*, Jimmy mused, sucking the last soggy crust. At least here they were out of sight.

So go ahead and buzz off, spade-o, he thought,

and nodded at the other's shadow wadded up at his feet. Who needed the heat brought around?

"Somebody been lookin' for you." The black gazed into the distance, the passion that had sparked when he'd looked at the freeway now ebbed away. "Askin' about you," he said. He rubbed the back of his hand across his nose.

"Who?" Jimmy folded the empty tray around the crumpled cellophane and bread wraper.

"Hey, man, I don't know your friends. Some skinny dude." The black pointed to the freeway underpass. "Was pokin' around your stuff. Said he wanted to talk to you."

Jimmy cradled the ball of trash between his legs. *Who the hell*—the thought pricked along the back of his neck. It was always trouble coming when you got told somebody was looking for you. It meant you'd fucked up, and the man—cop, officer, daddy, mommy—was going to lay it on your ass. Explain just how you'd fucked up, in some way you didn't even know about. Those kinds of lessons always hurt, left you wrapped around the slowly unwinding ache in your gut, lying on the floor of a dark locked closet while the woman you called your mother trailed off threats in the ear of a bottle, or on the cold concrete of a drunk tank that always smelled of disinfectant and vomit. Sometimes he wondered why cops and moms and MPs couldn't just tell you something without putting a fist or the end of a club into your belly.

Somebody looking for you was always bad news—it meant you hadn't succeeded in becoming invisible, staying out of sight. Somebody had been able to pick you out of the dust and litter. And now you were going to pay for it.

"Cop?" He looked up at the black. The crumpled

cardboard and cellophane had become tight and damp
in his hands.

"What—"

"Was it the police?"

"Naw, man." The black shook his head. "This
guy was in the life. You could tell, lookin' at 'm."
He smiled suddenly, oddly shy. "See you down at
the mission?"

"Yeah, sure. Maybe."

"I'll get a pint and sneak it in. Then those fuckin'
chairs won't be so hard."

After the black had walked on and disappeared,
Jimmy went on staring down the road at the freeway.
Going on downtown would be the simple solution,
even if he had to sleep tonight in one of the alleys
down around Sixth and Hill. He knew he was grayed
out enough that some bunch of punks wouldn't mistake him for a newcomer, some guy come to L.A.
looking for work, and try to roll him for money or a
set of tools rolled up in his coat. *Screw it,* he thought.
Whatever dude was looking for him wouldn't be able
to find him in the middle of all the other gray men.

The catering truck folded its aluminum sides, started
up, and drove toward the onramp. After a while the
work crew got up and put on their hard hats. Jimmy
watched them, but none of them glanced over in his
direction. He'd always pitied them because they only
knew the freeways and the spaces wrapped inside
them by the dull light of day. They didn't know.

For a while longer he gazed at the concrete and the
distant figures. Then he stuffed the trash in his hands
into the gutter. He stood up and started walking,
slowly, not toward downtown but back to the nest.
His home.

* * *

Bedell set the phone down and switched on the answering machine. For a couple of minutes he ran the machine through its cycle, turning the volume up to hear his own voice on the little speaker, asking anybody who called to leave their name and number, then rewinding the tape back to the start. The last thing on the tape in his head was the sound of Tyler's voice, the anger leaking through the tightly wrapped bindings.

The machine was ready and waiting. He looked down at it, nodding in satisfaction. *All right, you son-ofabitch*, he thought, smiling at the red-lit dot above the machine's ON button. *You're going to call back. And then we're gonna talk.* There was no way he would miss Tyler's return call; the machine would see to that. Now the hook was set, and he'd be able to set it deeper and reel him in with the gentlest of tugs over the wire.

He folded his arms, a good day's work—more than he'd accomplished in a long time—done in just a couple of phone calls, and looked across the room. The phone and answering machine sat on the book-shelves against the wall. Those, a set of file cabinets, and the IBM Selectric on a table in the back room he used as an office were the visible remnants of his writing career. The table was a buff-colored utility model, forty-nine dollars at the discount office furniture store, with folding steel tube legs. It reminded him of setting up for meetings held in the basement of a public library he'd worked at when he was in college. When he'd first brought it home he'd even remembered the little knack of lifting one knee and flipping the opened table upright so that its weight landed in just the spot he wanted. The table with its mottled composition surface that soaked up spilled coffee into permanent stains had come stalking out of his past on its skinny tube legs, chasing away the desk of lustrous fine-grained teak that had vanished along with the rest of the rental furniture. Behind him, as he faced the front window, the rest of the house's empty rooms stretched away, bare to the walls.

Out toward the street Bedell heard a small, unmufflered gas engine sputter into life. *Shit*, he thought, rubbing his eyes as the racket snarled into the sound of a metal blade chewing into grass and earth. The gardening service had shown up on their weekly rounds.

Bedell leaned forward to dig his wallet out of his back pocket and checked to make sure that there was at least a twenty-dollar bill inside. A month ago, the gardener, a stolid Korean whose wife usually came along to trim the hedges, in an old-fashioned poke bonnet to shade her face like something off *Little House on the Prairie*, had suddenly insisted on being paid in cash. Bedell had never bounced a check off the guy, but somehow that little secret, the blood trace of hemorrhaging bank accounts, had leaked out, been detected.

He got up and pulled aside the living room curtain, just enough to see the gardener's GM pickup at the curb, narrow wooden planks leaning against the tailgate for the mower and other equipment to be trundled down. Along the sidewalk a random spark flew as the edger blade struck the cement. The gardener, the bill of his Dodgers cap lowered as he watched the quick efficiency of his hands guiding the machine, didn't look up to see Bedell behind the window. He let the curtain fall back into place.

The little bites of cash that the gardener took were

the least he had to worry about. And you couldn't do without one. If you let the front yard go, then everybody knew. The inside could go hollow and be hidden, but the outside had to stay trimmed and clipped. Or everyone would know you were bleeding to death.

He turned around and looked across the living room: his worktable, the file cabinets, the aluminum and plastic-webbing lawn furniture he'd brought in from the weed-choked backyard—those at least he'd paid for with cash, and had remained behind when the black and buttery leather couches, the chrome and smoked-glass tables had evaporated back onto the truck that had first brought them. A mattress on the floor of one of the bedrooms, books stacked up in the hallways, including a box half full of the ones with his own black-and-white photo on the back. All the cups he owned were spread out on the kitchen counter, each with a dried brown sludge at the bottom—he had to scrub one out every time he went to spoon out the instant coffee.

And the gardener outside: a happy household. Bedell closed his eyes in the little surge of quiet when the clamoring engine shut off. He found his hands trembling and sweating as the silence filled the house. When he opened his eyes, he saw the red light on the answering machine, the tiny sip of electricity showing it was on. His fingers wanted to grab hold of the dead time between now and when Tyler would call back, and tear it closer.

Come on, motherfucker. Call.

Outside, the deeper rasp of the mower kicked on.

THREE

Later, as the day wore on, he got another call. Tyler had washed the few dishes stacked up in the sink, rinsed out the coffeepot, eaten lunch—a sandwich cobbled together from plastic-wrapped cheese and lunch meat—and was facing the usual downward slope of his afternoon hours, until it was time to go and open up the theatre, when the phone rang.

"Hello?" Tyler set the half-empty glass of water on the coffee table. In his palm a pair of capsules tapped softly together.

"Mr. Tyler?" A voice he didn't recognize, cool, professional.

"That's right."

"My name's Silberman, Mr. Tyler. Larry Silberman. I'm the attorney—one of them, at least—for your ex-wife, Linda Tyler. Hope I'm not interrupting anything."

"No, it's okay." He rubbed one of the blue and white caps between his thumb and forefinger, feeling the thin ridge where the two halves fit together. Somehow he had been expecting this little intrusion into the day's emptiness. It was impossible for her to remain a photo in the newspaper spread out on the couch. "What happened to what's his name . . . old Minosian?" That was the defense lawyer Linda's

42

parents had originally hired so long ago, a silver-haired legend straight out of the ritzy precincts of the Jonathan Club downtown. "I was expecting to hear from him."

"Mr. Minosian died about a year ago. I kind of inherited this." The voice on the line sounded embarrassed. And younger; younger than himself, Tyler realized.

"So what can I do for you?" *Some young hotshot*, he thought. He felt old, a relic of the past; the gulf of just a few years between himself and the attorney was filled with more than time.

The other cleared his throat. "I've been down at the women's detention center most of the morning, Mr. Tyler. Talking with my client."

He sat down on the couch. "Find out anything?" The capsules' skin had softened with the sweat of his hand. He laid them down by the glass.

"A little. It's going to take a while pulling all this together. She's in quite a state—I left one of my associates down there, trying to work out bringing in a private doctor to see about some kind of medication for her. They don't usually do that at the detention center, but I think we can get it."

Tyler nodded to himself. It sounded as if Linda's parents were already bringing the weight of their money around to bear on the situation. He could imagine the phone line down from Santa Barbara being pulled tight with their voices and orders.

"The reason I'm calling," Silberman's voice went on, "is that Linda gave me a message for you. She wants to see you."

Tyler said nothing.

"She wants to talk to you. She was very . . .

insistent about it. I had to promise her that I'd get you to come."

"No kidding." He studied the still life of medication and glass on the coffee table. "She's an insistent kind of person. You'll find that out."

"I guess so," said Silberman. "That's why I was hoping you'd agree to go down there and see her. You'd be doing me a big favor."

"Did she tell you what she wants to talk to me about? Anything important, or just for old times' sake?"

Another fragment of silence before the other answered. "She said to tell you that it's about your son, Mr. Tyler. She said you'd know what she meant."

The silence seeped from the phone line and filled the room around him. He could hear the traffic outside, the street noises buffeting the window, but as though from a distance that took years to cover. He was alone in the room except for the uncoiling thread of memory.

"Mr. Tyler?" Silberman's voice scratched at his ear again.

"Yes," he said. He was safe for now. The medication had laid its usual transparent barrier between himself and the cutting edges of the past.

"Maybe I shouldn't have called and asked you. But I didn't know what else to do. If you could . . . it might help. You know, calm her down so we can get on with the preparation."

"I don't know." He picked up one of the capsules from the table, gazed at it. "Maybe."

"Whatever you decide. I've got you down on the attorneys' list. As long as you bring some kind of I.D., you shouldn't have any trouble getting in to see her. Probably can't do anything over the weekend, but Monday, if you're free . . ." Silberman rattled off his office number.

After he hung up the phone, Tyler saw that the cap had crumbled apart in his other hand. Gritty white powder leaked from the thin shell and down his thumb and forefinger. For a moment he looked at it, then brought his hand to his mouth. His tongue curled with the chemical taste.

Maybe the guy was gone by now. Jimmy sidled past the chain link fence and mud-encrusted blades of the bulldozers on the other side. He peered beyond the silent machines to the darkness under the freeway. The city crews that moved the equipment in and out of the yard had all packed up and left—he figured that made it about three o'clock, because they always started so early in the morning, and there was a gap of a couple hours before the rush-hour traffic started knotting up the freeway lanes above. Since the black dude, whatever his name was, had told him there was someone looking for him, Jimmy had killed time just walking and sitting, the sun warming his back as he squatted on the parking lot curb, drawing circles in the gutter's silted-up dust with his heel. Never getting too far away from the underpass where his nest was hidden, he kept an eye on the deep shade and who-ever might be waiting for him in it.

Maybe he got tired of waiting, thought Jimmy. He stood at the edge of the underpass, a big square-cut cavern, and blinked as his eyes adjusted to the shadow. The traffic drumming overhead masked any sounds that might have revealed someone else hiding in the dark. *The guy gave up. Whoever it was.* He laced his fingers in the chain link fence between him and the dirt banks sloping to the concrete ceiling and pressed his face to the wires. He couldn't see anybody up on the narrow shelf at the top of the slope.

If you waited long enough, everybody went away eventually. That's all it took. Just the waiting, and then you could be alone again, nobody bothering you.

He set the toes of his shoes, canvas sneakers he'd bound up with shiny black electrician's tape where they'd started to split from the rubber soles, into the fence and climbed.

There he was. Rooting around in his stuff; *fucking sonofabitch*, thought Jimmy as he crouched down in the powdery dust underneath the freeway. From this one spot he had a clear shot through the concrete pillars to his carefully concealed nest several yards away. All the treasures were scattered about the intruder in a rough half-circle, his back curved as he squatted on his heels and sifted through them. Jimmy watched the guy's shoulders stretching taut the thin leather of his jacket, greasy lank hair dangling over the collar—not greasy because unwashed, like most of those Jimmy lived with under the bridge. He puts something on it, decided Jimmy, to keep it all shiny and dark like that. Points of the dim underpass light glinted off the intruder's hair, as though the jacket hunched up against his neck had taken root and grown, becoming part of him.

Fuckin' A. Jimmy felt a sharp sting of resentment at the bridge of his nose. (*Not fair*, shouted a voice in a memory-distant playground, a child's voice, his own, the taste of asphalt and blood in his mouth, the bigger and older kid towering over him as he shouted where he fell, *not fair*.) He could see past the intruder's back to his pale hands sorting through the little precious cache of papers and photos, holding each one up to the slanting light and his cold inspection. It's not fair. Jimmy felt the resentment spread hot across his face, blurring his sight, the intruder swimming in salt crescents at the bottom of his eyes. *He doesn't belong here.* He mouthed the words, leaning forward to balance his squat with his hands in the soft dirt. This is for us, this is our place, we're not bothering you, *leave us alone.* The injustice of it burned; he'd tried to do it right, to hide up here in the dark where they didn't have to see you—and why should they? He didn't mind that, or sidling around behind the supermarkets to go through the bins of stuff they didn't want. But then they come after you anyway. Fuckers.

Obviously the same guy the black dude had told Jimmy about. He felt it; better if it had been another one. Two different guys in a row could mean nothing, just the random usual workings of the world. People came and went; once a newspaper reporter, complete with photographer trailing after, had poked around in the underpass dens, talking with some of the inhabitants. He'd scurried farther back to the darkest part and stayed unnoticed. Some kid who'd been there only a couple of days and left a couple days later had yapped on and on about life under the freeway; that had satisfied the reporter and the photographer and they'd left finally. Things happened; they meant nothing.

But some guy come round looking for him twice—that persistence implied reasons. Jimmy worked the equation over in his mind. Wants to find me; me in particular. That's why he came here again. Or never left. *Not fair.*

The intruder finished looking through the pictures and other stuff and rocked back on his heels. It wasn't that the guy was so big—*I'm bigger than he is*, thought Jimmy—but he had that thin coiled look, like a snake stuffed into a bag, that always meant trouble. They had ways of hitting you so it really hurt; and fast, faster than you could get out of the way or do anything about it. The guy reminded him, just from his back, the way his spine arched deeper than normal, of those little fuckers you meet in army barracks, either small black city dudes or southern farm kids with their hair pasted down shiny like that, a fringe of dark grease on their foreheads, and who could leave you down in the corner of the showers where nobody could see, writhing about the imploded pit of your gut, the smell of soap and steam in your face like a blanket. And the more you tried to stay out of their way, as though walking around a snake hole, the more you found yourself bumping into them. Because they liked getting that sharp-edged and bright-eyed smile. And showing you what a big stupid fool you were. As if you didn't know.

And that would be the ultimate unfairness of it. He could see it all coming down the line toward him. You already knew what was going to happen, and still you'd have to go through with it. He was going to have to confront the intruder, face the guy about going through his stuff. And he'd get the shit kicked out of him; that's how it worked. (Or he could just leave, just slide down the slope to the roadway underneath the freeway, and just walk. Wind his way through the streets around the maintenance yard, break clear, and head downtown to a nice warm shelter. Or even find another underpass, another nest. There were dozens he knew about, with their little colonies of people like him. Room for one more, anywhere around L.A. And just leave this.guy behind. And his own stuff. Just junk anyway. Not good for anything. Memories of getting beat up, mostly. Leave it. Just walk.

(But if he did that, he knew, he wouldn't have anything. And he saw those ones who had nothing, not even the last little scrap of paper with their names, or anyone's, on it. In the shelters, holding trembling paper cups to their lips, a dribble of brown coffee into their chins' gray stubble. Their eyes fell away, red-rimmed holes staring at some faded church poster on the wall. And he didn't want to be one of them. Not yet. That was a little further away, still.)

He started his slow crawl, roundabout to the nest. Not straight on through the narrow space between the pillars; if the intruder heard anything behind his back— and he would, Jimmy knew, the slightest sound catching at the ears with the shiny black hair tucked behind—then he'd be able to turn and spot him while he was yards away. And there wouldn't even be the brief satisfaction of landing one sneak blow on the intruder's unsuspecting neck before the inevitable shit-beating began. *Quiet*—the unspoken caution to his legs and arms as he maneuvered hunched over, fingers prodding the dust. *You big dummy. Keep it quiet. Or he'll catch you first.*

The intruder was lost to his sight as he crept up the slope, the rumbling noise of the freeway traffic overhead growing louder as he approached the concrete roof of the underpass. The row of pillars blocked his view of the violated nest. He tried to swallow his breath but his heart hammered it back into his mouth. The toes of his shoes dug in and pushed him farther up the slope.

The gap between the last pillar and the freeway's underside formed the entrance to the scooped-out hollow, the center just big enough for sleeping curled around a half-buried cache. Jimmy pressed his shoulder against the rough-textured column and—slowly, quietly—looked around into the nest. The treasures of papers and photos lay spread out around the dirt-embedded blankets, the plastic-wrapped scraps of food still tucked into the sharp angle of concrete and packed dirt. But the intruder was gone. Two wedge-shaped indentations facing the spread-out bits of paper, as though fists had been pounded into the soft, loose floor—the shoes of a squatting man, all weight balanced forward as he'd inspected the cache, had made the deep marks.

Shit. Now what? On hands and knees, Jimmy looked around the space, the soft edge of the slanting afternoon light tracing the curved edges. *Sonofabitch is gone.* The twin indentations of his feet proved he'd been there, though. So the comforting notion of a dream, seed planted by that loony black dude, the sort of thing seen in the darkness out of the corner of your eye and you try not to look at straight, for fear it might really be there, that was denied him.

He crept into the nest, silence wrapped in the roaring noise of the traffic overhead, and looked down at the photos and papers, as if the intruder had spelled his name in the semicircle arrangement. As if he, dumbly, could read it.

Then he felt his head snap down to the ground, the slick surface of one of the photos pressing against his face. And the weight on his back, flattening him.

For a moment he couldn't breathe; he realized an arm was around his neck, the hard edge up from its wrist digging into his throat. The arm lifted him up from the dirt; from the corner of one eye, looking over the black straight edge of the photo stuck by sweat to his cheek, he could see the narrow, bright-eyed face examining his own.

The intruder swung him about and threw him onto the nest's sloping wall. His breath came back into him hard enough to press the top of his head against the freeway's underside. He looked down and saw the crouching figure coiled onto his haunches, watching with a thin smile. Some of the strands of shiny black had been tossed forward by the jump from the hiding place between the rows of concrete pillars; they looked like thick ink strokes on the pale brow.

"Sneaky, huh?" The smile widened, breaking into words. "Why'd you sneak around like that? Huh?"

Jimmy dug the heels of his palms into the slope's loose dirt, to keep himself from sliding down the couple of feet between himself and the intruder. The other's presence filled the nest's small space, pressing him up against its soft walls. He shook his head, eyes locked by the bright points across from him.

"Why you go sneaking around? Come on." The intruder leaned forward, bringing his breath close enough to be felt. "Tell me. You come sneaking up on me, and I want to know why."

The motion of his head stopped, frozen along the lines of his sight.

"Come on, motherfucker. Why the sneaking around? Why'd you do that?"

The words tapped at him, pressing him back against the slope. There was no place to go, to get away from them. Where the bright eyes weren't watching and waiting.

"Shit. Forget it." The intruder looked away in disgust, shaking his head. Moments passed, the rumbling of metal overhead filtered throught the layers of concrete. The other gazed across the distance to the

sunlit edges of the underpass, as if watching for
something at the edge of the other world hidden by
the daylight's glare. Jimmy looked at the sharp-pointed
profile and waited for the next words. There were
always more.

The bright gaze swung back around to Jimmy. "What
do they call you?" asked the intruder, voice a little
softer. "Jim or Jimmy?"

His name was on the army discharge papers, and
some of the other stuff scattered around the nest—
that was how the guy knew his name. "Jimmy," he
said. He stayed back against the edge of soft dirt,
keeping the few feet of distance between himself and
the other. The guy had known, like anybody else
would, that nobody like him was ever called James.

"Jimmy," echoed the intruder. He smiled, regarding him. "You live here, Jimmy?"

"Yeah." *You know that, you spooky shit. Why's
he go on asking stuff he already knows?* His hands
clenched into the loose dirt.

The intruder shook his head, still smiling. "Smells
like piss up here. You know that, Jimmy?"

Nothing to say—he kept on watching warily.

"You don't know that, do you, though? Because
you smell the same. It smells like you in here—that's
what it is." The intruder settled back on his haunches,
the easy rest of some sharp-muzzled animal. "You
know what my name is, Jimmy?"

He shook his head. "No."

"Slide. You call me Slide." The intruder leaned
forward, the bright eyes tracking along the invisible
line fastened to those watching him. "Okay, Jimmy?"

He felt the dimly lit space contract around them,
the dust-filtered shaft of sun holding their faces close.
He could smell the other's breath again, sharp and

acrid. The smile had changed to something different, the same on the white skin's surface, but pulled by something tautening beneath. "Okay," he said. The smile widened. Some other, unspoken agreement had been initiated.

"You like it here, don't you, Jimmy?" Slide looked around the concave nest, his eyes lifting for a moment to the concrete just above their heads. "It's nice. Nice and private. I can dig it. Nobody bugs you here. Because they can't find you, can they? Can they, Jimmy?"

"No." He had already learned. He had already learned that was how you stopped the voice's soft, insistent blows. You said what it wanted you to say. You did what he wanted. That was the agreement you went along with, your own voice going step by step, following where the other led.

Slide leaned even closer forward, one hand sinking for balance in the soft dirt. Jimmy could see the little triangles of blood at the corners of his eyes. "You can do something for me," said Slide. "Here. You want to, don't you, Jimmy?"

He drew back, away from the bright, red-pointed gaze and the sharp-smelling breath. "Like what?"

The eyes narrowed as Slide shook his head. "No," he said softly. "You want to. Don't you? Don't you, Jimmy?"

No escape. The other's gaze and breath filled the nest's entire space. He knew, with the words stilled inside his head, that the only room left for him was inside that gaze, the other's breath now deep inside his own chest. The nest and everything in it now belonged to this new thing that had claimed it.

He nodded, seeing the motion of his head reflected at the dead center of Slide's eyes.

Slide leaned back, still smiling. "Don't worry."
Kindness now, or the skinned bone of something like
it. "You'll like it. You won't get hurt."

The words were another voice in memory, one
that whispered instead of shouting. Words in a dark
space. *It won't hurt.* A grown-up looking over the
child, then close, right against, in dark warmth. *It
won't hurt you'll like it won't hurt won't hurt.*

The centers of Slide's eyes were hollow, not even
holding the reflection of his mute face now. The gaze
let him go, and he felt his cheek roll into the soft dirt
of the nest, the crouching figure watching him.

FOUR

He knelt in the apartment hallway, at the door of the closet, lifting the stack of old newspapers from the cardboard box beneath.

Hardly a month went by that, at some time, Tyler didn't have the book in his hands. Skimming through the words that he'd read so often that he could've closed the book and recited them off the incised scar tissue of his own heart. Thumbing through the slick-textured center section of photographs, gazing at faces long dead now, or as good as, including his own. Stopping at some gray paragraph that included his own name and reading it, and the ones that followed, page after page until another hour had been killed, carving the interior braille a fraction deeper. No pain; those nerves had died.

Yet he still kept his copy of the book buried in the box at the bottom of the closet. As though it were some private vice, another illicit drug, and like the ones before it, compounded of more parts shame and regret than any initial pleasure. It was his third copy, having thrown two others out before in spasms of disgust, the first the one Bedell had inscribed *To my friend and inside source* and sent to him while he'd still been locked up.

He straightened up, letting the stack of old newspapers and Steff's pack-rat stash of Christmas gift-wrapping subside back into the bulge-sided carton. The book's dust jacket, a slanting tear across the back, lay cool in his damp palm.

Rituals of protracted time, to be gotten through before the act itself. *Sign of somebody with not enough to do, and too much time for it,* he told himself as he stood at the window, watching the angle of street visible from this point. The book lay on the low coffee table behind him, as it had lain on other tables or the thin mattress of the prison's hospital ward bed before. *You've always got time to kill.*

Tyler sat back down on the couch, leaning forward over the coffee table. The dust jacket's faded primary colors splashed up at him. Red for blood; a lot of imagination from the publisher's art department there. And the wide black letters that spelled out *INSIDE THE NIGHT.* In smaller letters below: *The Wyle Group Murders.* Across the bottom: *by J. Alan Bedell, with Michael Tyler.* One corner of the jacket was stark white, as though it had been held there to dip it into the red that had soaked through to the back.

With one finger he tilted the book up onto its spine; it fell open at the photo section in the middle. The level gaze of Liam Wyle, the same calm studio portrait that had been used for the back covers of all his books, looked up at Tyler. He'd owned all those books once, the fat academic tomes filled with psychoanalytic jargon, the thin paperbacks with their—now already faded—hip vocabulary, the offset and mimeographed leaflets even more impenetrable, code words for the initiates. He'd had all of Wyle's books, a complete collection sitting on a single bookshelf like a shrine, right up until the Group's last days, just before the police raids finally put an end to the welter of blood. Wyle's face, all the copies of it caught in frozen black-and-white time, had curled and twisted into ash at the center of the small bonfire he'd made of the books.

Some collector had tracked him down through Bedell, looking for anything that might not have gone into the fire. Some of Wyle's rarer stuff, the insanity confined to print runs of a couple hundred for the chosen few, were worth a lot of money now. To certain people with a taste for that sort of thing. Tyler had kicked the guy halfway down the apartment building's stairs.

Wyle's face was, for Tyler, now nothing but an arrangement of ink dots on slick paper. Those eyes, which looked so calm and understanding in the photo, were now probably staring at the beige walls of a prison psychiatric ward. In the last chapter of Bedell's book was the note that after confounding the doctors with their own jargon—who better at their own game? —Wyle had lapsed into a contemptuous silence, unbroken yet.

Whatever he's thinking, thought Tyler, *inside there, I don't want to know*. Perhaps Wyle was thinking of him and all the others who had been in the Group. Or perhaps Wyle had made the leap, had gone beyond the blood and everything else, and was now in the cold, wordless landscape of the terminal schizophrenics he'd admired so much. *I don't want to know*.

He turned the page over, to other familiar slices of dead time. His own face looked up at him, the camera having caught the sharp point held in his eyes, fringed by his untrimmed hair falling across his forehead. The look of one who'd already seen too much. His wrists were handcuffed behind him as he looked over his shoulder at the camera flash; one cop's hand was visible, clamped tight on his arm and pushing him along.

Below that, Linda's face, the same photo he'd just seen in the newspaper. In some ways, he realized, the best picture he'd ever seen of her; no wonder they always used it whenever the Wyle Group crept back into public notice, at the anniversary of one of the killings or in one of those pious meditations on violence and TV or drugs or sunspots or whatever that showed up in the magazines. She still looked beautiful in the shot, maybe even more so, her face cut leaner and harder, the high cheekbones like curved knife edges. And in her wild eyes the whole history of the Wyle Group could be read; her gaze had burned throught the camera lens as if it could have ignited the film. The photographer, the same one, had got around in front of her; you could only tell from her thrown-back shoulders and the cop close behind her that she was handcuffed.

Their wedding picture was also in the book's photo section, included by Bedell's clumsy sense of irony. Surrounded by all the cheesy pomp her parents had paid for, he looked uncomfortable in the rented tux, she smiled happily over her bouquet.

Tyler slid his forefinger between the last page of the photos and the rougher surface of the text behind. With one small motion of his finger he was past the other pictures, the other Group members, the location shots of the university campus and tidy suburban homes, anonymous except for the dangling POLICE INVESTIGATION—DO NOT CROSS strips roped across the front walks. And the photos of the victims, alive and smiling, then sprawled in their own blood, reproduced on the pages in the blackest of inks.

For a few moments his eyes scanned across the

words without reading them. Outside, beyond the apartment's silence, he could hear the traffic's noise, sparse at this hour on a side street. On the main arteries, like Sunset and Santa Monica, it would be as thick as always, twenty-four hours a day. He turned the pages until one word—*Linda*—caught his eye. The section he'd been looking for, that he'd known was there. He picked the book up from the coffee table and settled back into the couch with it.

. . . *were about to find out. Even though all the others arrested so far, including her husband, Michael, had been held without bail on the exact same charges, Judge Bellamy was informed that the district attorney's office considered Linda Tyler suitable to be released awaiting trial. The same power that had delayed Linda's arrest for three weeks, and might have delayed it forever if the* Times's *Benelli and Royce hadn't traced her to her parents' Santa Barbara ranch, flexed its influence again. In a city where the name Mueller was to be found on everything from Spanish land grant parchments to the boards of directors of more corporate wealth than most countries, it was not likely that the daughter of that kind of money would spend much time locked up. Or any time at all, as it turned out.*

The bail request took Judge Bellamy enough by surprise that he summoned Welbeck from the DA's office, Linda's attorney, Aram Minosian, and—as reported in the morning edition of the Times, *but not the evening final—Linda's father into his chambers. When Bellamy emerged a bare twenty-five minutes later, the price for the conditional freedom of Mueller's daughter was revealed: a cool quarter million. If the judge was going to bend the rules for his old tennis partner, he was at least going to make sure that a respectable price was paid. . . .*

Poor old Bellamy. Tyler could see the judge's face even without looking at the photo in the book. He had finally come to feel sorry for the old man. The face had gotten older and grayer as the trials had gone on, each piece of evidence repeated over and over, the autopsy reports, the blood-spattered police photos blown up big enough to put on an easel and show to the jury, each little bit taking another bite out of him. Six months after he had handed down the sentences, five months after he had announced his retirement from the bench, old Judge Bellamy had been dead. *The last Wyle Group victim*, thought Tyler. He flipped through the book's pages, stopped, and read again.

. . . awaiting trial. Oddly, Tyler was finding jail to his liking. The relative peace and quiet of the isolation unit—as with the other Wyle Group members, he had been given protective custody arrangements, to prevent any other prisoner from gaining prestige through the harming of so notorious a figure—afforded him the first real opportunity to sort out the events of the last two years, to separate reality from murderous fantasy.

The court-appointed defense attorneys wondered at the time about the apparent fatalism that had set in, his lack of interest in the preparations for trial. There was no way he could tell them; no way, after the horrors he had seen, that imprisonment could hold any fear for him. Lying on his bunk after lights-out, staring at the ceiling and finishing up the daily pack of Salems—a teenage habit that had reemerged in jail and lasted until the trials were over—he watched the images of death come up out of his memory, seeing them as if for the first time. If sleep came at all, it was only toward morning, when the first light would chase away the phantoms.

During the period while the court was working through the attorneys' pretrial motions, Tyler received a mixed assortment of news. Judge Bellamy approved the motion forwarded by both the prosecuting and defense attorneys that the Wyle Group members be allowed to start on the course of psychotropic medications outlined in the notes of the army research team that had originally investigated the "Host" drug and its effects, then supplied by the German pharmaceutical firm under the code name 83 Blau. The army scientists had abandoned the research project and their hopes of finding a military use for the alleged "shared mind" effect provided by the drug, due to the negative side effects—effects which were dramatically illustrated by the aftermath of the Wyle Group's illicit use of it. The "pseudo-virus" nature of the drug had the unforeseen consequence of making its effects apparently permanent, the result of basic alterations in the brain's chemistry; the drug, in essence, bonded itself into the central nervous system of anyone who was exposed to it. Relatively simple medications, taken on a regular basis, could, however, alleviate the hallucinations and other abnormalities. The unfortunate enlisted men who

were the subjects of the original tests responded
well to a combination of . . .

Tyler's eyes glazed over the dreary list of tranks
and other drugs that Bedell in his picky, fact-obsessed
way had shoved into the book. The names were all
familiar to him from the labels on the orange plastic
containers in the kitchen cupboard. They weren't
made any more interesting surrounded by Bedell's
leaden prose. A dud like that had to write about
murder to get anybody to read him at all.

. . . even clearer. He had experienced the "group
mind" effect—or the delusions of it—diminishing
from simple lack of contact with the other Wyle
Group members. Now, with the medications
brought round four times daily by the nurses
from the jail's medical section, Tyler found his
mind to be his own again, after two years.
Though his apathy about the outcome of the
trials continued, defense attorneys noted a marked
improvement in his manner.

Then, during the pretrial period, a combined
blow. Only after a county psychiatrist had judged
him stabilized on the new course of medications
had it been considered safe to tell him . . .

He closed his eyes. The next few paragraphs were
too painful to read again. Reading them once had
seared the words onto his heart. He turned the page
before he lifted his eyelids.

. . . part of her attorneys' defense strategy.
They had already managed to split Linda's case
from that of the other Wyle Group members;

*now they wanted to make the distance even
greater.*

*Tyler sent word back that his agreement to the
divorce petition was dependent upon being granted
a special privilege in the jail. He wanted unlim-
ited access to books brought in from the outside.
Although Linda's attorneys would have offi-
cially had no control over such a matter, the day
after his consent to the divorce was given, his
first list was delivered to his cell, to replace the
paperback* Good News for Modern Man *that he
had already gone through a dozen times. Perhaps significantly, a King James Version headed
the list. The rest . . .*

The titles were just words to him now. He had
wound up donating them to the jail library after his
sentencing.

There's a limit, he thought, *to what you can learn
from books. Even one with your life story in it.* He
weighed it in his hand, the broad spine filling his
palm.

Kinross made coffee for himself, heating the water
in a loose-handled saucepan to pour over the instant
crystals. The pan was one that his wife had left
behind for him when she'd divorced him. He'd never
bought a new one, or a kettle—hot water was all he
ever used the pan for—even after he'd retired from
the LAPD, and there was time and money for im-
provements. Because there wasn't time. Not yet. As
he poured the water into the cup, the steam rising
across the deep ridges of his knuckles, he thought of
Linda Tyler. And all the other things he thought
about each and every day.

He took my baby. The words rattled around in his skull, went on making their circuit as he carried the cup over to the table and set it down beside the pink and white mayonnaise and bologna sandwich that was every day's lunch. *Slide took my baby*.

That was just like them. He chewed methodically, tasting nothing, watching the tape in his memory, Linda's face breaking into tears before she was led away. Asking him for help . . . They always did. He nodded to himself as he swallowed. They always, at the end, wept and pissed all over themselves, asking you to help them. And they're sorry. They're always sorry they killed all those people. And won't you help them now? *He took my baby*. Kinross drained the last of the coffee from the cup. *Fuckin' bastards*, he thought. *All of them*.

He pushed away the empty cup. From the other side of the table he drew toward himself another unvarying object in the rigid sequence of days, and months, and years. The book opened flat, the spine having broken from his handling long ago. He had thrown away the bright red dust jacket when he'd first bought the book, like a butcher's paper wrapping that had become soaked with blood.

There was nothing in the book, nothing that that fat asshole Bedell and Tyler—another murderous loony—had converted into smooth, Vaselined bestseller prose and into money to line their pockets, that Kinross didn't have in another, more complete form, neatly stored away inside his own head. All the contents of the manila folders stacked up in cardboard boxes around the room, the police reports and transcripts, all the thousands of pages he'd Xeroxed— against regulations—and collected here, before he'd retired and lost his official access to them. Though even then, the careful accumulation of paper on top of paper hadn't stopped. Some of the younger guys still on the force, who'd worked with him on the Wyle Group stuff, kept him supplied with copies of everything that went into the LAPD files. A steadily diminishing stream, as the years went by and the loose ends still attached to the whole business became more tattered and easier to forget. There were those who didn't forget, though; others like him.

The arrest of Linda Tyler was the first new event to add to the file for some time. His old LAPD connections made sure that he was notified—against regulations—and on the spot for it. As if he had never left the force. Which, in his own mind, could have been the case: he had just reached that point where he could spend all his time thinking about Wyle and the little bunch of lunatics that had gathered around him, and what they had done. The article from the *L.A. Times* about the arrest had already been carefully clipped out and added to the file, in the manila folder with her name lettered on it.

He leafed through the book until he came to the photo section in the middle. There was Linda Tyler's face, the same file shot used in the newspaper today. He knew whose was the hand gripping her arm in the photo, moving her along the corridors of the police station: it was his own. The ring on the finger, catching a spark of the photographer's flash, had been his wedding band—still on his hand now. He had never bothered to pry it over the thick wad of his knuckle and get rid of it.

Millions of people, everyone who'd bought Bedell's book, or the paperback edition of it, or some foreign edition—once, in Tijuana just before he'd retired, on the cush job of picking up a witness and driving him back up to L.A., he'd spotted a cheap Spanish-language version, the bloodred cover embellished with a typically Mexican grinning skull—all those people had seen his hand in that photo. A real cop's hand, doing its job. That was all they needed to see of him. That big hand, big even when he'd been a skinny thirteen-year-old boxing in the Police Athletic League's Golden Gloves tournaments, gripping that thin arm connected through a hunched shoulder to the face with its witchy tangle of dark hair and eyes glaring like a cornered animal's. *Which she was*, he thought, looking down at the picture of Linda Tyler in the book. *Is. Only she's broken now.* When she'd been arrested last night, she finally rolled belly-up to him, pleading, those eyes that had been like the hard edges of knives now all soft and wet with tears.

His name was in the book's index, too—Kinross, Gerald, Det. Sgt.—with four page numbers listed after it, referring to one stage or another of the original investigation and arrests of the Wyle Group. The district attorney, who'd gone on to write his own book about the Group and was now on the City Council, had a whole column of numbers after his name. The disparity was satisfactory to Kinross. Police were meant to work in grim anonymity. As he still was working.

He tapped his finger on the flat image of Linda Tyler's face. *Got you, bitch*, he thought. *Got you at last.* He could taste the satisfaction in his mouth, like his own blood welling under his tongue.

She glared back at him from the black-and-white depths of the photo. There were other pictures of her in his files. Her and the others. And of their victims. Bedell had used some of them in the book. But the publishers, in their commercial wisdom, had left out the worst photos. The ones where it took the eye a moment to recognize that the thing in the center had been human. What there was left of it.

But not done yet, thought Kinross as he turned the page and the rest of the book's photo section. His eyes skimmed across the orderly crawl of words, not looking for anything new, anything that he hadn't written into memory long ago, but letting the old knowing stoke a fire under his belly.

There was still that fucker Tyler. And all the others. None of them had paid enough yet.

His hands stopped, pressing the book flatter against the table. He started to read.

. . . in the summer heat. What Detective Sergeant Kinross found underneath the swarming flies would have made most other men uncontrollably sick. But with characteristic professionalism, he made his way back up the ravine's side to the road and radioed a call, logged at the station at 12:47 P.M., for the coroner's team.

Later, when the pieces were finally disentangled from each other, Kinross would be credited with finding the sixth and seventh victims of the Wyle Group. The dental charts put together by the coroner's office would eventually identify Kim Nygren and Jeffrey Wallace, two more university students.

But on that summer afternoon, as Kinross watched the investigation team combing the bushes around the site, he had no way of knowing that there were five more to come, and that he himself would find number nine a mere five hundred yards from this spot. That was still a week away.

*In the meantime, on the campus, a pair of
jeans spattered with blood and grass stains lay
wrapped around a Case knife with a freshly
nicked blade, at the bottom of the trash dumpster
behind the Sciences Building. If the Mac-D Rec-
lamation Company, which had the contract for
disposing of the university's rubbish, had picked
up on Friday as usual, the jeans and the knife
inside them would have disappeared the next
day into one of the county's landfill sites. But
Friday that week fell on the Fourth of July; the
trash pickup was made on the Thursday before
to allow the men on the route the holiday off;
and the red-stained bundle was still there until
next week, waiting to be found. . . .*

Kinross nodded in satisfaction over the book. That
had nailed them; the knife and the jeans had been the
tiny thread-end that had unraveled the whole thing.
Naturally, a bunch of snotty university types wouldn't
have thought of the garbage men taking the Fourth
of July off. Even before they had gotten into that
Host shit, and the drug had convinced them that they
were all little tin gods with the power of life and
death over mere mortals, they had probably thought
that anybody without a set of initials behind his name
was just some drudge to haul away their dirty laundry. That was what the real world and everybody in
it was for, to wipe their asses with. If they had been
able to tell what day it was at that point, Wyle and all
his disciples would probably have sneered at the
corny middle-class hokum of the Fourth; they had
had their own little rituals to attend to.

That's what you get, thought Kinross, *for shitting
on the real world*. The real world would, inevitably,

find a way to pay you back. Simple justice: if you left things that had once been human beings on a hillside where stray dogs could nuzzle the loops of uncoiled intestines and flies could hollow a nineteen-year-old girl's cheek until the sun-dried face looked like a melon left too long in the field—then you belonged to the real world, and not to the ivory tower you and your friends had built around your almighty guru. And to the machineries of that world's justice, the police and the courts and the prisons where you weren't put to death anymore, the way rabid animals were mercifully dispatched, but left alive so you could spend a long time thinking, nothing but thinking. About the real world.

And when that machinery screwed up, when the smart-ass lawyers finally poured enough grit and sand out of their fat, heavy books and into the fine-tuned workings of the court's gears? And psychiatrists with four-hundred-dollar suits that they paid for by going from courtroom to courtroom and explaining how murder wasn't murder, death wasn't death (*then what was that thing that smelled like the back of a butcher shop and was covered black with flies and he could still taste his own vomit, held at the back of his throat, thinking about it*) and the payback for what they had done was more drugs, handed out as medicine in nice cozy mental wards. Drugs that kept you from thinking about what you had done.

And if you were one of the lucky ones, whose lawyers were clever enough to convince the old fool of a judge that you hadn't really done any of those nasty things, you had just seen them being done by the others, and then had just helped your friends by keeping your mouth shut about the bodies rotting on the hillsides and in the trunk of the Volvo parked in the campus lot and stuffing a denim-wrapped knife in a dumpster and all the other little deeds that had wrapped the Wyle Group around itself for protection . . . until the rotting things stank too bad and couldn't be hidden any longer . . .

If you were one of the lucky ones, you could talk and talk in your cozy hospital room about all the interesting things you had seen, and let some fat-butt writer get it all down so he could put it into a book. That everybody would read, because nothing was more interesting than a carefully extracted heart rolled down into a gully like a red softball. And after the helpful psychiatrists said you were cured, and you were let out after a quick two years, then there would be a nice pile of money waiting for you—

What kind of payback was that?

Kinross closed the book and squeezed it in his hands, as if he could crumple it into a wad of ink and paper, small enough to fit into his fist.

The noise of the mower and other equipment was farther down the street. The gardener was tending some other residence on his route through the green and manicured, rolling suburban streets. Bedell lay on his back on the carpet, listening to the distant racket of the little gas-powered motors, holding his working copy of the book at arm's length over his head. The only book that mattered. *From whence all money flows*, he reminded himself from time to time. Or had flowed; that had been another time, which he had thought would never end.

Still the favorite child, though. Not that there were many other books by him with which to compare it. He looked up at the neat rows of words above him, his own words that he had marched onto the pages out of the chaos of tape recordings, interviews, police reports, newspaper morgues . . . He knew he looked, if someone outside peered through the curtains at this moment, like a parody of a traditional daddy-and-baby snapshot, dandling the beloved offspring aloft.

More likely, he thought, as if standing in the doorway to watch his own silly behavior, *shaking it to see if any more money falls out*. If they knew the state of his finances, that's what they'd think. *And they'd be right*—he gazed up at the words, which he'd written, and read and reread so many times, as if there were some new, unnoticed secret that could be spelled out of them.

The phone rang, cutting through the overlay of the gardener's noise. Bedell rolled onto his side, listening to his own voice on the answering machine's cassette reel off the canned words. The edge of his belt buckle dug into the soft roll of his stomach, as he raised his hand over the phone, ready to pick it off its place on the bookshelves.

"Alan? You there?"

The voice on the other end sounded worried. Or annoyed; maybe that was it. Bedell pulled himself up, leaning back against the wall. The fuzzy distance that three fingers of scotch had put between himself and everything beyond the drawn curtains slid the phone from his hand; he had to pin it against the carpet before he could get it to his ear. "Yeah, right. I'm here. What's up?"

"That's what I'm asking *you*." His agent, the one who'd taken over last year from Barry Ephrem, after the *Esquire* assignment fiasco and all the hard words that had followed. Bedell fumbled in his memory for the name—Jeff something or other. That was it.

Some wise-ass kid. "Did you talk to that Tyler character?"

Shit—Bedell twisted the phone against his ear to look at his watch. Two P.M.; so five P.M. in New York. He'd told the agent this morning, getting up before eight to make the call while the long-distance rates were still low, that he'd get back with Tyler's agreement to the proposal this afternoon.

"Yeah . . . yeah, I did." He rubbed his forehead, as though trying to massage the sluggish blood inside into motion. "He sounded . . . interested."

"How interested?" A definite trace of annoyance filtered across the line, all the way through the wire and electronics from New York. The note of strained patience, carefully held back. *You little shithead*, thought Bedell.

Time. That was what was needed: time and money. Bedell tilted his head down with the phone, turning away from the curtained window, as though concealing his words from someone listening there. "He's hot on the idea. Very hot. The guy's got a lot to say. About his ex-wife, and everything. I think he's going to do it."

"When's he gonna let you know?" The agent's voice pressed against his ear. "We gotta have a definite on this if we're going to line this deal up."

"He's thinking about it." *Don't push me, man.* "He needs a little time." *Time . . .*

"Maybe I should talk to him? We just want a straight business arrangement with the guy. That's my job."

No no no no. His own voice shrilled inside his head. He had to stay in the middle, between Tyler and anybody else; after that fuckup last year, any business agreement reached could also reasonably exclude him. Easy enough for this little bastard to throw him over, put together a deal for some other writer (*who could be depended upon—shut up shut up*). They were like that; no faith in you at all, to weather through the hard parts. Take their 10 percent and split, just when you need them the most—like that fucker Ephrem. For a moment Bedell saw before him his old agent's lean, gray-sideburned face above the perfectly knotted tie, the collar with its discreet points of gold (*which my money paid for*): in the corner booth of the New York bar after the *Esquire* and the Knopf editors had got up and left, taking with them all their deals and money. He saw Ephrem shaking his gray head, sadly, over the thin sheaf of pages, the product of one night's frantic work, coffee until his hands had trembled against the Selectric's keys; the tail end of six weeks staring at the blank paper in the machine, drinking and not drinking having equal results.

"Well?" The new agent's voice at his ear brought him back, dispersing the memory track. He realized he'd let seconds—how many?—of not talking indict him over the long-distance line. "Should I get hold of him?" asked the agent.

"No. No—I don't think that's a good idea." Bedell's tongue moistened his dry lips. "Tyler's kind of a, a difficult character. But I know him, right? I can work with him. I can handle him."

A distant sigh. "Look. Try to get him nailed down as soon as possible." The voice did a parody of patience, signaling the opposite. "That woman getting arrested has brought the whole Wyle stuff back into national news. We're not going to be the only ones shopping some proposal around to the publishers."

An edge of good news there; Bedell's mind clicked

over, calculating. The Wyle Group being in the papers and magazines again might revive sales of the first book. Even so, the money wouldn't show up in the publisher's royalties reports until six months or a year from now; far too late, given his present hemorrhaged condition. *Time. Time and money*.

Forget that. The thing to do, at this moment in real time, with the phone clamped to his ear, was to keep this snotty little agent working for him. Instead of stealing the new book idea—*Fuckers! They're all that way!*—and putting it together with some other guy. And to keep Tyler, and through him Linda, under wraps, his exclusive material to hammer at the typewriter like a forge, into a new book, new money. That was what had to be done. To keep the whole thing from slipping away from underneath his fingers.

"I'll get back to you, man." He moistened his lips again, his tongue tasting the trickle of salt sweat at the corner of his mouth. "Soon as I know. Probably tomorrow."

"I hope so." The agent hung up.

You little shit. Bedell reached up to put the phone back into its cradle on the shelves. His other hand, he saw now, still held the copy of the red-jacketed book, one finger still holding his place in the middle. *INSIDE THE NIGHT. By J. Alan Bedell*. There were other copies of the book in the house, pristine, unopened, like a trophy in the glass-fronted cabinet he used to have across the room or stacked in the half-full cardboard carton in the closet of the bedroom he used as an office. But this was his reading copy, his working copy that he underlined and filled with marginal notes, all his ideas for squeezing another book out of the basic raw material of blood and murder. Rapidly fading into history, a period piece, pushed into the back of everybody's minds by the new murders, the new blood that came washing against them every day from the pages of their newspapers, out of the TV screens switched on to the news at six and eleven. Pushing him back there, too, with his book, his one lucky break of being at the right place at the right time, sinking in that red ocean like a raft beneath him.

All those scribbled ideas, slanting alongside the printed words, amounted to nothing. Compared to a hook like Linda being found and arrested. And having the exclusive line on her through her ex-husband, Tyler. Bedell had already heard that she was asking for him. The real key into that spooky cave of her mind.

He opened the book on the carpet before him. Like a lucky omen, Tyler's name leaped up at him. *I got him*, he thought, the scotch's afterburn firing into exultation. *I got him before, squeezed him right down into words on a page. He's mine. Always mine.*

Leaning over the book, he started to read.

. . . interesting problem. For the prosecution team to have split so profoundly, this late in the trial, over basic questions of strategy, indicated the confused legal territory on which they were walking. What to do in regard to some of the Wyle Group members was obvious: in the cases of Paula Josephson and Dennis Meyer, where the hard forensic evidence connected them directly with the killings, the prosecution went on pressing the multiple-murder charges. Wyle himself, before lapsing into an arrogant silence, had made no denial of having instigated the crimes. Beyond that, from the dovetailing testimony of

the other Group members, it was clear that he had been at the site of at least six of the killings, either during or shortly after the events. All of the killings had been reported and described to him; his manifesto-like Ikon Anarchos, unfinished at the time of his arrest, confirmed this. The ragged typescript was now one of the prosecution's main exhibits in the trial.

But what of Tyler and the other Group members, who had been able to demonstrate their awareness of the killings, had even confessed to knowing about them—yet whose knowledge of the crimes could only be explained by the alleged "shared mind" effect created by the Host drug? If the prosecution team denied the existence of the shared mind, they would be forced to come up with some other explanation for how various Group members, some at a distance of over two thousand miles, knew the minutest details of the killings, as they happened. In the cases of Bonnie Rees, flying back from Boston at the time of the Delahay murder, and Glenn Williamson, at the university dig site in the Yucatán peninsula during the Nygren/Wallace/Bowers spree, even the remote possibility of telephoned descriptions of the killings was ruled out. Yet, in the carefully dated "contact diaries" that they and all the other Group members kept, and which the prosecution team had also entered as evidence, details as small as the plastic-capped safety pin that Kim Nygren's sister had given her for the temporary repair of her bra strap had been duly noted.

The other half of the double bind that the prosecution attorneys found themselves in was

just as bad. If they admitted the defense's argu-
ment about the existence of the shared mind,
they opened a Pandora's box of psychiatric
testimony about the Host drug's effects. Dimin-
ished capacity, temporary insanity, the whole
quagmire. The arguments raged through the night
in Welbeck's office and in Judge Bellamy's cham-
bers. Could the concept of criminal conspiracy—
"combining or acting together"—be maintained
when the only way to demonstrate the defen-
dants' shared knowledge of the crimes would
also admit the existence of a single mentality
behind the crimes, acting through, rather than
with, the individuals involved?

In the end, as so often with cases bogging
down under their own complexity, compromise
was seen as the wisest choice. The district attor-
ney, facing a rigorous reelection campaign, could
ill afford either the majority of the Wyle Group
being found not guilty on the various psychiatric
grounds, or a lengthy and costly retrial during
the current county budget crisis. The initial con-
tact that led to the opening of the plea-bargaining
process came from Welbeck's office in the form
of a handwritten note, early on Monday morn-
ing, the 21st. . . .

The drug; it always came down to the drug. Bedell
sat cross-legged on the living room carpet, the book
in his lap, as he massaged the back of his neck. *What
the Host taketh,* he thought, *the Host giveth back as
an alibi.* Lucky for Tyler; he and the others had
found themselves in the deepest of deep shit, way
over their little university-educated heads. And what

had gotten them in, got them out. The Host. It all got blamed on the drug. *The Devil made me do it—honest.*

And lucky for him, too. Bedell nodded to himself, stroking the book's slick dustcover. The whole "shared mind" business had lifted the Wyle Group murders from the status of faded Charles Manson–LSD–Sharon Tate's baby reruns, good for a fast fade in *Time*— more wacky doings in wacky Southern California— into something different. A new angle: something to justify the great book-buying public's perennial interest in knives and dismembered torsos. For them as well, the Host was an excuse.

No wonder the Wyle Group had worshiped the substance, made it their sacrament. The blasphemous pun of the name they gave it: Holy Communion echoes from Wyle's own Roman Catholic childhood, mixed with the figure they all claimed to have seen, which smiled and welcomed them into the transfigured night. The hallucinatory image they also called the Host.

What must it have been like? In all his research for the book, all the long hours of interviewing Tyler and any of the other Group members who would talk, he had come as close as words could take him. But no further; the final secrets were still locked up inside their heads.

He spread the book flat on the carpet, bending over it again. Back to the section in the first half, where the pages opened on their own.

. . . remarkable similarity. Even though no contact had ever been shown to have occurred between any of the enlisted men in the original army study of the drug and any Wyle Group member, descriptions of the hallucinatory figure

*experienced by those exposed to the drug over-
lap in significant detail. The enlisted men and
the Wyle Group came to identify this characteristic manlike image with the drug itself, referring to the figure as the drug's "spirit" or
"guardian," in a manner similar to the hallucinated "Mescalito" figure reported by Carlos
Castaneda and others writing about the use of
peyote. The Wyle Group regarded the appearance of this figure—"the Host"—to an individual as a sign that the drug had in some way
accepted the person, thus not only providing
access to the "shared mind" effect but also
opening up an entire transformed world to the
person.*

*Descriptions of the Host image invariably made
reference to the animal-like pointed teeth of the
figure, generally bared in a smile, and its im-
pressively dark eyes. The nighttime was associated with the Host, its spectral appearances
generally occurring as distortions in the visual
field triggered by the absence of light. . . .*

Bedell lay back on the carpet, resting the book on
his chest. Even now, after all this time, the words
fascinated him. His own words, describing something he had never seen. But he could imagine it;
they had all told him so much about it. The Host.

Fascinating—and scary, with that thin edge of danger and dark, dark secrets. A whole secret world,
overlaying this one, that Tyler and the others had
moved around in. He felt the sharp pang of his envy
at the base of his stomach. *The lucky shits*. Even
when they had been sitting in their cells, leaning
toward his cassette recorder microphone, after the

blood had finally seeped through the numbness and their voices had cracked around the bleak recital of what they had seen . . . Even then, he had been able to detect the little note of awe and mystery when he pressed them for more about the Host, the drug and the figure out of the night; silence, and a distant gaze that looked beyond him and, past the jail corridors, to a point beyond his reach. Beyond the reach of anyone who hadn't been in there with them, in the Host's world.

He opened his eyes and flipped back to the book's photo section. To the scariest and most fascinating picture of all. Lifting his head from the carpet, he gazed at it. Not a reproduction of a photograph, but of a piece of paper with a crude drawing on it. The only thing found in Dennis Meyer's cell except for his own body dangling by the neck from the knotted rope of his clothes.

With his finger, Bedell traced the outline of the image in the picture. Something like a man, thin and spectral, the trunk and limbs barely wider than a child's stick figure. The face was only two jagged lines, the points of its grinning teeth, and the two circles of its eyes, drawn so black that the pencil point had torn holes in the paper.

Poor Meyer, thought Bedell. In a file cabinet drawer he still had the cassette of his last talk with him, the shaking voice claiming that *he* hadn't killed them, it had been the Host whose sharp-pointed teeth had torn apart the bodies . . .

The others hadn't said anything when Bedell had repeated Meyer's words to them. Just looked away, silent. They had their little secrets.

So did he. That he hadn't put in the book or told the police. Something else that Meyer had told him, that had sent him out in the middle of the night when nobody could see what he was doing. He had driven out to the hillside in the range at the city's edge and found the piled-up stones, and had dug up the Thermos bottle beneath. Had taken it home, here, unscrewed the cap, and pulled out the rolled-up plastic bag from inside. Onto his palm he had shaken out the six clear capsules with the white powder inside, the Group's holy sacrament, hidden before the arrests had come down.

The night world that the Host stood guard over, concealing its mysteries, had lain in his hand, almost weightless. Then, carefully, he had hidden them again. His little secret.

Those smug bastards. Tyler the worst of them. He knew they despised him, deep down, all of them. They despised everybody who wasn't in on it, their private world. Even after it had all come crashing down around them; they still had something nobody else could have, nobody else could get into.

But I could, he thought, sprawling out on the carpet. *Anytime I wanted to. Easy enough*. They didn't know; they were all so fucking smart, but they didn't know that. Anytime. And then he wouldn't be on the outside any longer, waiting for a jerk like Tyler to call him back. He'd be on the inside, at last.

That'd make a hell of a book. The ultimate in research; no goddamn Mailer or Capote could claim to have to have gotten *that* far inside a criminal's mind.

He smiled at the thought, until he closed his eyes and saw, against his eyelids, the scrawled figure with its teeth and dark eyes.

* * *

. . . triggered by the absence of light . . .

Tyler closed the book, holding his place with his finger. There was no need, never as long as memory lasted, for him to look at the photos at the center or read the words surrounding them. They were all, like the drug, bonded to his central nervous system. The medications he took were as much to keep the past at bay as to keep the drug's symptoms—the bitter taste in his mouth, the blue light edging objects in the night, the excitement ticking the blood faster in his veins—from seeping back out of his contaminated bloodstream.

And the final symptom, the sight that would mean that he had been pulled into that other world. The sight of a smiling face, the teeth sharp points below the dark eyes, dark enough to fall into, and never come up again. The Host welcoming you, a long-lost friend, a blood relative, flesh of His flesh.

Triggered by the absence of light. That about summed it up. The final diagnosis: the past was a substance that, once it had touched you, the rest of your life was spent taking the medicine that would keep it from coming back. If any medicine could.

He pulled his finger out of the book and laid it on the coffee table. He'd had enough. Still bright outside, the day working its slow progress through the sunlight. Hours to go before he had to do anything, drive over to the day-care center and pick up Eddie, have him here for Steff before he went down to open up the theatre. The small details of life, such as it was. That's what the pills and capsules, four times daily, were for: to keep it that way.

Plenty of time. Hours and hours of it. Time enough to call back the lawyer and set up a little appointment. A little piece of the past. Just enough to prove that you weren't afraid of it, afraid of the dark anymore.

He pushed himself up from the couch and went into the kitchen. Taking the phone from its hook, he started to dial.

FIVE

Eddie was up and dressed, ready for the day-care center, ahead of schedule. Enough time for his mother and Tyler to have their morning coffee together. Few words spoken; Tyler's gaze shifted alternately between the brown depths of his cup and the living room's far window. In his fingers he rolled the crumpled ball of aluminum foil that had held his morning dosage, carefully sorted out and wrapped up the night before to prevent any mistake in the bleary hour when he first awoke, the aftereffects of the previous day's chemicals filtering through his system.

The silence was no affront to Steff. She knew what was on his mind: what appointment he would keep today, who he would see. After he had told her about it, it had gone undiscussed, if unforgotten, all through Saturday and Sunday. Enough that he was this far out of the past's hold, to sit here with her at all. She watched Eddie running a plastic truck along the top of the sofa.

Tyler looked up when the buzzer sounded from the front gate of the apartment building. "That's him, I suppose. See anything?" he called to the other room.

Eddie was at the window, where he had a clear shot at the driveway between the buildings. He drew his nose back from the glass. "Just a BMW. That's all."

" 'Just a BMW,' " said Steff. "I like that." Her son had a spotter's eye for cars, aided and abetted by Tyler. The two of them had a favorite drive, down Santa Monica Boulevard toward Century City. Past the Rolls-Royce repair shop—oddly tacky and greasy-looking to her—and the edge of Beverly Hills where they sometimes spotted a particular red and black Lamborghini, slinking down like some exotic preda-tor from the hills above the city. That being one of the cultural advantages of living in West Hollywood: the constant smell of money.

"A definite note of disappointment," agreed Tyler. He drained his cup and carried it to the sink. "Give the guy a break," he called to Eddie. "He's probably only a junior associate; they get issued their cars with their three-piece suits."

Steff followed him to the living room. "So how long's this supposed to take?" she asked as she watched him pulling on his coat.

Tyler grimaced sourly. "Believe me," he said, "not very long. I don't know what *she's* got to say to me. But I don't have anything to say to *her*."

"Who?" Eddie, truck in hand, looked up from between them.

"Nobody. Somebody Mike used to know." She reached down and pushed him in the direction of the bedrooms. "Go get your jacket."

The gate buzzer sounded again. Tyler waved it off. "Let him wait. I'm doing him a favor. What's the schedule today?"

Her classes, wedged in around the different shifts at the restaurant, required a military precision to pull everything off. Not Mike's fault if he couldn't keep

them straight; she had a hard enough time herself.
"I'm dropping Eddie off and going straight over to
the college." She nodded her head at the textbooks
on the coffee table; four black plastic wheels from the
toy truck were scattered across them. "And then I'm
going to take the afternoon shift. I just wanted to
make sure you'd be back in time to pick up Eddie
from day-care."

"Yeah, no problem. Back in plenty of time. Believe me."

She kissed him at the door and watched as he
descended the steps to the front gate. She felt her son
push into the space beside her. "Where's Mike
going?" he asked.

"Never you mind. You know where *you're* going."
She looked down. "What did you do with your
shoes?"

"I want you to know I appreciate this." Silberman
had on his sincerest manner. He radiated it like a heat
lamp. Tyler kept his shades on, as much to shut out
the serious expression as against the bright sunlight.
"I'm glad you made the time for it."

Tyler shrugged, leaning back against the car's seat.
"I just like going for rides in German iron. You
know? It's so smooth." The lawyer's smooth demeanor
irritated him. It brought out his own bad attitude. "I
used to know this little punk chick, right after I got
out, and she loved driving around in Mercedes. But
she couldn't stand the square way they looked. So
she had her daddy buy her one, and then she and her
friends beat up the outside with sledgehammers. Until it looked like it was made out of old toast. And
they all went cruising down Sunset like that."

Silberman looked at him for a moment, then went

on steering the BMW through traffic, heading for the nearest freeway onramp. Tyler noticed that he had a stash of Doors cassettes in the bin underneath the dashboard stereo. *Ah, the man's a classicist*, he thought, nodding a silent approval. *Into the primeval L.A.*

"Linda's family appreciates it as well."

He tilted his face against the headrest to study the young lawyer. "What's that mean?" The thought of his former in-laws triggered a certain wariness.

Now it was the lawyer's turn to be cool. He one-handed the car around a corner. "Doesn't mean anything," he said. "Just that Mr. Mueller is a man who knows how to show his gratitude."

"Really?" The last time Tyler had encountered Linda's father, the gray-haired magnate of parking lots, and any other way of converting inherited Southern California acreage into money to pile on top of more money, he had been brandishing a corny silver-headed cane in the corridors of the Los Angeles Superior Court. That being the emblem of wealth and power he had picked up from a childhood of B movies, the store from which so many of his generation had furnished their interior lives. Brandishing it, and swearing—more melodrama—to make sure Tyler wound up in the deepest, darkest corner of the state penal system. There to be buggered into abject contrition over what Tyler had done to the old man's fair, innocent daughter. Until Mueller's lawyers had had to pull the shouting, red-faced old man away.

"And what, say, is Mr. Mueller's gratitude worth?" Tyler rested his arm along the windowsill, letting the warm L.A. air flow up to his shoulder.

Silberman shrugged. "Well, I don't really think we're talking money here. I don't think that's appropriate in this situation. And you don't really need it, do you? Let's just say that Mr. Mueller is a good person to have in your corner. Say, if anything happened. Where you got into trouble or something. Very handy to know someone like that.''

Well, you little shyster. Tyler regarded the lawyer's profile, eyes straight on to the traffic ahead. The nature of business had come out at last. "Don't screw with me, jack. I've gone through a lot rougher school than you ever did, learning about how threats are made." The lawyer's gaze darted over to him. "What's old Mueller going to do if I don't cooperate? Get my parole yanked or something?"

"Nobody's threatening you, Mr. Tyler." The lawyer's voice stayed smooth. "But you know how things can happen.''

"Things don't 'happen.' They're made to happen. That's what I know. And you or Mueller or anybody, you got no handle on my parole. I'm a clean sonofabitch, Silberman." *You're a tame rat now.* "It's what I know how to do best.''

Silence for a few seconds between them, then: "Just as long as we understand each other, Tyler." A simple, cold announcement.

"Oh, we do. Believe me." The adrenaline sparked into his bloodstream by the words, his own as well as the other's, diluted the medications in his body. Just enough so that the L.A. street scene the car passed through, tinted dark by his sunglasses, vibrated with an electric blue edge around the buildings. The last stretch of Sunset before turning up to the freeway; one of the hookers, at the end of her night's prowl at her corner station or just starting a morning's work, turned to inspect them, as she did with every car that went past. For a moment Tyler saw a face from memory, no longer female or even human, grinning at him with pointed teeth. Then, as fast, it was the blank, bored mask of lipstick and mascara, the studied doll's face that anyone else saw.

He tilted his head back; in the corner of the rearview mirror she could be seen receding on the sidewalk. Already looking away, toward the next car sliding toward her.

They drove the rest of the way to the women's detention center in silence.

After being searched—more thoroughly in Tyler's case; they knew who he was—he sat waiting in one of the little rooms at the front of the building. The institutional beige paint on the walls and the plastic-molded chairs bolted to the floor were all familiar to him. He had done his voyage through this compartmented world, absorbed it, made it part of himself. The same room, like the others beyond it in hospitals and every other kind of lockup, was a windowless space underneath his heart. Where the regulation clock high on the wall, white face in black circle, ticked on without relation to time outside.

He had learned to wait in rooms like this. That had been the major lesson of his time inside.

Silberman came back into the room, the door pushed open by a policewoman with a key running on a lanyard to her belt. She closed the door after the lawyer stepped through.

"Linda wants to see you by yourself."

Tyler looked up at him. "Does she?" He smiled. "That's very willful of her. You're in for a fun time, working on this one."

"I'll want to know what she tells you," said Silberman.

"Don't worry." Tyler pushed himself up from the hard plastic chair. "Her father's paid enough to get me in here this far—I'll give you a complete report."

The same policewoman on the other side of the door led him to another room identical to the first, except for a table and two chairs in the middle. A few minutes waiting, and he heard the policewoman's footsteps returning down the hall, with another set echoing out of rhythm. The door swung open; he looked up and saw his ex-wife.

"Please keep your hands up on the table." The policewoman sat down in the solitary chair by the door, equidistant from Tyler and Linda on opposite sides of the table, and became part of the room's sparse furniture.

Her hair was shorter than when he had seen her last, years ago. Then it had reached down to the middle of her back. Now it was pulled into a short ponytail held by a plain elastic band. Even a few thin lines of gray near the temples. No makeup; he could see straight through to how much older she had become. *And what do you think you look like? We went into it all as nothing but kids, and this is how we came out. If we ever did get out.*

"Hello, Linda." His hands lay flat, unmoving on the table, a distance of blond wood between them and hers.

She plucked nervously at a thread hanging from the cuff of the faded, standard-issue blue blouse. "Michael—you've got to listen."

Inside himself, he felt the small room like this one, with the clock going through its meaningless cycles on the wall, fall into a deeper silence. And all the other rooms beyond the blank walls; nothing spoken, nothing heard. Because he could see in the dark centers of her eyes, as she leaned across the table toward him, that she was still there, in that mute space. Had never left. She was the one who had skipped; he had gone to prison and the hospital along with the others. And he and some of the others had eventually found their way out. She had vanished on the eve of the trials, and hadn't gone in. And she was still in there, in that timeless room. The dark spaces under the lashes were observation slots into that chamber; he could see in, but she couldn't see out. He wondered if she saw anything at all, to what fragment of the past, fringed with electric blue, she was talking.

From somewhere in his own memory, Tyler heard Wyle's voice speaking. A lecture, to one of his little groups of disciples; before things had slid down into blood. Quoting Jung, one of the few relics from psychology's past to have escaped Wyle's withering, incendiary disdain. Something about schizophrenia: *. . . and from that point on, no new thing enters the mind.*

He studied his spread-out hands for a moment, then looked back up at her. "Listen to what?" Already, as if no years lay between, they were back on the line that would always run between them.

"*Slide took Bryan.*" Her fingers arched, the tips digging futilely at the varnished wooden surface. "Where I was living—where they found me—Slide got in and took him. He's got our baby."

Tyler leaned back, watching the tears that had begun to well in Linda's eyes. She lowered her head, the palm of one hand pressing at her cheekbone as if to keep the face from dissolving into pieces.

The one word, the name, had dropped another fragment of the past in front of him. He could see the face, with its smile pleased with his own cleverness, and the eyes bright as some enameled metal. Slide had been the only other Wyle Group member, besides Linda, to have disappeared, slipped out of the legal net tightening around them all. Gone to ground, as though he were some ferretlike animal with its secret burrows and tunnels beneath the dull earth's surface. Which had always seemed somehow appropriate to Tyler, when he'd thought about it while lying on some prison bunk or hospital bed. Slide had been the Group's link to the dark, spooky world of drugs and money and the people who changed each into the other. Not some academic jerk, teaching university courses and hankering after a little latter-day consciousness expansion like an affair with some fresh-faced student crossing her legs in the front row of class. Slide had brought with him the chill air of a different world, thinner and harsher. He'd known what to do when the bottom had fallen out of their little playpen, soaked with blood; trouble with police was nothing new to him, not like these poor campus types in over their heads; he'd simply faded back into that dark, hard world he'd come out of.

And now here was Linda, saying that Slide had their son. The ferret had crept into the nest and stolen the small, fragile hatchling. He studied the weeping figure across the table from him. "How do you know it was Slide?"

"He—he called me." The eyes, now reddened and damp, looked up at him. "On the phone. *It was him.* He said he took Bryan, and he told me to look, and he was gone. Bryan's gone. And he just went on laughing. Slide just kept laughing."

The words had come out like dead snippets of tape, pieced together into a cracking voice. *She's*

hysterical, realized Tyler. *But they gave her something*.
The screaming, and the flailing until her small fists
had spattered blood against the concrete walls of
some holding room, had all taken place last night.
And had been taken care of by the competent, efficient policewomen working as guards, taken care of
with the soft flannel ties at each wrist and ankle. It
was the usual policy, as Tyler had had enough occasion to observe, to let someone scream it all out,
until exhaustion provided a certain anesthesia. But a
father such as Linda had could get a private doctor
in, and the comfort of a needle and subsequent pills
sent over to the detention center's nurse station.

He knew that the words were being screamed at
him, that inside her skull the fists were still beating
the red staccato message about a lost child. Only the
chemicals in her bloodstream kept the words soft and
understandable, kept the soft ties off her wrists, and
inside in her head where they were the most effec-
tive. *Blessed be the chemicals, that give the appearance of sanity, when it would be saner to scream,
and go on screaming*. The thought of his own tinged
blood produced a small, mirthless smile. He was
long past screaming—that was in those dark years
behind him—but still the chemicals kept the wolf
(*that face with the longer, sharper teeth, that devour-
ing smile*) from his own mind.

"Bryan's with Slide, then."

She nodded in her insulated misery.

He felt the room inside himself go cold, as though
the icebound mass of his heart had touched its walls.
"What do you want me to do about it?" he said
quietly.

"He's your *son*." Linda's voice broke, pleading.
"Our baby—I know, I know, I know . . ." The tears

started again. "I know I took him, you haven't had him or seen him, all this time . . . I was going to let you know, tell you where I was, but I was afraid they'd find me . . . But still—"

Tyler stood up, shoving the chair back, and leaned across the table. The policewoman by the door started to rise, then stopped, watching them intently. His voice dropped even lower: "I'll do what has to be done. Linda—you know that, don't you?"

She nodded dumbly.

"Okay, there's another man who's going to come back later and talk to you. His name's Silberman; he's your lawyer. All right? You understand? You do whatever he says, and you tell him whatever he wants to know. Okay?"

Another nod. "Michael—"

The cold had filled the small room inside, and the one that held them, and all the ones beyond. His fury could have sent the flat of his hand against the crying woman's face and sent her sprawling across the floor. Instead, he pushed himself away from the table and toward the door.

"What did she say?" Silberman stood up from one of the waiting room chairs.

Tyler jabbed one finger into the lawyer's collarbone, just beneath the perfect silk knot. "Look, fucker." He pressed the finger in harder, forcing the other back a step. "You get me out of here, and then you can come back, and you won't have any more problems with her. But I don't want to see you or hear from you again. Got it?"

Silberman studied him for a moment before nodding. "All right," he said. "But you're only throwing away your own advantage. Linda's father—"

"Fuck you. And Mueller." Tyler pushed past him,

heading for the next set of doors that led out to the
parking lot.

She came out of the building and saw him waiting
for her. When the anatomy class ended, Steff had
fifteen minutes to eat the carton of yogurt she'd
brought with her, and get a plastic cup of coffee from
the vending machines that lined the quad area, to
brace herself for the ninety-minute lab grind ahead.
But straight through the bodies of the other students
rushing or dawdling across the concrete space, she
spotted Michael sitting on the low edge of one of the
planters, leaning forward with elbows at his knees.
Watching with brick-wall patience for her to emerge.
He stood up as she came over to him.

"What are you doing here?" Steff hadn't even
known that he was aware enough of her class schedule to find her. Maybe he had tracked her down, and
lain in wait, by some animal instinct. The grim set of
his face worried her.

"I got done early," he said. "With her." He
didn't have to say the name; there was only one
possible.

"How'd it go?" She shifted the weight of her
books in front of herself.

"Oh, it went fine. Just fine." Around them, the
students milled and flowed, their laughing conversa-
tions a backdrop to the bitterness of Michael's low
voice. "She told me all sorts of interesting things."
At the center of his eyes was a darkness that held
her gaze; the voices and laughter surrounding them
faded from her hearing.

Steff said nothing, waiting. From the corner of her
eye she saw him rolling an aluminum foil packet in
his fingers. The shapes of the capsules inside could

be seen, though it was already past noon and the clockwork ritual of his swallowing them.

"You want to know what she said to me? You'll love it."

"Mike—" The sharp edge of the anger that had leaped, uncoiled from the bitter voice, pushed her back a step.

He grabbed her arm, gripping it tightly above the elbow. "Come on. I've got something to show you."

She made no protest about the rest of her classes as he pulled her out to the street at the edge of the campus. This was the worst she had ever seen him; the things that she knew he kept bottled inside himself had burst out through a crack in the rigid wall. The fright that she felt was kept pace by the worry, keeping her from wrenching her arm free of his grasp and running back to the crowded security of people and noise.

A parking ticket had been slid under the Chevy's windshield wiper. Michael yanked it out and threw it away before pushing her into the car. A moment later, he was jabbing through the lunch-hour traffic.

"You know what she told me?" he demanded again. He braked, swung viciously into a gap in the next lane, and sped up.

She shook her head, keeping the books up to her breast like a shield between them.

"I used to have a little boy." Michael held her gaze, uncaring of the traffic. "You didn't know that, did you?"

"I—I don't know." She couldn't remember, couldn't summon the knowledge from her brain. He'd never talked about, never said anything about a child. But something . . . something about the way he looked at her own Eddie, in moments when he was silent and brooding, unaware of her watching him from the light slanting out of the kitchen doorway . . . Maybe she had known. But she had kept from asking, from finding out any more than she already did about loss and pain.

"Just a baby." His gaze went back to the hurtling shapes beyond the windshield. "Named him Bryan, after my grandfather. Linda told me she's had him all this time, with her while she's been hiding. What do you think of that?"

Steff kept silent, watching him.

He leveled his gaze across the traffic he was cutting through, as if measuring each driver in a gunsight. "She told me that somebody took him. Somebody we used to know stole our son, kidnaped him, just before she was arrested. And now she wants me to find him and bring him back."

"Can you?" she said. "Can you find him?"

"Find him?" His laugh battered the inside of the car, forcing her against the door. "Of course I can find him! I know where he is—I've always known where he is."

He jerked the car over to the curb and slammed it to a halt, twisting the key in the ignition to kill the motor. The books spilled from her arms onto the floor as he dragged her across the seat toward the open door on his side.

"Mike—please. That hurts . . ."

He ignored her pleading as he pushed her along, grip digging deep into her arm. The traffic roared, streaming behind them. He pushed her through a wide stone gate framed by palm trees.

For a moment, in the quiet on the other side of the thick, high walls, she thought she was in a park somewhere in the middle of the city. The green manicured lawns stretched away to another gate at the far side. Outside the walls, the evenly spaced ranks of palm trees—old ones, so tall they bobbed wandlike against the sky—surrounded the block. Only the dimmest murmur of traffic penetrated.

She looked down at the grass at the edge of the curving path. Small rectangles of polished brass or marble dotted the green, with words engraved in them.

Near her, a metal cup, half sunk in the ground, held flowers, wilting in the dry air.

Michael dragged her a few yards farther, into the green quiet field, then let go of her. The shove of his hand sent her sprawling off the path. She pushed herself up from the grass.

In front of her a brass plate read BRYAN MARK TYLER. The year of birth and year of death were the same.

She twisted about and looked up at Michael. He stood above, shadow cast across her and the grave marker, his pulse visible at the corner of his temple. She couldn't tell if he saw her, or if his gaze stopped at any point above the small coffin in the ground below her.

SIX

After she put Eddie to bed, she came back out to the living room. Michael was still sitting in the dark, the thin blue light from the streetlamps outside slanting across the chair he had dragged over to the window.

"Steff—"

She turned at the sound of her name. Her shadow stretched from the kitchen doorway toward him. All evening she had gone back and forth from the kitchen to the bedrooms at the back of the apartment, zones of light, fixing dinner for her son and watching the little black-and-white TV on top of her dresser with him. The brooding quiet in the other room had seeped along the hallway, a dark radiating. Oppressing even Eddie's usual chatter, so that he'd buried his face in his pillow, turning from her good-night kiss.

"I'm sorry," said Michael. Only his hands were visible, pale in the blue light as they rested on the chair arms. She saw his face turn toward the window, the profile etched in cold silver. "I was all fucked up. From what she told me . . . and all the rest. It just sort of ticked something off. I really didn't know what I was doing."

She said nothing. The memory of the child's grave had lain across her sight, even when she'd looked down at her own child's head resting against her arm on the pillow. (*His son . . . His son is all cold. All night, in the dark grass, the black palms whispering outside the stone walls.*) Tired, she leaned her shoulder against the doorway, glancing for a moment at the unwashed dishes piled on the counter, then back to him. A sparkle of light on the floor beside him: a scrap of aluminum foil, empty and crumpled into a tiny ball, on top of a book, the red cover black in the darkness.

His voice sounded dead, as if the words had been measured out and cut long before. "If you want me to," he said, "I'll go. I don't want you to have to be worried. About something like that happening again."

For a moment she stood watching the figure sitting in the dark. Then she walked over and stood by him. Looking out the window, she could see an angle of the brighter lights, the backlit plastic bar signs and the traffic out on Santa Monica Boulevard. The cars slowed down for the light at Fairfax; it almost seemed as if she could see the faces inside, scanning intently across the sidewalks ahead for whatever they were seeking. The headlights opposite drained the faces of all color, giving them the appearance of long-toothed masks. She drew back, even though she knew no one could see her in the apartment's dark window, when a solitary face in a car turned in her direction.

She rested her hand on Michael's shoulder. "I'll think about it," she said.

He reached up and put his hand on top of hers. Already she knew what the answer would be. In here the darkness was for a moment; it could be dispelled with the switch on the wall. Outside, the traffic slid along the streets, unceasing, eyes and headlights peering into a dark that none of them wanted to end.

*　　　*　　　*

. . . received the news with an apparent lack of emotion. The guards in Tyler's wing of the jail initially took this as proof of sheer cold-bloodedness on his part. Only later, after he was granted permission to attend his son's funeral, and collapsed, still handcuffed and surrounded by four police officers, by the grave site, did the fact of the infant's death seem to penetrate the numbness. . . .

He set the book down in his lap. He hadn't been able to sleep; he'd left Steff curled up on her side of the bed, the brush of freckles underneath the strap of her thin cotton nightgown palely visible through the loose strands of her hair. Quietly, so as not to wake her or the sleeping child in the next room (*that other child would never wake*), Tyler had come out to the chair still left by the window overlooking the street.

The lamps outside were bright enough for him, tilting the book toward the blue radiance, to make out the lines of text. *What's that old song?* he thought. *Something, something about you don't need the light, their address can be read by the moon.* The first Leonard Cohen album, with that grim Jewish-Canadian face on the front cover doing its suffering-Christ imitation, and the lady in flames on the back. Which LP, for a time in the sixties, had been mandatory furniture in every hip collegiate apartment. Along with *Surrealistic Pillow* and Big Brother's *Cheap Thrills*, and among the more aggressively hip, *The Velvet Underground and Nico*, with the Andy Warhol banana peel still intact. All of which he'd had.

He rubbed his eyes. Reading in the dim light had stitched a salt thread under the lids. Though he'd left his watch on the table beside the bed, he knew it was well after 2 A.M.; the bar traffic along Santa Monica had ended, leaving the relative quiet of the cars heading for farther destinations. Whatever transactions, financial or carnal, that hadn't been completed on the street would have to wait until tomorrow night. The distant, steadily rolling traffic sounds lulled his heart quiet for a moment.

(*Other memories, connected only by the thread of the street. A gay friend of his announcing that, as he put it, he was "going to stop cruising for chicken" on Santa Monica Boulevard: "There's nothing you can say to them except 'Now you do me.' " Loneliness and AIDS, all they could possibly leave behind. The next time he ran into the guy, he'd bought a condo with a long-term lover, the traditional progress into gay middle-class respectability.*)

Tyler pushed the random thoughts out of his mind. Underneath, the memory of his ex-wife ticked away. In the past, years ago, and then less than twenty-four hours ago. The woman in the little room at the detention center was the same one he'd married back at the university. And had a child by. Bryan slept in his small grave tonight, as every night. But this night the child's mother, the woman he'd followed into madness (*led?—no, we went together, hand in hand*) no longer sang her lullabies to the baby she thought was still with her, still alive. (*What song?* He tried to remember a soft voice in another apartment, smaller than this, long ago. *Rock-a-bye . . . hush-a-bye . . .* He couldn't remember, couldn't bring it back.)

Into the madness, and then out of it, at least for some of them. Rudy Yates worked out of a Christian evangelist mission in Freeport, Kentucky; every Easter Tyler got a card from him, full of Bible-thumping messages, and no reference to the red past that lay between them. For a couple of years Tyler had derived a sour amusement at the thought of old Rudy, the Group's most scathing cynic, back in the sort of flock he'd always jeered at. Wyle's earliest books were to have been the final blow against all the old tyrannical superstitions—or so they'd all thought. Now Tyler wondered if what he felt, when the annual card with Jesus' face on it came in the spring, wasn't a certain melancholy envy.

And others, who had been at the fringes of the Group and had been only spattered, not immersed, with blood. But a few, like Linda and himself, who had gone all the way into the red core, and back out. All broken or changed in some way; no one came out the same as they went in; that wasn't possible. There was Bonnie Rees, still living here in L.A. (Most of the others, when they'd gotten out, from hospitals or prison, left for other places, where the goad of remorse would be hopefully duller.) He had two pictures in his mind of Bonnie: a long time ago, her stringy blond hair falling across a knife that had been handed to her, gazing at the wetness on the blade as though some revelation were written there. And the last time he'd seen her, behind the cash register at a small bookstore, with the eyes of a laboratory rat who had been given too many electric shocks to try going through the maze again.

Ken Ruhman worked in the Hollywood recording studios as a sound engineer. The Wyle Group, with its narcissistic video cameras and tape machines—which the district attorney had been so hot to get his hands on—had been a sort of job training for Ken. At least some small benefit, for someone, had come out of the business. He was the only one Tyler had seen much of; he had even, through his film industry

connections, gotten Tyler the job managing the run-
down, slated-for-demolition movie house—a bullshit
position that demanded few hours and paid almost
nothing, but kept his parole officer satisfied about his
having gainful employment and not just living off the
book money.

There were others. Tyler made no effort to keep
track of them. That was for people like Bedell, the
self-appointed historians of mass craziness.

Now Linda, the gap in that history, had reemerged.
Dragged out of the darkness she had disappeared
into by the LAPD. He had to hand it to them: they
had the true faith of cops, never giving up until the
job was done. Like the mill of the gods, grinding
slow but fine. *And not so slow, either*, thought Tyler.
They'd moved fast enough to throw everybody else's
ass in jail, when the time had come.

Out of the dark, but not out of the madness. Linda
was still in there. All these years, with a hallucinated
baby. Had she imagined Bryan growing up? Sending
him off to school someday? Tyler stared out the
window, his heart growing leaden in his chest. Maybe
the machinery of delusion had finally broken down
for her; there was no small boy in whatever hidey-
hole she had dug out for herself. And the wreckage
of one hallucination had spun out another, as hallucinations do. Calling upon the specter, old spooky
Slide, to crawl up out of the past as boogeyman and
steal the child away. Fairy-tale stuff, out of, perhaps,
the darker Hans Christian Andersen, the stories they
didn't let children read anymore. Plenty of blood and
craziness there. He watched the gray traffic rolling in
the distance.

That was what the medication kept him from, he
knew. That was why the capsules and pills were

locked and bolted down into daily ritual, the doses at their appointed hours. The darkness, and the going into it and never coming out . . .

A hallucinated child, stolen by a hallucinated kidnaper. That was the upshot of all of Wyle's fine theories, fine rhetoric against the conditioned bourgeois mind. The second delusion was the proof of the first; Bryan was gone, wasn't he? And Slide gets the blame. Tyler shook his head sadly. Slide was probably dead by now, or doing time in some Deep South prison under his real name, for some other crime—he'd had a soft cracker accent, amphetamine-eroded. A genuine professional criminal, not a wide-eyed naive ideologue like all the others Wyle had pulled into the game.

In his lap, the pages of the book were shading from the streetlamps' blue to steel gray. Dawn soon; the first traces filtering into the sky over the silent bars. He had sat by the window for hours, brooding on these sad things. About poor mad Linda, not because any trace of love for her was left—that had all been burned away—but from the simple grief for things lost in the dark.

He closed the book and, without switching on the light, carried it back to the hall closet. Lifting the stack of old papers, he slid it back into the box at the bottom. *Don't read it anymore*, he told himself. *Just forget*.

The door to Eddie's room was ajar; he pushed it open and looked in. A small shape curled under the covers . . . Bryan would have been older, but not much. Still a child. Tyler stood in the doorway, watching.

Easy enough. He took one step into the dark room. He could see the child's lashes on the soft cheek. It was easy enough to see another child sleeping there. *It's not Linda that's lost. It's me.* She still had her child, their child. Even if stolen; the child was still alive somewhere. In the dark, you could find the things you thought you had lost.

"Bryan . . ." he whispered in the room's silence. He closed his eyes, steadying himself against the doorframe. Indulging in madness; he knew it. This was how it started. But still, just for a moment . . .

He looked again at the small figure tucked under the blanket. In the half light that filtered down the corridor from the living room window, the child's face now looked different. He stepped closer, bending to see, one hand reaching to touch, holding back an inch from the sleeping face. "Bryan . . . ?"

The lashes were all fringed in blue, each one separate and electric.

The face turned up to him.

No longer a child's face, but with a sharp, long-toothed smile, the eyes open wide in laughing recognition.

Tyler jerked back, his hand flying to the switch by the door. Light poured across the room.

Eddie lifted his head from the pillow, frowning, one fist rubbing at his eyes. "Mike?"

"Shh. It's okay. Everything's okay." His heart pounding, Tyler stepped beside the bed and gently pushed Eddie back down. He felt the sweat from his hands soak into the shoulders of the child's pajamas. "Go back to sleep." He reached behind himself to switch off the light.

Outside Eddie's room, he leaned back against the wall. The morning gray was lighter now.

Don't do that again. His own warning, delivered

to himself. *Don't mess around like that. Your son's dead.*

He'd have to remember. There was nothing in the dark but the darkness.

She lay in bed with the light off, listening. Steff had felt him slip out of the bed, and had heard him pad barefoot out to the hallway. The surreptitious rummaging through the junk in the closet, careful so as not to wake anyone, had followed, Mike retrieving the thing he kept in the box at the bottom.

Out there in the front room, reading. She knew that was where he had gone. The book. The book that her own curiosity had pushed her to dig out of the closet when he hadn't been around, and that she had shoved back under the old newspapers, unread. Her curiosity was bounded by the edge, black against white, of things she didn't want to find out, knew she didn't want to know. She gazed up at the dark ceiling, listening to the apartment's silence.

Once she had asked him, as they had lain together, what it had been like. To be locked up. Dead minutes had dragged by, with her biting her lip and wishing that she hadn't said anything, before he had answered. He'd said that it was all right, it was no big deal. Some people made it out that it was worse than it was, because they wanted your pity or because they liked getting into more of the same sort of trouble that had landed them in there in the first place. But if you just kept your mouth shut and did what you were told, and went where they told you to and sat there and waited for as long as they told you to, then it was no big deal. There was lots of time to think inside those places. That was, sometimes, the worst part of it. You just had to think.

She hadn't asked him anything more about it, about the past that filled the unread book. She had just wanted to know, not even that, but anything. Any small piece of the past that swallowed up the light behind him like a cavern.

Then weeks later, again at night in the bed, he had started to talk in a quiet voice, as if the thoughts circling in his head had finally worn through the bone and leaked into the bedroom's dark space. The past had become a substance that pressed against them, a constant weight like the air itself. She had listened while he told her in his soft monotone, not about the things that had happened, the murders and other things he had seen, but about how it was possible to see those things and not know that you had gone crazy, that everyone around you was insane, and that all of you together had become figures in a distorted landscape sinking under a tide of blood.

There had been the drug that he and his friends took, that they had all thought they were so clever and enlightened for putting inside themselves. Stuff like that could make you crazy—she had known that already. A six-pack of beer, sometimes, had been able to make Eddie's father into a slouched form gazing heavy-lidded at the TV, waiting for her to drop a dish so he could come into the kitchen and beat her into the narrow space between the refrigerator and the wall, only stopping when she no longer tried to raise her hands to shield her face from the blows. Or the whites that he had bought from his buddies in the refinery's parking lot, to get him over the hump of going on the graveyard shift, only he had liked the little pills so much that he would still be chewing them when he came home and she would know, just looking at him in the doorway, that she would be tasting her own blood in her mouth while he drove his weight between her bruised thighs and the only sound that would come through the ringing in her ears would be the baby, named after his father, crying somewhere in the apartment's distance. She knew, and could believe, a lot about small things people swallowed, and they made people crazy. She knew all about it.

But Mike had gone on talking, his voice winding softly in the bedroom's stillness. About a name she had somehow heard even when nothing had come in from beyond that other apartment's walls, when all she knew about had been the manic climate of her husband's moods and her baby in the other room, a whole world inside the other one. About what it was like to be so flattered and pleased, to be accepted into the great man's inner circle, to go from being a university teaching assistant to hobnobbing with one of the intellectual elite, world-famous author and heavy thinker—all the way inside, right at the hot cutting edge of thought itself. *Like being loved*, she had thought while he'd told her, *for the first time, the only time you could remember, so you didn't even care how that love showed itself, as long as it didn't stop, didn't leave you alone like you were before*.

And about what it was like to be so in the shadow of someone else, so dominated by another personality that you couldn't even tell your own apart any longer, and you couldn't tell that the other person was crazy, and you had become crazy, too. She had known all about that as well. At the shelter, with the other bruised wives rocking their kids in the day room, where their husbands and boyfriends couldn't find them because the address was a secret known only to women's centers and hospital emergency rooms, she had heard about one of the former residents. The woman who had gone on for seven years with a husband who once a month or so would look up from his breakfast and she would know that it was one of the days when he would take her out to the garage, lock her inside the trunk of the car, and take the bus to work, letting her out when he came home so she could fix his dinner. The story could be believed because they could all look around the circle of threadbare donated couches and folding chairs and see, underneath the bruises that had finally driven them here, the older marks that hadn't. (At night, in the little room she had shared with Eddie, then two years old, she had wondered if the woman had cried or tried to sleep, tucked into a ball in the space smelling of tire rubber and gasoline; if she had thought anything at all, or just been numb.) There was a lot of things that Mike had talked about that she could understand.

Maybe, if she had known everything there was to know, she would never have hooked up with him. One of the counselors at the shelter, who still wore a spinal brace from her marriage, had said that she hadn't even been aware that men had walked on the moon until after she had left her husband. So complete and enveloping was the little world you could find yourself in, so constant was the ache in the flesh that no longer produced tears. Mike's face, as with the others in the Wyle Group, had had its moment of evening-news notoriety, nightly bulletins to match the Manson Family that she remembered from her high school days, and she had known nothing about it. Somewhere else, while she was having her spine slammed against the wall, someone else was being murdered. Somebody was being murdered all the time; that was no big deal. But Mike, the man she slept with now and who picked her kid up from day-care and farted around with model cars for the child's amusement, had gone to jail, to the kinds of hospitals they didn't let you leave when you wanted to, all because of murders, a whole bunch of them. Even if he hadn't done them. She knew that much from a "Where Are They Now?" article she had come across in a magazine at Eddie's dentist; Mike was down for concealing evidence and obstruction of justice and that was all, that was all—the smell of them somehow came faint from that black space behind him, that the talking in bed late at night had been her only glimpse into.

If I had known. Now she gazed at the dark ceiling and wondered again. Maybe she would have let the past decide, let everything that would ever happen to her be the same as what had happened. That was what they had told her at the shelter she shouldn't do; when the counselor had asked her what she wanted to do now, and she had blurted out the wildest thing possible, only it had been true, and the counselor hadn't laughed or said it was impossible, but had started pulling the junior college catalogues from the shelf, telling her how long it would take, working and going part-time, and even if she didn't get all that way, because that was hard though not impossible, she would still be better off. Just for trying. The past became just the past then.

And what was it for Mike? She wished she knew. Eddie was her souvenir from that other world. Mike had the book, and the picture of his ex-wife in the paper, and all the other little reminders that came creeping out of the hole.

She heard him in the hallway and closed her eyes,

imitating sleep. Another door opened, Eddie's bedroom. She could hear Mike's whisper, words she couldn't make out. Then Mike softly telling her son to go back to sleep. *Maybe a nightmare*—Mike was good at stroking the child's sleep-troubled brow smooth again.

The blanket lifted from her shoulder as he slipped in beside her. In the dark, she pressed against him, letting the thoughts, still circling, fade until she couldn't see them.

ƧEVEП

"**Ƨ**o that's what you decided?" The therapist leaned back, clasping his hands behind his head. "That she was crazy?"

Tyler nodded. He rubbed the wood grain on the edge of the desk. "What else?" he said. "She was crazy before. We all were. Nothing's changed for her. That's just the way it is."

"For some people."

The shrink was young, balding, and wore contacts that kept him blinking wetly, like an owl with hay fever. Tyler sincerely hated Goodrich and his bland, carefully weighed words. For which he paid a nice little sum every week: Tyler mailed the check in, not trusting himself to write it out in front of the little twerp without making some acidic remark that would blow the equally bland, equally careful cover he'd built up over the last three years. It was either this or weekly group-therapy sessions at the county medical center. As long as the book money enabled him to, he was glad to pay to avoid going to those. They were even more deadening—sitting in a circle of folding chairs, listening to one moaning whine after another, coaxed out of the terminally depressed by some grad student putting in the hours necessary for his MSW degree, while you tried not to be too obvious about sneaking glances at the wall clock. A blessing when Herlihy, his parole officer, had approved the switch to the private sessions with Goodrich. Psychiatric counseling of some kind being part of the price of his freedom, one of his parole conditions; hence his faithful (*you're a tame rat now*) attendance.

The shrink also renewed Tyler's prescriptions. *Better living through chemistry*; he tried to remember that. He could put up with any amount of twaddle for the sake of those tiny substances that stood between him and madness. (*Sharp-toothed smile in a child's bed*.)

He wondered if he was supposed to say something now. Maybe it was a deliberate pause on Goodrich's part, to show how deeply the shrink was mulling things over.

A pencil point danced on the desktop between them. "You know," said the therapist, looking at the marks his hand had made on a sheet of paper, "it might have been a good idea to have called me. About what this, uh, lawyer wanted you to do."

Ah hah. Here it comes. Tyler looked at the wet, wide-open eyes. *Into the shit.* "I didn't think it was that important."

Goodrich nodded. "Well . . . you should've called me. I'm not sure I would've let you go down there and see your ex-wife. Not until I'd at least had a chance to talk with the staff who're, uh, treating her." He swung his chair around to face Tyler straight on. "It was certainly a very stressful situation for you. Probably more than you realize."

Your ass, thought Tyler.

He plowed on. "We've made a lot of progress, Mike. You can be proud of yourself. And I know it hasn't been easy—nobody can go through the kinds of things you've gone through, and come out . . . the same, I mean, the same as they were before. But still, I mean, we're really doing pretty good here, right?'' A smile underneath the blinking owl eyes. ''But that's why you've got to be *careful*. You don't want to mess all that up.'' The watery gaze went up to the ceiling, searching for something. ''You know, the mind's like a sheet of glass or something. You don't really *see* it all the time, so you don't worry about it. But it's really kinda fragile if you put the wrong kind of pressure on it. Right?''

Tyler held his face from turning into a sneer. Inside, he heard his own voice saying, *You fool*. There had been a time when he'd been in the inner circle around one of the finest minds ever to have attempted to take apart the human soul like a pocket watch. Wyle's books, the early ones that came out of the top university presses and then were recycled as blue-spined Penguin paperbacks—staples for the hip bookshelf, Janis Joplin on the AR turntable—they were still cited in academic papers. Impossible to ignore; classics of the field, right up there with *Moses and Monotheism* or *Mysterium Coniunctionis*. Tyler had been part of that small band of initiates who had gone with him all the way, wherever that path had led, past the breaking of the conditioned mind and into the pure freezing wind of the absolute. Where murder was the final act of the free, where blood was sacred enough to be poured on the ground. Wyle was still out there, all that unconditioned world inside his skull in some small locked hospital ward; Tyler, afraid like the others, had finally turned back. *But at least I was there once. At least I know.*

And here was some twerp with his degrees carefully arranged on his office wall, handing out some bullshit metaphor on the mind. This was what he had to put up with.

"I guess you're right," said Tyler. No sense in blowing his credit with the therapist, after he'd put in so much time building it up. He hadn't told him about dragging Stephanie out to Bryan's grave; that would've really caused the alarms to go off. If he wasn't careful, he'd be keeping his appointment inside the hospital again. One word to Herlihy and, bingo, parole violation. "I thought maybe I could help—that's why I went."

Goodrich nodded again. "Sure. That's cool. But talk to me about it next time. That's what I'm here for. Okay?"

He set his blank, emotionless gaze between the wet eyes. "Sure," he said.

Slide had told him to wait. So Jimmy waited. Something had to be done in the dark; Slide was going to come back with something important then. That's what he'd told Jimmy, leaning forward in the nest's small space, so that the bright, eager eyes had held inches away. Voice in a smiling whisper: *Something important. Wait till it's dark.*

He spent the time picking up the precious scraps of paper and photos that Slide had scattered about the nest. Carefully, he wiped the powdery dust from each one against his shirt. Some of the things had gotten stepped on during the quick, hopeless scuffle; those he straightened out against the overhead concrete, pressing them flat on the freeway's underside. All of them he wrapped up in a tattered plastic bag, and stowed them again in their violated hiding place where the dirt and concrete met.

After that he squatted on his heels and went on waiting for darkness and Slide's return. He was getting hungry. *Maybe he'll bring something to eat back here.* Jimmy hoped so; it'd be the right thing for Slide to do, to repay him for following orders and waiting so patiently here, not moving from the nest no matter how his stomach growled. It was like going in the army or the rescue mission: if you did what they told you to do, they had to feed you. That was the deal. He could wait.

Jimmy listened. You could tell a lot that way about what the other people were doing. Tucked away in the nest, he could hear the rattle of the chain being unlocked and dragged through the mesh gate of the construction crew's storage area, then the heavy equipment being driven in. The workmen's voices faded away as they walked out from the overpass and headed for where they had left their cars.

After that, the rumble of traffic filtering down from the freeway lanes over his head grew louder and denser. A continuous roar, like one big machine: rush hour. They had homes to go to, and cars to get there in. Beneath their wheels, Jimmy crouched, listening through the yards of interwoven concrete and steel to their frenzied passage.

Then dark again, the light draining away red from the sunset beyond the edge of the freeway. And quieter; he could hear anything that moved in this concrete-roofed world. Now there was nothing but his own breathing.

''Jimmy—''

His back jerked into a bow at the whisper next to him. He scrabbled away into the dust at the rim of the nest, then fell, sprawling backward.

Slide's soft laughter hung in the space for a moment, before a flashlight's beam swam around on the overhead concrete. The glow sparked in the bright eyes as Slide dug the butt of the flashlight into the dirt at the nest's center.

"I'm back, Jimmy." The cone of light made a circle on the concrete above; the nest was filled with the dim reflection. "I said I'd come back. Didn't I?"

Jimmy could just see him crouching a few feet away. His forearms rested on the taut fabric of his jeans, his hands dangling a white paper sack with shiny grease spots across the bottom. The warm odor of meat brought a thick flood across Jimmy's tongue.

"Didn't I?"

He looked up from the paper sack to the eyes with the flashlight's pinpoints in their centers. He nodded. "You did."

Slide smiled and tossed the sack over the flashlight to him.

"I'm glad you waited," said Slide. He'd watched him tear into the first hamburger in silence. "See what you would've missed?"

Jimmy nodded as he unwrapped the second hamburger. Thick and greasy, the bun pressed into a paste at the bottom. He'd forgotten how good something warm that filled the mouth, unlike the shelter's thin soup, could be. The meat was red in the middle, swelling in his throat with its salt taste. He wished he had something to drink, but went on ripping and chewing.

"Good, huh?" Slide rocked back in his easy, hunkering crouch. "See, you don't have to worry about finding something to eat anymore. I'll take care of that. So you don't even have to leave here anymore. You can stay right here where it's nice and warm and comfortable. That'll be nice, huh? You'll like that, won't you?"

Jimmy looked up from his shiny fingers to the eyes watching him. "Yeah," he said. He knew that was what he was supposed to say.

"Because I got something I want you to do for me. I want you to do a favor for me. Okay, Jimmy? You wanna do me a favor, don't you?"

He crumpled the empty waxed paper into a ball and dropped it into the dirt between his feet. "Sure," he whispered.

"Don't you?"

Louder, nodding his head: "Sure." There was no choice, by this point. Whatever was asked.

Slide's smile came back. "I want you to look after something for me. Right here in your little hole. You'll just stay right here and take care of it. That'll be easy. You don't have to go anywhere anymore."

He felt the soft walls of the nest contract around them, as though the night outside was pressing him closer to Slide's breath. "What," said Jimmy. "What is it?"

"Something important." One of Slide's hands flicked upward to the hiding place at the edge of the overhead concrete. "Not like your stupid trash. Something *really* important."

Jimmy watched as Slide turned about and crawled just beyond the flashlight's circle. He came back, half pulling, half dragging something with him.

It lay so still against the banked dirt at the nest's edge that for a moment Jimmy thought it was a doll, a big one, like in a store window. Then the eyes opened and he saw the child looking back at him. A little boy; the hair was all tousled, and a smudge of dirt on one cheek.

"His name's Bryan." Slide turned his face to the boy and pointed across the flashlight. "This is Jimmy. He's going to look after you."

The child's grave, wary gaze went from him to Slide and back again. For a moment Jimmy felt the closeness of the others, their breaths all mingling in the little space. Like a family, camping out, their fire in the middle, throwing their long shadows into the night. Without looking to the side, he knew Slide was watching him.

"Hello," said the little boy.

"Tyler!"

Halfway through the shopping center's parking lot, he heard his name shouted. Surrounded by rows of cars, Tyler turned and squinted through the bright sun at the figure advancing toward him.

It took a moment before memory clicked. Then he recognized the old cop. *Kinross. Great,* he thought. *All I need.* Though he should have expected it; Linda's face in the paper was a key to wind up a lot of people.

"What do you want?" He stood and let Kinross, wheezing from a rapid walk, come up to him. The policeman looked smaller than when he'd last seen him, the brown suit—that was the same as before—hanging looser on him. As though he were being slowly eaten by it, like a tide-pool fish caught by one of those gelatinous sea creatures that are all soft folding mouths. Tyler's mother and a couple of aunts had looked like that—consumed, made smaller by something that ate from inside—before they died: cancers ran in Black Irish families, the abandoned Catholicism having its genetic payback down the line. Maybe it was in Kinross' lungs, signaled by the shortness of breath. Tyler could smell stale tobacco smoke on him, embedded in the brown suit's fibers as much as from behind the yellow-stained teeth.

With Kinross, though, the consuming thing inside hadn't weakened him. Standing in the parking lot, Tyler could see that: the cop was smaller because everything else had been stripped away, thrown into the furnace at the core, revealing the pure obsession. *It got him, too*, thought Tyler. That's how it worked for anyone who came too near.

"Let's have a talk," Kinross' wide, calloused hand, as if from long habit, closed above Tyler's elbow.

He let himself be steered back along the row of cars and pushed inside an aging Chrysler. The prescription that he'd just got from Goodrich slid back into his coat pocket—the shopping center's pharmacy was where he'd been heading. He was indulging the old policeman. The jailhouse line on retired cops was that they all wound up killing themselves with the guns the force let them keep.

The ashtray in the dashboard was stuffed with cigarette butts. Tyler reached to roll down the window and let some air into the musty-smelling interior, and found the window handle missing. He leaned back and stared through the dusty windshield at the multicolored ocean of parked cars.

"This has been like old home week for me," said Tyler. "Just one face out of the past after another."

Kinross laid one hand across the top of the steering wheel and regarded him. "I know," he said. "You've been busy. You and your friends."

Tyler kept his face blank under the other's gaze. He knew the outlines of Kinross' obsessions; had known since he'd first gotten out that the old cop was watching him, keeping track of him. Even without feeling those hard eyes, the whites stained yellow as the crepe skin around them, locked onto his back. There had been confirming tip-offs: Herlihy had questioned him about some anonymous reports that had been sent to his desk. Possible parole violation stuff, if Tyler hadn't been able to explain them away. But enough scraps of information to make him realize that he was under surveillance; like walking around in his own private police state. Herlihy, a bit miffed at someone trying to do his own job for him, had asked around and confirmed the name Tyler had already been sure of: it had been common knowledge among Kinross' old LAPD cohorts that his brain had locked onto the Wyle Group business and had never let go. Tyler had seen across the courtroom, while the judge had been reading the sentence, those hard eyes staring at him. And had remembered. The same eyes were looking at him now.

"What's that supposed to mean?" he said.

One corner of the mottled skin twisted into a sneer. "Did you have a nice talk with your wife?" said Kinross.

"Linda's not my wife anymore. You know that."

"Yeah, right. You've got a whole different shack-up now, don't you? That skinny broad. Your tastes don't change much, do they?"

Tyler looked across the parking lot, then back to Kinross. "If this is all you wanted to say to me— fine; you've said it. Okay? Happy now?"

"Which one of them are you in with?"

He sighed. "What the hell are you talking about?"

"Your old friends, Tyler." Kinross' hand closed on the steering wheel and squeezed it. "You and Linda. And Slide."

The last name had been spat out. Now, twice in two days, he'd heard it spoken aloud. "I still don't know what you're talking about," he said after a moment.

"Did you have a tiff? A little falling-out?" Kinross' voice twisted, mocking. "What was it—you and Slide got pissed off at Linda, so you turned her in? Or maybe both of you are on his shit list now."

Tyler said nothing.

"Come on," said Kinross disgustedly. "You know how it works. You can tell me, and then we can go down and make it official. The first one who talks always gets the best deal. You don't want Linda to beat you to it. She's screwed you over enough once already."

He found breath enough to speak. "What was that about Slide?"

Kinross looked at him with something like pity. "Maybe you don't know," he said. "Maybe he didn't tell you what he was going to do."

"Slide—" Tyler realized what he was being told. *Slide did it—*

"That's right. Your old friend Slide called up the police and told us where Linda was at. Right down to the button. Nothing to do but drive on out and pick her up."

He's here, thought Tyler. He looked back out across the cars, to the city streets beyond the parking lot. *She told me the truth. He's here somewhere.*

Kinross' voice drew him back. The ex-cop's eyes had narrowed around a seed of triumph.

"You're in a world of shit now, Tyler." Gloating. "You're ours now—just like you've always been. I hope you've had a good time on the outs, because you're going straight back in. And not to some cozy little bug ward, either. We'll make sure of that. This kind of parole violation is gonna get you hard time, asshole. Because there's going to be new charges on top of it. Aiding a fugitive—that's a good one. Whatever your fucking ex-wife got you to do, to help her stay free, now you're gonna find out what that'll cost you.''

"Up yours." He felt a wave of nausea, the car's narrow space, filled with Kinross' sour breath, closing around him.

Blood pumped up into Kinross' face; red and sweating, he went on. "What were you and Slide up to, anyway? Class reunion?" The corners of his mouth were bright with spittle. "Some bright idea of getting your little bunch together again? Well, I'm going to make sure you get the chance, Tyler. I'm going to make sure you go back in. Then when we get Slide, the two of you can sit at Wyle's feet all you want. And you'll have a long time to do it.''

Tyler found the door handle and pushed it open. The air outside pulsed into his lungs as he swung his legs out and stood up. "You're the one who's fucking up," he said quietly. He leaned into the car, holding the door open with one hand, his anger squeezing his knuckles bloodless against the metal. "Because you got me wrong—I've got nothing to do with Linda, Slide, anybody. And you got yourself wrong. You aren't no fucking cop anymore, Kinross. Better remember that. You can't do shit to me." He slammed the door shut and started walking.

The other's voice followed him. "I'll see you around," shouted Kinross. "I'm looking forward to it, Tyler."

He felt the eyes on his back, their yellow gaze

pressing against his spine as he passed one car after another.

"Are you all right?" said Steff.

It took a moment before he looked up at her. "Sure," said Mike. "Yeah, I'm fine. Just . . . you know . . . thinking about stuff." He managed a smile.

He was sitting by the living room window, in the chair that he had pulled over to it the night before. She had come home from a half shift at the restaurant, toting her books from her morning classes, and had found him already there. As though watching for something, his deep silence absorbing like a black hole the noise of Eddie zooming his plastic cars around on the carpet in front of the TV's evening news. At least Mike had remembered to pick Eddie up from the day-care center; that proved there was still some connection with the real world to cut through his brooding.

The station at the window had lasted all evening, Mike shaking his head when she'd asked him if he wanted any dinner. "Is Mike okay?" Eddie had looked at her from his small bed. She had paused, her hand on the light switch, before making some vague, comforting remark. *Smart kid*, she thought as she looked at Mike by the window. *You can't fool them*.

"I'm going to bed now," she told him.

He nodded, his gaze already having returned to the dark vista outside.

With the bedroom light off, her face against the pillow, she could hear the silence of him sitting in the other room, watching.

* * *

You're really blowing it. Tyler could see himself reflected in the window. There was no expression on the face looking back at him from the dark. *You're acting like a complete shit*, he thought. *Why don't you just tell her to kill herself? Maybe that would make you happy*.

The street, the short stretch of Santa Monica Boulevard that he could see at the end of the block, was dead, the colors of the traffic's lights and the bar signs dulled by the medications in his blood. Nothing to watch for, and if there had been, he wouldn't have been able to see it. The evening's dosage had sealed that other, bright-edged world from him, leaving him locked inside the circling depth of his thoughts. And sorry, underneath, that he had given Steff the big zero, the silence that couldn't be broken through, could only be walked around like some gigantic parcel filling the apartment to the walls. That was unfair to her; maybe after this night was over, with its attendant thoughts, he could successfully apologize to her, return to normal, or as much so as was ever possible. He went on looking out the dark window.

Slide. Not so much a thought as just the one word, the name he'd had spoken to him twice in two days. That had chilled him. Not that Slide, old spooky Slide out of the past that the tightly held door kept slipping free from, was actually out there, walking around in the night. There was no proof to that. A couple of hours after being harangued by that bastard Kinross, when the adrenaline of Tyler's anger had dissipated, his thoughts tore that belief to shreds. The cold melancholy he felt was for Linda, and even Kinross. *They* believed Slide was out there; Slide had come back and was walking around in their heads.

He wondered if it was a matter of the hallucination traveling like an infection from one brain to another. First Linda, living with her hallucinated child (*our child*) (*sleeping he won't ever wake up*) and then dreaming up the phantom Slide to steal the nonexistent baby; and Kinross catching that second delusion from her. Certainly the retired cop was nuts enough to believe anything about the Wyle Group's old members; it would just take Linda saying that she had talked to Slide for Kinross to fall into that part of her insanity—even if he was still straight about the child being dead and buried. Or else the business about Slide was just the intersection of two separate delusions, Linda's and Kinross', both of them keeping Slide alive in their minds, seeing him around any corner in the dark.

Or else—Tyler saw the corner of a wry, self-mocking smile on his reflection—Slide was out there. Here.

Don't screw around with that stuff, he told himself. He remembered the flash, the quick glimpse of the Host's sharp-toothed grin, he had seen superimposed over Eddie's face in the dark bedroom. There were consequences to playing around, indulging in tiny hits of craziness. Nobody knew that better than he did. The fun part, the little shiver of gooseflesh up the arms, runs out soon enough. And then you're not playing anymore. You were just crazy.

But if Slide *was* out there . . . *What if*, thought Tyler.

The phone rang.

He turned away from the window, toward the sound shrilling across the apartment from the kitchen.

It rang again. If he didn't answer it soon, Steff would wake up.

(*Dark outside. He'd call at night—if he was out there.*)

Again, cutting through the still apartment.

He pushed himself up out of the chair, strode rapidly to the kitchen doorway, reached around, and grabbed the phone in mid-ring. "Hello?"

For a moment, silence. Then, at his ear, he heard the voice with the thin smile in it. "Hello, Tyler," said Slide.

Something woke him up. Jimmy stayed curled in a ball, listening to the rumbling noise of traffic from above. The sound grew thinner late at night, but it never stopped. That wasn't what had penetrated his sleep.

He raised his head from the rolled-up jacket and looked around. His sight had adjusted to the darkness behind his eyelids; easy enough to make out the nest's small confines and everything in it by the edge of street light seeping between the pillars.

Slide had left some food with him. There was still a big plastic bottle of Coke and half a package of cinnamon rolls, the soft ones pressed into squares on a shiny cardboard tray, in the supermarket bag. He could smell them through the brown paper.

Maybe there's a rat, thought Jimmy. They came under the freeway sometimes, down from the tops of the palm trees and the thick beds of ivy where the houses were. You had to watch for them: they didn't bite, but if they got into your food stash they'd shit where they had nibbled at it. *Fuckin' rats.* He listened carefully, through the constant rumble from the nest's concrete ceiling, but couldn't hear any soft scratching of claws against paper. He heard just his own breathing, then another's, falling out of rhythm with his.

The kid. *Bryan*, he thought. That was what Slide had called him. He had almost forgotten the kid, the task Slide had given him. *You're going to take care of him. Aren't you?* The smiling voice and the bright, watching eyes. *Aren't you?*

Maybe the kid had cried out in his sleep, and that had woken him. Kids did that sometimes; Jimmy knew that. From being scared, from nightmares. He'd heard the old men cry out, too, during long nights in one of the shelters downtown. Not fright, but sad wails, sometimes with toothless mumbled words, names. And a muttered chorus echoing from the benches and folding chairs. If he himself cried like that, at least under the freeway there was no one to hear him.

He listened to the child's soft, regular breathing. On his hands and knees, he crept across the nest to check on the small figure wrapped in blankets.

"What do you want?"

"Mike . . ." Slide's voice parodied hurt feelings. And always, behind the words, the sharp-edged laughter about to break through. "Is that any way to talk? After all we went through together?"

Tyler felt the phone's plastic growing warm in his grip. He kept his voice low, tightly controlled. "How'd you get this number?"

"Ahh, come *on*. I'm good at finding things out. You know that, Mike. We found out a lot of things together, didn't we?" A measured beat of silence. "Didn't we, Mike?"

"Shut up."

"You sound like you're not happy to hear from me, Mike."

Tyler stood in the unlit kitchen doorway, thinking. Putting together the pieces of the last couple of days. *So he is out there,* he thought. *He did find Linda, wherever she was hiding, and got hold of her.* Good at finding things out; that was true. A ferretlike intelligence, slipping through darkness, nosing things out. Maybe when Slide found her, he'd watched her for a while, and latched on that she was living inside her hallucination that Bryan was still alive. The image came to him of Slide listening at a door to a woman's voice that came through it, talking to a child whose replies made no sound. And that had given him the hook, to catch her on and torment her, for whatever bent purpose seeped through Slide's brain. Pretending to steal the kid, who didn't exist except in her muddled brain; that showed a certain psychological mastery on Slide's part. He had turned out to be Wyle's best student, after all. Tyler could hear Wyle's voice, a tape out of memory: *Whoever controls your delusions,* an old lesson, *controls you.*

And then an anonymous phone call to some LAPD detective, just the way old Kinross had told him. Slide operated just as well in the real world.

"Well?" Slide's voice again, pulling him to the present and the phone in his hand. "Aren't you happy?"

"Why did you call?" said Tyler. There were things he had to find out before Steff heard his voice and came out here. "I want to know what you want."

"You know . . . that's the same thing Linda asked me." Slide's voice curled around his own self-pleasure. "When I talked to her. Everybody wants to know what *I* want. That's kind of you."

"Cut the shit." His grip tightened on the phone. "If there's something you want, then say it, asshole. If you're just fucking around, if this is your idea of a good time, you can just hang it up. And don't call here again—there's nothing I want to talk to you about."

The smile at the other end of the line dropped, Slide's voice turning hard as it came over the wire. "Yeah, there is. There's something you want to talk to me about. You want to talk about your little boy, don't you? Don't you, Mike? Because you want him back. That's what you want."

So that was it. That was how far madness, the delusion, had spread. From one to the other, a disease. "My son's dead," Tyler said quietly. "He's been dead a long time. You know that, Slide. You can't give him back to me. Nobody can."

"Really?" The mocking tone again. "You sure about that? Sure the kid's dead? It'd really be something if you were wrong."

Madness—or cleverness. With Slide it could be either way. "Forget it. You can pull that shit with Linda. But she's crazy." Somewhere else in the night, in one of those little rooms (*back in the dark*), if the sedation hadn't put her out completely, she'd be weeping for the child she thought had been taken from her. Stolen by the voice that was at his ear now. "It won't work with me."

"It won't, huh? I think you're wrong. I think you're wrong about a lot of things, Mike. Maybe Linda's not the one who's crazy."

Tyler made no answer. In the gap of silence he could hear the current singing on the line stretching between him and the other.

"And you're gonna think about this," Slide's voice

continued. "I know how your mind works, Mike. 'Cause we were all there together once—weren't we? Those were good days, Mike. Everybody had a lot of fun back then." The words arched, the smile behind them. "We could all have some fun again. Couldn't we? But first you're gonna think about some stuff. Think about your kid. That's what you're gonna do."

"Slide—"

"No. *You* listen, fucker. You think about it, and then when I call again, you won't act so shitty to your old friends. You'll want to talk to me then."

With a sharp click, the line went dead. Slide's voice was replaced with the dull hum of the dial tone.

Tyler replaced the phone on its hook. Slowly, he looked over his shoulder and saw the window across the living room, the empty chair in front of it. The darkness outside was ringed by the blue of the streetlamps.

Jimmy reached down to smooth the sleeping child's hair. *Bryan,* he thought. *That's his name.*

A different face looked up at Jimmy. Bending over the sleeping child, he could see, like faint white triangles in the dim light under the freeway, the sharp-pointed teeth of the grin. The eyelids opened, and the gaze locked onto his, freezing his breath in his throat. He couldn't move, couldn't pull away from it, but went on falling into the dark-centered eyes as the grin grew wider, the teeth longer as they drew apart.

Light flooded from behind him, throwing the shadow of his outstretched arm against the nest's sloping bank. There was no sharp-toothed face looking up at him. The child's lashes lay on the soft, round cheek, trembling against the sudden brightness.

Jimmy turned around and saw another smile, behind the beam of a flashlight. The glare made Slide's eyes even brighter.

"How's he doing?" Hunched over against the concrete ceiling, Slide moved across the nest. Standing beside Jimmy, he put his hand over the light, dimming it so as not to wake the child. "Looks just fine. Just fine."

The narrow face was just a few inches away from his own. "Where'd you go?" said Jimmy. He realized he didn't like being alone in the nest anymore. Alone except for the little boy. He could feel the weight of all the steel and concrete, and the cars and trucks above him, pressing down, squeezing the small space into the dust.

Slide, his face etched into shadows by the glow leaking around his fingers, looked around at him. Still smiling: "I had some business to take care of," he said. "Had to make a phone call." He leaned closer. "Why? Anything happen while I was gone?"

I got scared. He wanted to say that. But he knew there was no point to it. He was supposed to be scared. That was how Slide liked things. "Different," he mumbled, dropping his gaze. "Looked *different.*"

He felt Slide still watching him, not even glancing around at the sleeping child. "Yeah? Like how?"

"Teeth," said Jimmy. "They were all sharp. And he . . . looked at me . . ."

Slide's other hand reached around Jimmy's head, the fingers splaying through the matted hair. He tilted Jimmy's face up to his, coming even closer, as if to kiss him.

"Great," said Slide. Jimmy could see his own face, tiny and half-shadowed by the flashlight, in the center of his eyes. "That means it's close. Real close."

When she woke up, the bed was still empty beside her. "Mike?" said Stephanie. She brushed her tangled hair away from her face. The covers were all askew—she could barely remember a dream fragment where she had been running, calling—and dangling to the floor on her side of the bed; she knew from that that he hadn't come in beside her during the night.

Barefoot, she padded down the hallway toward the living room. The gray morning light came in through the window, the shades still pulled back. The chair in front of it was empty.

"Mike?" she called again. For a moment, as she turned about, it seemed as if the apartment were empty. Then she looked behind her, down the hallway. Through the doorway at the end, she could see the rumpled sheets and blanket she had thrown aside. Before that, halfway down the hall, the door to Eddie's room stood ajar.

Mike didn't hear her push the door open. The back of his head was to her as he sat on the corner of Eddie's bed.

From the doorway, she called Mike's name again softly. Eddie was still asleep; she could see his breath raising and lowering the blanket pulled under his chin.

He didn't look around at her. As if he didn't hear her at all. He went on watching the sleeping child.

EIGHT

From the coffee shop booth, he could see Tyler walking toward him, easing through the shopping mall's crowds. Bedell fingered the rim of his cup, the second he'd had while waiting for him to get here, and leaned back.

"Hey, good to see you." He gestured to the other side of the booth as Tyler walked past the cash register counter. "Been a while, hasn't it? You want some coffee?"

"No," said Tyler. His face was held expressionless as he slid into the seat.

"Sure you do. Ungodly early hour. Sweetheart—" He signaled to the waitress. He could feel Tyler's eyes burning into him. *Tough shit*, he thought. He knew the fucker wanted something; when Tyler had phoned, he didn't even let him say what it was, telling Tyler to meet him here instead. Time for some face-to-face dealing.

"You know," he said, leaning across the table, "I really like this place. One of my favorite places in the world. You like shopping malls, Mike?"

Tyler glanced behind him, then back around. "Not especially."

"I dig 'em. Big contribution to civilization." He pointed to the coffee shop's glass front and the wide

135

spaces beyond. Up here on the top level, he could
see the mall's corridors branching off toward the
department stores at either end. Under a vaulting
central dome, an abstract spiderweb of steel cables
stretched through the open space beyond the railings,
crisscrossing above the heads of the shoppers on the
ground floor. "You can do a lot of market research
in a place like this. They got three different book-
stores in here. There's a B. Dalton just below us on
the third level, a Walden on the first, and something
that moved in when the Brentano's folded." He sipped
his coffee and nodded. "When the book came out,
and then the paperback edition, I used to come over
here—'cause I live so close—and see how it was
doing. Check the racks and see how it was doing.
You know?" A smile. "Thinking about all that
money."

Tyler said nothing. His own coffee stayed un-
touched in front of him. Easy to see that he knew he
was being gamed, screwed around with. *That's life
on the hook*, thought Bedell. When people wanted
something, then you had them.

"You're really screwed," said Tyler quietly.
"Aren't you?"

That set him back. "What do you mean?"

"Broke. Against the wall."

He shrugged nervously. "A little tight." He worked
a smile onto his face. "Just goes to show, doesn't
it—a writer should stick to his typewriter. Start mess-
ing around in real estate and those stock options,
amazing how fast the money can go." He still barely
believed it himself. There had been so much of it.

Tyler's set gaze measured him.

"So," he said. "You been thinking about my
little, uh, proposition?"

"Maybe."

"Maybe what? Maybe yes, maybe no . . ."

"Maybe I'm still thinking about it."

Bedell studied his reflection inside the cup. "Don't think too long," he said, looking up. "It's not an indefinite offer. We gotta nail things down while it's still in the news."

"I'll let you know." Tyler spread his hands on the table. "There's some stuff I thought maybe you could tell me, though."

"Like what?"

"Linda's address. I mean, where they found her."

Bedell kept his voice cool. "Why do you want to know that?" *Careful*, he thought. *Just reel him in.*

"No big deal," said Tyler. "I just thought . . . if she'd been living close to me all this time, or somewhere I went by a lot—I don't know. Just struck me as intriguing. Maybe an angle for you; who knows?"

"Yeah, maybe." He rubbed his lip, trying to figure out what Tyler was edging around. "What makes you think I'd know where they got her?"

"Come on. That's your business. Isn't it? You got contacts and stuff."

He laughed. "I guess so. Hang on a sec." He took his notebook from his inside coat pocket and leafed through it. "I don't know if you would've gotten over by her very often, though." He wrote down the address on the back of one of his own business cards.

Tyler nodded as he looked at the card.

"I think it's a good idea, though," said Bedell smoothly. "A good hook—her being in the same city all this time, and everything. So, uh, you want to . . . get something down on paper about this? Work out our split?"

The other's level gaze came back up. "I'll let you know."

"What's that mean?"

"It means," said Tyler, getting up from the booth, "that you can go fuck yourself."

Bedell tried to grab his arm, but missed. Before he could get out from around the corner of the table, Tyler was already past the register, striding toward the mall's distant exit.

"Shit." He took out his wallet and laid money down. Outside the coffee shop, he gripped the waist-high rail and glared down at the lounging teenagers and strolling housewives on the floor below. He couldn't even remember where he had left his car; the mall was angled into a hillside, with parking lots outside the entrances on both the top and bottom levels.

Bottom, he figured. He remembered looking up at the artsy-fartsy tangle of steel cables when he had walked in.

Working his way down the escalators, he stopped at each bookstore, going right back through the paperbacks to where *Inside the Night* could be found. Not caring whether any of the staff was watching, he shoved the books next to it over to make room, and turned the copies of his book around so the bright red cover faced front. So they could be seen.

First he had to go by the theatre. To do the little bit of work he was paid to do—the employee time cards had to go into the chain's central office this week—and to sit in his office behind the cashier's window and think what he wanted to do. Bedell's card with the address scribbled on back flipped back and forth across the edge of his hand.

He tossed the card onto the cluttered desk. The address was already sealed in his memory. Not the greatest of districts; he recognized it as one of the dividing lines between the gentrifying gays and what was left of the heavy Chicano neighborhoods in East Hollywood. A good place to hide, lots of old places tucked up in the hills, no rich people to demand a lot of police patrols.

When he stepped out of the office, closing its door behind him, the kid from the concessionaire looked over the top of the candy counter in the lobby. He was wiping congealed grease—supposedly butter-flavored—from inside the workings of the popcorn machine. "What's up?" he said as Tyler walked down the corridor. "You look kinda weirded out, man."

He caught his reflection in the glass over the Coming Next poster on the wall. The same eyes looked back at him as before. "Working too hard, I guess."

"Yeah, right," said the kid. Jobs in the chain of movie houses were well known for their low pay and idiot requirements. He began reassembling the dispenser's chrome pan.

"You going to be here much longer? I was thinking of locking up until this evening."

"Just finishing, man." He closed the machine's plastic door and gave it a wipe with an oily paper towel. "I still gotta hit the Four Star and the World."

"If you see Louie over at the Star," said Tyler, "tell him he still owes me a box of carbons for the projector. And I want that key back, too." Minor thefts—"borrowing" with no payback—from each other was how the theatre managers scraped through their operating budgets.

"Whatever." The kid dropped his spray bottle of soapy water and roll of towels into the box of candy and lifted it onto his shoulder.

After Tyler wrapped the heavy chain around the push-bars of the front doors and snapped the padlock shut, he fetched the Chevy from the alley behind the theatre. In a couple of minutes he'd turned left up La Brea and was heading for East Hollywood.

Poking about in the narrow streets that snaked up into the hills above the far end of Sunset, he found the address Bedell had given him. He pulled the Chevy over to the opposite curb and killed the engine. A concrete retaining wall bordered the sidewalk beside him; the musty smell of leaves decaying under the warm sun drifted down from above it. The angular lettering of spray-can *placa* spelled out *El Rattler con Li'l Mouse por vida.*

The address was one of two small apartments, detached from each other, sharing a driveway. Tyler leaned his elbow on the car's windowsill, studying them. *Forget it,* he told himself. *Just drive away. There's nothing here.* He went on looking at the small stucco-walled buildings.

Slide's voice, thinned leaner by the telephone line, had stayed in his ear from last night. *You want to talk about your little boy, don't you?* Even after he'd finally pulled himself together enough to get through the usual morning rituals of seeing Steff off to her morning classes, Eddie in tow to drop at the day-care center, the mocking words (*really be something if you were wrong, wouldn't it?*) had gone on twisting farther into the side of his skull. Even after the morning dosage of his meds had dulled the edges of the real world, memory had gone on cutting toward his blood. *You're gonna think about some stuff. That's what you're gonna do.*

Insanity—that was the explanation. For Linda, and Slide. Tyler worked the equation back and forth in his mind as he gazed at the apartments. Linda definitely crazy; he had seen that in her face. But a matter of degree when it came to Slide. How much of the words in that laughing, coiling voice had been due to madness, and how much had been just trading in it, like a coin that could be passed from one person's hand to another's? Slide wanted something. He'd always wanted something; even back in the Wyle Group days, Tyler had known that Slide had had his own separate agenda, different from the one everybody else shared. And now Linda's madness, the delusion of the dead child being still alive, had become part of his operating method to get what he wanted. Whatever it was. And passing the madness on, spreading it, infecting Tyler with it—that was also part of it, he had realized. *He wants me back in there*, thought Tyler. *In the dark, with her.*

So get out of here, he told himself again. *Don't mess around with this stuff.*

His hand dropped to the key in the ignition switch. For a minute longer he went on gazing at the apartments. Then he pulled the key out and pocketed it as he got out of the car.

In the narrow driveway between the apartments, Tyler looked about at the numbers painted beside the doors. The second one had been Linda's, according to Bedell, at the very end of the cracked asphalt strip. He stepped up and peered inside through the screen. The front door behind it was open; he could see through to the light shining in from the kitchen window at the back. Someone was inside. A sharp smell of ammonia and soapy water touched his nostrils.

He rapped with one knuckle on the screen door's thin aluminum frame. "Hello!" he called. "Anybody there?"

In the kitchen doorway he saw a woman appear, almost stocky enough to block the light from behind her. In one hand, a sponge dripped spots of water onto the linoleum floor. "Yeah?" she shouted. "What do you want?"

He shaded his face with one hand to see better. Dust sifted down from the screen where he'd brushed against it. "Are you the apartment manager?"

"Naw, I own 'em." Tyler stepped back as the woman unlatched the screen door and pushed it open. "Me and my son do." She had a soft barrio accent, and several layers of blue eye shadow expertly shaded together. Her flowered plastic apron had cracked with age. "You from the police?"

For a second he wondered if the lie would prove of more use. "No," he said.

"Good." She took his interruption as the excuse for a break and dug a cigarette pack out of the apron's pouch. "Cops been driving me crazy. Crawling all over the place, got it all wrapped up in their stupid yellow ribbon 'cross the door, won't let me go in—" The hand with the cigarette in it waved smoke into the room behind her. "I gotta get the place cleaned up. Ain't making any money with nobody in it."

"I guess they finished," said Tyler. "The police, I mean."

"Yeah, yeah." The woman nodded. "You her brother?"

He shook his head. "Just a friend. A long time back."

"I thought maybe you were, 'cause you look kinda like her." She leaned forward to peer closer at him. "Maybe not. I only saw her once or twice, back when she first took the place. I told the cops that, too." Gray ash dribbled down the apron. "Did you come to get her stuff?"

"No. I just—"

" 'Cause the cops, they took it all. Dragged it all away. Everything except the phone. Guess 'cause the phone belongs to the phone company, huh?"

Tyler could feel the sun against the back of his head. The street was quiet enough, tucked this far into the hills and away from the freeways, that he could hear the faint rasp of a motorcycle winding through distant curves. "I wondered if I could . . . look around a bit. That's all."

"Sure, sure. No problem." She stepped back, with one heavy arm holding the screen open wider for him. "You looking for a place?"

He stepped into the apartment's cool shaded interior. "Sorry," he said with a faint smile.

"That woulda saved me putting the ad in. I got a regular ad I run in the *Pennysaver* when somebody moves out. They give you a better rate than the *Times*. The *Times* thinks you're trying to rent out City Hall or something." She cupped her hand to catch the next quarter inch of ash. "That's how the lady came here; she answered the ad."

"How long was she here?"

"Like I told the police: six months. I looked at my receipt book, and that's how many I sent her. I don't charge no first and last, just the security deposit."

Tyler slowly turned around. The doors leading off

the small living room were all open, with the windows revealed beyond them pushed up to air the rooms. A gas heater had been covered with the same beige paint as the walls; the fabric on the arms of a couch and chair were worn thin enough to see the white cotton batting beneath. He stepped over to the hallway. A mattress and frame, stripped of sheets, could be seen in the bedrooms at either end.

With no idea of what he was looking for, Tyler crossed in front of the landlady to the kitchen doorway. There the musty smell of old paint was mixed with the years of cooking grease that had seeped into it. He could see that the cupboard doors had been covered so many times with the ubiquitous beige— even the hinges—that most of them no longer could be closed all the way. A four-burner range, the newest-looking thing in the apartment, was too small for the niche it stood in; around its corners were the rust-brown indentations of the one that had been there before.

"It's a nice place," said the landlady from behind him. "It's clean."

He heard the yapping bark of a small dog. Another screen door at the back, beside the vintage refrigerator, bowed with the force of a tiny Yorkshire terrier hurling itself against the mesh.

"That's not hers. That little guy's mine." She walked over and bent down to tap at the dog's nose through the screen. A glossy ribbon had been tied on top of its head. "Be quiet, you."

He looked outside the door and saw a small yard, mainly weeds and dried yellow grass, sloping down to a dark-shaded gully. On the porch a gray square, a cardboard box flattened out, lay under two plastic bowls. One had flecks of cat food still in it.

"Did she have a cat?" said Tyler.

"Not supposed to. No pets inside, that's what the rental agreement says. They always pee on the carpets. But maybe she fed one out here. There's a lot of them that come around. People let 'em go up here when they don't want 'em anymore."

He unlatched the screen door and pushed it open. The Yorkie dashed in and began jumping around the bottom of the landlady's plastic apron. He slid the cardboard from under the bowls and held it up.

The side that had faced down showed the bright colors, still unfaded, of a Fisher-Price children's toy. The big cartoon eyes and wide smile of something called a Wiggly Worm grinned at him. A wheeled toy, a segmented worm with a saddle in the middle, that could be propelled by the child bouncing up and down on it. A Toys R Us price sticker remained on the flap that had been the top of the carton.

Tyler studied the picture on the flattened box for a minute before he turned around to the landlady. The panting Yorkie was cradled against her breast. "Did she have a kid with her?" he said quietly. "The lady who lived here?"

A shrug. "She said she did. She put down on the rental application one adult, one child. 'Cause it's a two-bedroom, right? That's what she was looking for."

"And you saw the kid? A little boy?"

"Nah." She waved her hand. "When she come by my house to pick up the key and look at the place, she was by herself. Who goes dragging a little kid around when they're looking at apartments? The kid's gonna live with you wherever it is, anyway."

Tyler nodded, looking at the flattened toy carton in

his hands. He glanced up at the sudden noise of
high-pitched barking. The Yorkie wriggled in the landlady's arms, yapping excitedly at him, the tiny points
of its teeth bared.

"You bad thing." She opened the door and set it
outside. It went on barking and throwing itself against
the screen.

"Can I keep this?" Tyler held up the cardboard.

She shrugged. "Just trash. Sure."

He walked back out to the living room. "What
about the other apartment? The neighbor—would he
have seen very much of the lady? And the kid?"

"Eh." She made a contemptuous gesture toward
the door. "That old fart. He drinks. The police, and
the newspaper guys, they tried to talk to him, but it's
no good. He don't know nothing, except when his
check comes at the first of the month."

At the door, he folded the cardboard in two.
"Thanks," he said.

"Sure." Holding the door open, she watched him
step down to the driveway. "Did she really do all
those things? Like in the paper—kill people and stuff?"

He turned around. "No." True enough; like him,
the worst she could have been nailed on would've
been some bullshit charge like obstruction. That was
enough.

"Well, you tell her Mrs. Ruiz has her telephone.
I'll keep it for her. When she gets out and she wants
her deposit back from the phone company, she can
come by and get it."

Across the street, he threw the folded cardboard
into the Chevy's back seat and slid behind the wheel.
So what'd all that prove? he thought as he turned the
key in the ignition. *She was crazy enough to buy a
toy for a nonexistent kid. That's all.*

He watched the apartments for a moment longer. Still quiet enough to hear the dog yapping on the back porch. The dog's teeth had been sharp little triangles set in shiny black.

(*Don't mess around with that stuff.*)

He dropped the car into gear and pulled away from the curb.

When he got back to the theatre, he found the chain missing from the front-door bars. Tyler stood underneath the marquee with the padlock key in his hand; through the glass he could see the chain coiled in a neat pile on the lobby carpet, just inside.

After scanning in both directions down the sidewalk and in back of him to the street's traffic, he leaned close to the glass and peered inside. No sign of anyone; the neat rows of candy wrappers in the cabinet at the back of the lobby were undisturbed. When the theatre had been broken into last year—not as neatly as this, but an early morning brick through the glass instead—the refreshments counter had been ransacked in the fruitless search for some kind of cashbox. He could see that nothing had been touched; the fluorescent tube underneath the countertop shone across neat rows of mints and gum. The carefully looped chain on the lobby floor, the links shining like the scales of a snake in its coil, was enough of a calling card. He already knew who was inside.

Tyler stepped over the chain and pulled the door shut behind him. The glass blocked out the street noises. He walked farther through the lobby's dim quiet, feeling his slow footsteps sink into the carpet. The faces in the wall posters gazed across him as he stopped in front of the counter and turned his head, tracking across the interior. Double doors, sound- and lightproof, on either side; beyond them, the rest room signs glowed faint green at the end of the short corridors. He stilled his breath for a moment and could hear the whisper of water leaking through one of the urinal valves.

His visitor had left no trail to wherever he was hiding. *He's still here*, thought Tyler. He could feel him nearby, somewhere. The skin prickled over his forearms.

He pushed open the padded double doors and let them swing shut behind him. In the theatre's silence, the rows of empty seats gazed up at the dark screen. He slid his hand across the mock-velvet fabric of the seat backs as he went past them, down the sloping floor.

Something skittered away from him when his foot struck it. An empty popcorn container, missed by last night's cleaning crew, rolled in a circle back under the seats.

A small, sharp noise came from above and behind him, but before he could turn around, light flooded off the screen, washing over him. He brought the palm of his hand up to block the sudden glare.

The projection booth window, high on the rear wall, was filled with the glare of the projector switched on with no film wound through it, bright enough to speckle the air with dust motes caught in the light. Still shielding his eyes, Tyler saw a blurred shape move in front of the burning white lens. He turned and saw the same motion enlarged and distorted on the screen: a hand's shadow, formed childishly into a rough mouth with fingertips for teeth. A wrist's neck stretched off the side of the screen.

The shadow mouth clenched, biting into the light.

"Hello, Mike," came the voice. Here, not over the phone.

Standing in the aisle, he tilted his head to look up. His hand blocked the glare, but he could see nothing past it. "I figured it was you, Slide." He raised his voice to call to the booth.

"Hope you don't mind my finding my own way in." The theatre brightened a bit as the hand drew back, leaving the blank screen.

"Some things don't change, I guess."

A laugh sounded from the small light-filled opening. "Yeah, it's just like old times," said Slide.

"Tell you what," said Tyler. His own shadow, cast by the reflection from the screen, stretched up the back wall. "I'll come up there and we can talk about 'em."

"No, why don't you just stay where you are. I can see you fine from here. I like that." Slide's voice curled, teasing. "Besides, you didn't sound too friendly the last time we talked. That's why I thought I'd come here and . . . talk some more."

"What about?" The light dimmed again; he looked behind himself and saw the magnified shadow of a hand slowly fanning across the screen.

The hand stopped, pumped into a fist a couple of times, then drew away. "Come on, Mike." The voice went lower. "What do you think we're going to talk about? What've you been thinking about all day?"

The skin on his arms tightened, as if squeezing the blood back to his heart.

"Huh, Mike?" The voice pressed, insistent. "Come on. What've you been thinking about? What is it? Come on."

He could feel another connection stretching be-

tween himself and the light streaming above. Something besides the words in the theatre's still air.
Come on. They were in his head as well, the thoughts
falling into sync with the other's. *Come on. Tell me*.

Behind him, he sensed another shape moving on
the blank screen. The light from it changed, darker,
even though he could see every detail, every stitch
and tear, in the empty seats' fabric. His own shadow
against the double doors crouched lower.

If he turned (*go ahead—you want to, don't I?*), he
knew he'd see it, the teeth sharper than the shadow
of Slide's hand . . .

(*Come on. You want to. I want to see it. Again.*)
"Come on . . ."

He turned his head, looking over his shoulder, the
darkening light streaming above him

(*Don't mess around with that stuff.*)

and dug his nails into his palms until the pain sang
up his arms. He tasted blood trickling from the inside
of his lip.

The screen was a blank rectangle of white light.

"Too bad, Mike." Slide's voice was barely audi-
ble. "You almost had it. But don't worry. You'll get
it soon enough."

He looked up at the projection window. "There's
nothing for us to talk about, Slide." Around him, the
theatre's seats had faded back into dimly lit space.
The musty, sweet odor of dried Coke and candy
ground into the stained carpet reached his nose. "Why
don't you take it on out of here?"

The laugh was harder this time. "What about your
little boy?" Slide called from the booth. "What about
him, Mike?"

Tyler let out his breath. "I don't have time for

this," he said, shaking his head. "You want to screw around with—"

"He's not dead."

Crazy. He looked around the theatre. *It's not just Linda. They're all crazy.* He brought his gaze back to the window and the glare-blurred silhouette visible behind it. "He is dead. My son is dead, Slide. I've been to the grave. A lot. This shit isn't going to bring him back."

"That's not your son in that grave."

He said nothing. (*Maybe . . .*) (Don't mess around with that stuff.)

The voice from the projection booth was softer, almost a whisper in his ear: "It can be like it was before. Even better."

That brought him out of his thoughts. "What are you talking about?" said Tyler.

"You know what I'm talking about. Don't you, Mike?" Slide's hand moved across the bright lens. "The Host. He's still there. Inside you. Inside all of us."

He didn't turn around to see what shape was cast on the screen. "You're crazy." A simple statement; the obvious. *It got him, too. Like Linda—that's how it spreads. From one to the other.*

"You felt it, Mike." Slide's voice went on, quiet and disembodied in the empty theatre. "You feel it all the time. You feel *him.* The Host is still there, inside you. He never went away. You can try and keep him bottled up, you can take that shit they give you, but he's still there. And you know it."

He said nothing, tilting his head to catch the other's words.

"And we're all in there together," said Slide. "Still in there with *him.* That's how I found Linda.

She couldn't hide from me. *He* showed me where she was. 'Cause it's time. Time to bring the Group back together, Mike.''

The words brought a quick laugh from Tyler. ''Won't that be kind of hard?'' he said. ''They're not letting Wyle out for a long time to come.''

''We don't need Wyle anymore. Not out here. But he's in with us, anyway; even under all the stuff they give him to keep him quiet, his brain's still working away, man. Like yours. You can't keep the Host out, Mike. 'Cause he's inside you already. He never left.''

Tyler felt the crawl of skin over his arms again. In an empty, darkened movie theatre, he listened across a fan of light to a voice with no face attached to it, just memory. And he was cold, a remembered chill that came with the dark where everything was visible, cold and edged with a blue light. *Inside you*, he thought. *Never left*.

''Don't you see?'' Slide's voice went up in volume and pitch. ''The kid—your *son*, Mike. He's the key to it, man. And now it's time.''

Tyler nodded. Now he understood: the perfect breadth and width of the delusion. He actually felt sad for Slide. Like a wild animal that had eaten the poisoned meat set out for it and was now vomiting it out again, along with its own guts. Madness that tailored itself to the desires of the individual; Linda wanted her child to be alive and not dead, and Slide wanted the old glory days, the days of craziness and blood, to return. And for both of them, the same delusion—the living child—turned the wheel to which they had bound themselves.

''And that's how you're going to do it?'' said Tyler, perhaps too soft for Slide to hear. ''You think my son's alive, and somehow that means you can put the Group together again.''

"We can put the Group together again." Slide's voice was as quiet, as though next to his ear. "It'll be just like before. We'll all be in there together again."

"And you want me to help you." An open invitation: join in the craziness. Eat the delusion, draw it down into yourself, become it. "I won't," he called up to the projection booth. "It's not true, my son's dead, and I won't—"

He stopped, listening to the silence in the theatre. Slide was gone; he knew he was alone now. He turned and looked at the blank, empty light shining on the screen.

"Check this out—nneee-yow!"

She stepped back, momentarily startled by the apparition that came swooping in a waist-high curve as soon as she'd come in the door. "Jesus, Eddie, you nearly made me drop this stuff."

With no contrition, her son held up the spiky-looking plastic model for her inspection.

Shifting her books in the crook of one arm and the Ralphs supermarket bag in the other, Steff bent down to look. "It doesn't have any wheels on it," she noted.

"Because it's a rocket ship," shouted Mike from the front room. "Intergalactic transport's got no wheels."

Bearing the model aloft, Eddie raced down the hallway. Mike looked up from the litter of paper and plastic bits spread across the coffee table. "Obviously," he said, "we're not finished."

"Obviously." She crossed to the kitchen and set

the bag down. "This more *Road Warrior* stuff?"
That had been a big craze with Eddie since Mike had
taken him to see it—to her dismay, when she found
out. Mike's defense had been that the movie was no
more than an extended Coyote and Road Runner
cartoon.

Eddie turned from his admiring the thing to give
her a child's stern look. "No," he said emphatically.

"There's no rocket ships in *Road Warrior*," explained Mike. He came up behind her and poked into
the bag on the table. "As it comes to all adults
eventually, the younger generation finds out that you
are a cultural ignoramus." He pointed Eddie back
to the living room. "We still gotta put the decals on,
ol' scout."

"He's got one on his forehead."

"That's just with spit." Mike peeled it off and
handed it to Eddie. "Don't lose that."

"Special occasion?" said Steff after the rocket,
her son attached below, had flown back to the living
room. "The two of you revised his birthday or
something?"

"Just taking an interest in his education. I don't
want any little morons growing up around here, thinking rocket ships got wheels."

"Your ass."

He stepped around her to the refrigerator and pulled
out a bottle. "And *voilà*—cheap German white from
the Trader Joe bargain bin. Everybody's favorite."

As she fixed dinner, Steff considered Mike's change
of mood. Or the simulation thereof; she had seen right
through this the first time it had happened, and every
time after. Steam drifted up into her face as she
emptied the package of spaghetti into the boiling
water, prodding it with a wooden spoon. From the

other room came the murmuring voices of the television's evening news.

The performance was an improvement in some ways, she admitted to herself. Even if she could detect the studied banter, the guilt behind the small gifts, her son at least took them at face value. *Maybe he does,* she thought, moving between can opener and sink. Or maybe he was just smart enough to. Kids were bright that way, she knew. She could remember her own father, and sitting on his lap when she was very small, as he watched the fights on a big old Philco black-and-white TV. Just to make her laugh, he'd sing along with the cartoon Gillette parrot when it came on between rounds in its straw hat and blazer; she remembered the smell of his workday sweat, like the sharp aroma of the quart bottle of Pabst Blue Ribbon by the rocking chair, and the tickle against her cheek of the hair curling over the neck of his T-shirt as she laid her head against his chest; the clang of the bell when the shining men came out from the corners of the ring again and swung their great pillowed fists at each other.

"Shit," she said, quietly so they wouldn't hear her in the front room. Lost in memory, she had poked a spoon at the canned tomatoes sizzling in the skillet's garlic and butter, and one had spat seeds and pulp across her apron. She dabbed at it with a paper towel.

She remembered the warm safety of her father's lap even now, long after other memories had been laid across that one, like transparencies in an anatomy text that built up layers of bone and organ into a body complete except for the concealing skin. (*Her mother in the kitchen—always there, that little world—and looking up, wondering, at the hands shaking as they peeled a potato at the sink, and her mother suddenly gazing down at her—what age? five? younger?—and the imprint of her father's wide hand still bloodless on the cheek wet with tears.*) Maybe the small gifts were some genetic program in the male of the species; she remembered those, too, the flowers wrapped in a cone of newspaper, the drugstore perfumes that were always too sweet for her mother to wear but always stayed on top of her dresser in their gaudy, odd-shaped bottles. Her mother never threw them out until after her father was dead. After the long-undiagnosed illness that had clamped down on the blood going into his brain, like a fist squeezing inside his skull, triggering those red-visioned rages, finally broke the fragile gray tissue and she found him, shoulder blocking the bathroom door, his hand still trembling against the electric shaver buzzing on the cold tile floor. (*Darkened hospital room, the green lines tracing notches of breath and heartbeat on the screen above the bed. Until the green lines were straight, registering nothing.*) She'd stayed home from high school all the week of the funeral, to be with her mother, and had found the perfume bottles, all of them, carefully broken at the bottom of the trash can behind the house, the faded scents mingling in the sweet smell of crushed flowers.

So what did it mean? She stood in her own kitchen now, her hands the ones that chopped and peeled and stirred, the simple inheritance of craft. The grave and memory had swallowed those others—her mother just a couple of years after her father—that she had watched, looking up at them and wondering, as they carried out their mysterious comings and goings, shouted angry words and burning silences. Now she lived in that adult world that went on just above a child's head. She wondered if she understood it any better now.

The question, the scary question, was always if you were living your parents' lives over again. That was another thing they had talked about at the shelter. And whether you loved someone because you understood that the thing inside them, the sickness with the sharp edge that broke through the careful control

(*the blood vessels clamping off the oxygen in the brain until all her father could see was red*)

(*the book Mike kept hidden in the closet, the woman's face in the newspaper photo, memories unspoken but as red*)

that thing was something different and not really them. Or whether—like those women who went on marrying one alcoholic after another, because their fathers had been alcoholics—that other thing was what you wanted, punishment or just the way you had learned to spell out love when you were a child. *I want a mean bastard, just like the mean bastard who married dear old Mom.* Scary to think about; it meant that the real sickness had somehow got inside of you, become a family pattern as much as the color of your eyes or the shape of your nose. And that the cure for it was to stop loving the person you did love.

That was how the past worked. You thought you were getting away from it, and it was there waiting on the other side for you.

Her hands had gone about their business, tearing lettuce into a salad, while she had been elsewhere in her thoughts. She carried the bowl to the table. Through the doorway she could see Mike, now watching the evening news while Eddie piloted the new rocket ship, wheels or not, across the carpet.

As she watched, Eddie sat back and held up the

model, pointing out some detail for Mike's inspection; Mike went on gazing at the TV screen as if he didn't see or hear Eddie, until he suddenly jerked his gaze down to the child. The expression on his face—almost fierce, as though snapping out of a violent dream—silenced Eddie's chatter, until Mike's face softened and his hand reached to tousle the child's hair.

A slipup in the performance there. *What's the next one going to be?* she wondered as she pulled rattling tableware out of a drawer. The question she didn't even want to let into her mind was what she would do about it.

The interruption from Eddie had been enough to pull Mike out of his dark meditation. He sauntered into the kitchen, giving her a one-handed hug as he looked over the steaming pot on the stove. "Looks like it's about time to open this sucker," he said, pulling the wine out of the refrigerator.

He bent over, gripping the bottle between his legs as he threaded the corkscrew in. His hand came flying up as the cork suddenly disintegrated, half of it still stuck in the neck. She glimpsed a welling spot of blood on his finger where the curved point of the screw had nicked him. Then glass and wine splashed wide across the kitchen. The splintering crash of the bottle as he threw it against the wall rocked her back against the counter.

"Wow," breathed Eddie, wide-eyed, from the doorway.

Mike whirled around, the blood pumped bright into his face. She reached for his arm, to grab him and hold him back from the child.

It wasn't necessary. Mike's face drained white as his shoulders dropped the hunch into which they had drawn his spine. His eyes were dazed for a second as he looked at Eddie, then the gaze swung around to hers and to the wall behind him. Sparks of glass slid through the wet to the floor.

He moistened his lips. "Guess we should be glad it wasn't a red." He managed a smile for Eddie. "Hey, scout. Get me some old newspapers from the hall closet, okay? Got a mess to clean up."

"Sorry," he murmured when Eddie had run off to get the papers. He sucked the blood spot from the end of his finger.

The performance went back into place, and ran seamless all through dinner.

As she washed the dishes, she glanced over at Mike sorting through the orange plastic medication containers on one of the cupboard shelves. He assembled his late-night dosage and wrapped it up in a square of aluminum foil.

"I'm going back to the movie house," he said, slipping the foil into his coat pocket. "Help 'em lock up."

"This early?" The wall clock read just before eight. Usually, when he went back to the theatre at night, he timed it so that he got there when the last showing was over and the customers were already filing out.

"I got some paperwork to catch up on. One of the distributors has been sending out these bullshit survey forms we all got to fill out."

"Hold on." She wiped her soapy hands on a dish towel. "I'll go out to the car with you."

Eddie was sitting in front of the television, the rocket ship installed on top. "Right back," she called at the hallway, and he nodded without looking around from the screen.

She slid into the passenger seat beside Mike. He put the key into the ignition and then waited, knowing that she had something to say to him. He was already prepared for it.

In the car's dark interior, the streetlamps' blue sliding through the windshield, she leaned closer to him. "Look, I know there's something wrong."

He made no denial, gazing down the sidewalk to the brighter flow of traffic at the end of the block.

"Since that picture was in the paper. You know, your ex-wife."

He nodded slightly, still not looking at her.

Then the harder part, the words she had been taking apart and reassembling all through dinner. "If it's going to be something that takes a while to work out—if you need time to be alone, to think about things—that can be arranged." She touched his shoulder. "I mean, I can pack up some stuff and take Eddie over to Pauline's—she'd put us up for a while. And if—"

Mike turned his face to her. The dim light coming into the car only caught him from the neck down. "You don't have to do that," he said. "It's okay."

She looked at him for a few seconds before she spoke. "I have to think about Eddie," she said quietly. "About what he sees."

He shook his head. "It'll be all right. Nothing's going to happen."

"Mike, it's *okay*. I mean, if you need the time. I know what it's like—"

"You don't know." His voice hardened. "You don't know anything." He looked away again, across his hands tinted blue on the top curve of the steering wheel, through the dark to the red streaks of taillights moving in the distance. "You haven't been there."

She watched in silence as he tilted his head back, kneading his brow with one hand. "Don't worry," he said, voice his own once more. "It'll be all right."

Standing on the sidewalk in the warm night air, she watched him drive off. The wind, or something else, rustled the thick ivy at the edge of the sidewalk. When the car lights had merged with the others, the hard bright river cutting through the dark, she turned and walked slowly back to the apartment.

NINE

He knew the bookstore closed at ten. So he had plenty of time. Tyler drove down to Melrose and east on it, past where the bright fronts of the clothes stores changed to the subdued lighting of interior decorators.

The store had changed since he'd last seen it. That had been a long time ago, in that other life before the Wyle Group. It had been converted from an ordinary house to start with, in good ecology-minded recycling style, a bit run-down from its closeness to a busy street. Pocketing his car keys, Tyler stepped up to the wooden porch. The hand-carved sign with its spreading-tree emblem swung over his head. That much had stayed the same; but where he had parked on the side, he had been able to see that the back of the house had been ripped out and a new construction of white stucco and broad, jutting roof beams, twice as large as the original house, had been tacked on. A large circular window colored the sidewalk with the light streaming through the modernistic stained-glass rose at its center.

A brass bell jangled as he pushed open the door. The girl behind the cash register marked her place in her book with her finger and looked up as he approached.

"Bonnie Rees working tonight?"

The girl nodded. She had on earrings made of small bright feathers, the same as on the glass shelves inside the counter, alongside the bits of polished crystal mounted in silver. "I think she's back in the office."

He followed the direction of her pointed finger. "Thanks."

Past the shelves lining the walls of what had once been ordinary rooms in an ordinary house, long since transformed into a cluttered maze by the rows of books lined from floor to ceiling, the wider spaces of the new extension could be seen. A few customers wandered the aisles. Tyler pushed past a balding, bearded type in Rajneeshee red cotton pants and shirt.

He recognized Bonnie from the top of her head as she looked over order forms spread across a desk. Her once-blond hair had darkened to a mousy brown, but was still pulled back and braided. She looked up when he knocked on the doorframe.

"Michael." She blinked at him in surprise. Her hands fluttered across the papers, as if suddenly detached from her.

"Long time," he said. He smiled, hoping to calm her. "Got a moment?"

"I should've known you'd be coming by." She lifted a stack of leaflets from an empty chair and let him pull it to the other side of the desk. "Everybody else has been here. Since . . . Linda was arrested."

"Like who?" He sat down and folded his hands in his lap.

Behind the woman's head was an antiwar poster, a Picasso dove, so old that the edges had yellowed and curled away from the wall. She shrugged. "Kinross—

of course. He's come around before, though. And that other guy . . . the one you wrote the book with."

"He wrote it. I just told him some things." Tyler tilted his head toward the rooms past the office door. "You keep it in stock here?"

Bonnie shook her head. "It's not really our sort of thing. People can always go to the B. Dalton to get that."

"I suppose. What about Wyle's stuff? Have any of that around?" He kept his voice level, easy.

The hands had come to rest, but the name spoken brought a twitch to them. She bit her pale, uncolored lip. "Some. Some of the early stuff. People still ask for it. They keep it in print."

"The early stuff. Right—for the real purists." His voice slipped into sarcasm. "Looks like business is all right. They've really expanded this place. I remember when it was a real hole in the wall, stuffed with every freeze-dried hippie in L.A. Could hardly see the books for the patchouli in the air. You the manager now?"

Her braid swung as she shook her head. "Just the assistant. But I fill in sometimes—the owners went with the manager to India for a month."

"Really? People still do that—I'm amazed. I would've thought by now they'd have come up with a simpler way of getting amoebic dysentery."

"Don't tease, Mike. Please."

He fell silent and regarded her. She was actually holding back from tears; even his words were too much violence for her. *Now, at least,* he thought. So much for the theory that, witnessed or committed, it hardened you. Her passage through the Wyle Group had left her fragile as thin glass. Once, along with the rest of the Group, she would've despised a place like this, with its muddle of Zen and Esalen, complete to the pot of herbal tea simmering beneath a hand-lettered HELP YOURSELF sign. Now it was a refuge for her; he could imagine the little route her world had shrunk to, a triangle between here and the Erewhon health-food store on Beverly Boulevard and somewhere a small cat-filled apartment. (*Your world's so much better?* His own voice mocking inside his skull. *It's small as the little room you thought they were letting you out of. But you don't mind. You're a tame rat now.*)

"I'm sorry," he said. They all had gone through the wars together; how each of them lived in the charred battlefield left afterward was a private matter.

"It's all right." She brushed a loose strand of hair away from her face. "What'd you come by for?"

"Nothing." He gripped the arms of the chair to stand up.

"You wanted to ask me something. Didn't you?"

"Forget it," he said. If she was as fragile as glass, she was also as transparent. *She doesn't know anything*, he thought.

"You wanted to know if I'd seen them." She drew up enough strength to say the names. "If I'd seen Linda. Or Slide. That's what the others wanted to know."

"You don't have to tell me anything." He knew he could have seen straight through to it if she had.

"I haven't seen them," said Bonnie simply. "I don't know anything about them. It's all a long time ago for me."

"I'm glad." He stood up and pulled open the office door. "You should keep it that way." He walked through the narrow aisles without looking back. On the sidewalk, the colored rose fell across him as he headed for his car.

After midnight, and the sound studio's lobby was as lit up as a law office's would be in the middle of the day. This was another world that went on all through the dark hours; studios of one kind or another, dotted all through Los Angeles, went on sleeplessly hammering out the fine details of their product.

The only difference was the locked door. You couldn't just walk in. Tyler pressed the button underneath the speaker grille. Through the glass he could see the girl break off her conversation with the fellow leaning on the reception desk. They both looked around at him.

"Yes?" Her voice crackled through the speaker. Insulated by the glass door, her lips seemed to move in silence along with the words. "Can I help you?"

Tyler imagined they got a lot of bums and weirdos coming by and eyeing the plush, soft-lit lobby at night. Or worse, teenagers of any sexual variety tracking down a street rumor of some idol having booked 24-track recording time. That explained the icy, formal hostility in the girl's voice upon sight of anyone she didn't recognize, the determination to keep those on the outside on the other side of the glass.

He leaned close to the grille. "Ken Ruhman's expecting me. I called him."

Deadpan bored, the receptionist worked some other buttons on her desk. After a moment, her mouth moved again, silent to him, then the door buzzed and clicked as the lock opened.

"Down to the end of the corridor and left." She pointed a pen toward a towering glossy-leafed plant and track lighting receding from the desk. The guy she had been talking to continued his lean on the counter, watching Tyler standing next to him. A thick package of hexagonal film cans bound with a padlock stood against his legs. "You'll see his name on the scheduling sheet on the door."

He felt their gaze turning and following him as he walked. From the street, the building looked like a warehouse, with a chain link gate protecting the cars parked in front, and had probably been converted from one. It was only when you got inside—if you got inside—that the deep carpets, cooled and filtered air, and bland, emotion-free abstracts under precise spots of light were revealed. *And soundproofing*, thought Tyler as he went down the corridor. It had struck him the only other time he had come here to see Ken: where the constructing of sounds was the business, those were the only quiet places in L.A.

The red bulb over the door was unlit. He pushed it open and stepped into the darkness on the other side. It took a moment for his eyes to adjust and to see the rows of plush seats facing an unlit screen.

The studio room was a miniature movie theatre, different from the usual sort such as he managed. Only about fifty seats arranged in a wide crescent, wider and plusher, with an elaborate system of buttons and a tiny light on a chrome gooseneck stalk built into the arms. And the screen was wider, not a boxy rectangle for black-and-white MGM revivals and grainy foreign expressionism, but a full 70mm projection sweep. Movies weren't watched here, except to have their final gloss tacked on.

A little crawl of recent memory, as he stood looking around the dark space: standing in an empty theatre, the screen blank and listening . . .

The voice came from behind him. "Hello, Mike. What's up?"

He turned and looked. Behind the last plush seats a curved half wall separated a recessed area from the rest of the studio. The other's face was lit by another one of the stalk lamps as he leaned across the top. His glasses caught the reflection of the dials and switches in the editing console below.

"You're working too hard, Ken." Tyler walked past the seats, his hand brushing the velvet backs. "You ought to try going out of here sometime. Don't you read the papers?"

Ken swiveled his chair around and pushed another toward Tyler. "Oh, you mean that stuff about them finding Linda. Yeah, I heard." He tilted the chair back to reach for a pack of cigarettes on the console. "They were bound to get her sooner or later."

Tyler looked about as he sat down. The walls of the recessed area behind the theatre seats were filled with the equipment with which Ken worked: big half-track tape machines, a bank of video monitors, a sound mixing board with row upon row of knobs and slide controls. Wire racks filled with metal film canisters and reels of recording tape, each with a neatly hand-lettered label, covered the back wall. A multicolored cable ran from a computer in one niche to a small music keyboard; incongruously among all the electronics, an alto saxophone leaned in one corner.

"Who'd you hear it from?" he asked.

Ken smiled. "Who else? Bedell, of course. That turkey was on the phone before I had a *chance* to see the papers."

"What'd he want?"

The glasses rode up on the back of Ken's hand as he rubbed his eyes, bloodshot from hours at the editing console. "Same thing he probably called you up about. He's running around, trying to put together some kind of deal. Going around, calling anybody he can think of." He straightened his glasses and looked at Tyler. "You know, I wouldn't advise it, if you were thinking of going in on something with him."

An overhead vent efficiently sucked away the smoke from Ken's cigarette. "Why's that?" said Tyler.

"Come on. The guy's a flake. He had his one lucky break with you, and he's blown everything since. He bounced by here—about a year ago, I think—and gabbled at me for an hour about some documentary he said he had a producer lined up for, wanted me to work on the sound track. Wyle Group stuff, naturally. I finally had to call security to get him out of here. Turns out this producer had already told his secretary not to put through any more calls from Bedell." Ken shook his head. "I'd forget him if I were you. You don't need money, do you?"

"No, I'm doing all right." He looked at his own hands spread against his pants legs. "I already told Bedell to take a hike." *Lucky break,* he mused. That was a weird way to put it. People get killed, and it's a lucky break for someone else. Maybe it was understandable that Ken would think that way; he had done all right through his involvement with the Wyle Group. Tyler remembered him as a clever nineteen-year-old, mucking about in the university's media department while humping sound systems at some rock dive in Costa Mesa, when he'd drifted in. Or actually recruited: the Group had needed somebody who knew what he was doing to handle all the fancy videotape gear that Wyle's continuing book royalties had bought. (Later, lying on a bunk in one of those small rooms

that became his world, Tyler had time to reflect on
the narcissism of madness. Back in the sixties, the
Manson Family had liked to record their little rituals,
too. The camera and microphone were toys for a
certain vanity. Or was blood so mesmerizing that
having once seen it smeared on your palms, you
could never see it enough?) The Group's elaborate
equipment had been the perfect sandbox for Ken to
play out his self-taught apprenticeship. Being on the
other side of the video recorder, watching it all, had
insulated him more than just legally; he'd gotten off
lightly in court and in a short stay in some private
hospital. And L.A. studios didn't care where you had
gotten your expertise, so long as you knew what
knobs to twist.

Miles of tape had threaded their way under Ken's
hands when he'd been in the Group. A few snippets
had shown up in the courtroom. Rumors went around
town about what had happened to the rest; screening
parties up in Beverly Hills mansions, film execs who
had seen everything, jaded by special-effects fakery,
ready for the real thing. If the stories were true, he
couldn't knock Ken for having converted the stained
relics of the Group into the kind of currency that had
gotten him the gig at the studio. He'd found the
money that came in from his share of Bedell's book
handy enough, if something he had never planned on
getting. The writer's microphone had just been a
handy ear in which to talk, and go on talking, until it
was all out.

"What'd you want to see me about, then?" said
Ken.

Tyler looked out across the console and the rows
of seats to the empty screen. "There's some other

stuff going on." He turned back to Ken. "About the Group."

"Like what?"

He leaned forward in the chair, narrowing the gap between them. "I want you to tell me something. And it'd better be the truth. Have you heard from Slide?"

Ken folded his arms across his chest and leaned back, pushing himself away. "What're you talking about?"

"You heard me," said Tyler quietly. "Slide—has he called you up? Come by here? Tell me."

"I haven't seen that fucker in years. Since back then." Ken started to fish another cigarette out of the pack. "And I don't want to see him, either."

Tyler waited until the other's gaze returned to him. In silence, he looked past the nervous twitch of the eyelids behind the glasses and into the dark centers. His stare lasted a few seconds, then he straightened up in the chair. He had seen nothing.

He stood up. "If you do hear from him, let me know."

Ken followed him to the studio door. The light from the corridor washed across his face, pale from night hours and more. "Maybe you'd better not come around here again," he said.

Tyler looked down the corridor. Around the corner and past the glass door, it would still be dark outside. "Maybe so," he said.

He lay in bed thinking. Tyler could hear Steff's soft breathing, her warmth next to him.

Doesn't prove a thing, he told himself. Staring up, he could make out the rough surface of the ceiling in the dark. All of his driving around that night, looking up old Group members, had been wasted time. Additions to the parade of faces from his own past, which had started with Linda's photo in the newspaper. And their voices—if Bonnie and Ken had been lying to him, in the words unspoken as well, how was he to know? *No way*, he thought. If they were in with Slide on this, if they and all the other Wyle Group veterans, both in and out of various lockups, were looking to put the group together again, they wouldn't tell him. The fact that he had to ask proved that he was on the outside. And when you were on the outside you didn't get told the secrets. Until it was too late.

He rolled on his side. Enough light from the streetlamps came down the side of the building to the bedroom window that he could see her profile against the pillow, the lashes on her cheek. She stirred, burrowing further into sleep, as he carefully lifted the blanket and slid his legs out of the bed.

Eddie's door was slightly open. He looked for a moment at the small sleeping figure, then padded barefoot down the hallway to the front room.

Tyler stood in the middle of the dark room listening. The chair had been pulled, by him, away from the window and back to its usual position by the couch. In his blood, the slow trickle of medications left the room's objects dull silhouettes against the unrevealing dim light through the curtain. His own shadow sank into the carpet around his feet.

He turned his head toward the kitchen. The telephone's looped cord dangled alongside the doorway. He waited, listening to his own breath in the silence. If the phone rang now, he knew who it would be on the other end.

And what would I say to him? There were other

questions he hadn't even asked of the ones he had spoken to this night, questions about a child and a grave.

But to ask those questions would be more than admitting he was on the outside, not in on the secrets.

He felt cold, as if a draft had penetrated the window and his skin.

Don't mess around with that stuff.

The warning no longer sounded like his own voice inside his head. His voice wanted to ask where his son Bryan was, if he wasn't in that small grave with the ancient stalky palm trees nodding over the night-dark grass.

And he knew that would be how it would start. By admitting that little possibility into his mind. *That's how you join them,* he thought, closing his eyes to the room. *In there with them again. First you tell yourself that it might just be true, it's possible . . .*

Then you wound up knowing it was true.

A drunken voice shouted something, faint from the end of the block where the bars were.

Don't. But underneath the warning, the whisper in his own voice: *But what if . . .*

He stood in the middle of the dark room, head bowed against his chest, as if listening, waiting for one small sound.

TEN

"**W**ell. This is bright and early." Bedell stepped back, throwing the door open. "Come on in."

Tyler stepped into the house. He had been pushing the doorbell button for a full two minutes. Out of the morning sunlight's glare, he scanned the sparsely furnished living room. There seemed to be an unusual amount of dirty coffee cups scattered about, some still half full, with cigarette stubs drowned in them.

"What brings you around?" Bedell extracted a cigarette pack and matches from the pockets of his bathrobe. He stood with his back to the wall's bookshelves. "I got the impression," he said coolly, "that you'd already made your decisions."

"Maybe not." Tyler tucked his sunglasses into his shirt. "Maybe I'm still thinking things over."

"Really." The other nodded, rubbing his pursed lower lip. He gave Tyler a half-lidded glance. "Maybe you'd better hope the offer's still open."

"Don't give me that shit." Tyler strode past him to where the room opened onto the kitchen. Beyond the greasy dishes stacked in the sink, and the empty frozen-dinner cartons piled on the counter with the brown triangles of used coffee filters, he could see out to the backyard. Beyond the uncurtained sliding

door, brown weeds crowded the concrete patio slab.
"You're not in a position to negotiate anything with
me," he said, voice hardening as he turned back to
him. "You might be able to put together a deal if
you can tell some publisher you've got me working
with you. But it's a sure thing you can't if you don't
have me in on it."

The pivot of Bedell's jaw worked, as if he were
chewing away the flesh from inside. "What do you
know," he said tightly. "My agent's got people on
the line right now."

"Bullshit." Tyler stalked around him, tracing a
wide circle across the marks in the carpet where the
furniture had once stood. "You're a joke all over
town. Everybody knows how much you've fucked
up."

The puffy flesh went pale. "All right," he said.
"Maybe so. But you didn't come by just to shit all
over me. There's something you need, too." His
eyes became smaller, bright hard points. "Isn't there?"

They were on the same wavelength at last. *No
more screwing around*, thought Tyler. Finished with
the pretense of friendliness, comradeship beyond their
names being on the same title page. *Now we can get
down to business*.

"Great." He stopped his pacing. His gaze ran an
unflinching line between his eyes and the other's.
"You get to use me. You tell 'em what you want.
Make whatever deal you can get. But there's something I want to know. And you're going to tell me."

Bedell folded his arms across his chest, waiting.

Don't mess—

He ground his teeth together, a red wash roaring
over the voice inside his skull. He could barely
hear the words sliding out of his own mouth.

"Is my son alive?"

The red faded as his blood slowed. He could hear, somewhere in the house, the idiot buzz of a fly tapping against window glass.

Bedell's eyes widened. "What are you talking about? You mean *Bryan*?"

Another name spoken out loud, the past battering at his head. He felt a dizzying hollow, dark at its center, open up in his chest. "Yes," he said softly, nodding his head.

A sharp, amazed laugh as Bedell rubbed his forehead. "You mean, like Linda thinks. You got the idea from her."

"It doesn't matter where I got it. I just want to know if it's true."

"That's wild. That's really wild." Bedell ground out his cigarette in an ashtray on the bookshelves. His gaze drifted into some private vision. "I mean, after all these years. You been walking around all this time, you know your kid's dead and buried—and then bing, just like that." He snapped his thick fingers. "Some loony babbles at you, and you fall right into it. I thought you were straightened out, man. Like all those pills are supposed to work, or something. But you're as crazy as she is."

He held the rising pulse of his anger down. "I want to know," he said evenly, "if the child in that grave is my son."

"Who the hell do you think it is?" shouted Bedell. "The name's right on the stone."

"Maybe," he said, "that's a lie. Like some of the other things."

"Shit." Bedell's hands fumbled at the cigarette pack, found it empty, and tossed the crumpled wad into the ashtray. "Look. If it's not your son Bryan, then who is it?"

He drew his breath deep inside himself. No sense in turning back, once having gone this far. "Remember Patty?" he said. Another name from the past. "What happened to her?"

"You mean Patty Wright? Jeez, Mike; I put it in the fucking book. She split before the busts. Nobody knew where she'd gone until they found her body up in Oregon. They thought she was one of the Green River Killer victims, then they changed the verdict to suicide. You know that."

"And what about her little boy? What happened to him?"

"Who knows? For Christ's sake, Patty was a god-damn junkie. She had needle tracks up her arms wide as your thumb." Bedell waved his hand at the filing cabinets on the other side of the room. "I can show you the autopsy photos. The body weighed ninety-six pounds when they found her."

"But her son wasn't with her. Nobody up there ever saw her with a kid."

"So what?" Bedell shook his head. "Patty had lost track of herself, let alone her kid. People who live like that aren't up for Mother of the Year awards. She probably sold the kid somewhere along the line to some black-market adoption agency, got enough for a week's supply of smack. If the kid hadn't died of pneumonia or malnutrition before then."

"Patty's child," said Tyler quietly, "was born two days before Bryan was."

"And that's your big theory about this? It was Patty's baby that died, and not your kid? And so it's not little Bryan they buried. You think he's still alive."

Tyler could feel the walls against his shoulders, as though the room had closed around them. Just space enough for him and Bedell's mocking voice. "I never saw Bryan dead. I was locked up when they told me what happened to him. They didn't even let me out for the funeral."

"You've worked this all out, haven't you?" He regarded Tyler with a smile of wonderment. "You've really thought about it."

"Easy enough to substitute one three-week-old baby for another. Patty and Linda looked enough alike to be sisters; the babies had the same dark hair. I remember that. And the way things were falling apart— toward the end, everybody in the Group was so fucked up they didn't know what was going on. Patty was already on to all that other stuff; she was so comatose most of the time, she might not even have known about the switch."

"Come on," protested Bedell. "There's identification methods, even for infants. They take their footprints in the hospital, right in the delivery room."

"Why don't you read your own book? *Those babies weren't born in a hospital.* Remember? Wyle had all those hip theories abut the birth process— Patty and Linda had their babies at the place up in the hills, that old estate where the busts were made. They had that Denny what's-his-name, that med student, for a midwife. And there was all that other crap about the Group raising the kids free of bureaucratic tyranny. Nobody went downtown to the records office. Bryan's birth registration and his death certificate are dated the same goddamn day. Aren't they?"

Bedell shrugged, and nodded. "All this doesn't prove anything. You can think up all the crazy theories you want. You can't prove they're true."

"That's why I came here," said Tyler. He stepped close to the other and laid the point of his finger against the bathrobe's lapel. "You're going to tell me."

He backed away from the fierce glare facing him. "You crazy? How the hell am I supposed to know about something like this?"

Tyler turned and strode to the file cabinets and jerked one of the top drawers open. Papers scattered in a white flurry as he grabbed a handful of manila folders and threw them on the floor.

"You've made this your whole career." Tyler's clenched jaw ground out the words. "The Wyle Group's become your life. You've dug up every little scrap of information, every photo, every rumor. Gone all over the country, digging up anybody who'd ever had the slightest connection with the Group. That's all you've ever done—because your book's been the only success you've ever had. And you need that to happen again; I know that. You've got stuff in here you've found out since the book; stuff nobody else knows. So if anybody would know the truth, some little thing that hadn't been told yet about the Group, you'd be the one, wouldn't you?"

Bedell returned his level gaze. "Maybe," he said. "But if I'd come across something—if I knew your son was alive, why wouldn't I have told you about it?"

"That's not how you work it. You like to have secrets. Keep something to yourself until you can get paid for telling it—that's how it's done, isn't it?" Tyler's eyes narrowed as he looked at the other's face. "That's how you keep people on the line."

Bedell looked at the files strewn across the floor, then back up to Tyler. "What if I told you that you were right?'' he said quietly. "How would you know that I was telling you the truth, then? Even if I showed you something, some kind of proof your son's alive, how would you know it wasn't fake? And that I was just telling you what you wanted to hear? Something that would hook you on to that line even harder.''

He could feel the pulse at his temples, blotting out the room, everything except the face in front of him. "Just tell me. *Is he alive?*''

"What's it matter—if I tell you the kid's alive or he isn't. You're fucked up, man. You've lost it. You've bought the whole story.'' One hand gestured angrily at the window. "Slide's out there with your kid, that he stole from Linda, just like she told you. That's what you believe. It doesn't matter what I tell you.''

Tyler could feel how the fleshy neck would fill his palms, how the small eyes would bulge from their sockets as he pressed his thumbs into the windpipe. He jammed his sweating hands into his pockets.

"You want me to tell you something?'' Bedell's voice rose in pitch. "I'll tell you something. For all the good it'll do you. I've heard all this before. I talked to Patty Wright up in Portland before she died. A long time back; she actually wrote to me. How's that? She told me that it was her baby that died, that your son was still alive, Linda had him with her—all of that. It's not a new story to me.''

"And you knew this? Why didn't you tell me?''

"Because there's no proof, Tyler. Because Patty was a strung-out emaciated junkie, who didn't know what fucking planet she was on. She mumbled all kinds of shit at me—Wyle was God and was going to take her to Paris on a crosstown bus. For Christ's sake; how much of the stuff *you* believed when your brain was blitzed turned out to be true?'' His hands plucked the empty pack from the ashtray, tore it open in their search, and threw it back down in disgust.

Tyler turned and stared out the window at the bright sunshine washing over the street. Behind him he could hear Bedell's voice going on.

''That's why I didn't tell you. What's the point in your screwing up your head with some loony idea? These are nuts talking, Tyler. You know that. You can listen to them, but you can't believe what they say. Not without proof.''

He faced Bedell, but said nothing.

''Come on.'' Bedell spread his hands placatingly. ''Forget this stuff. We got a book to do.''

Tyler shook his head slowly. ''There isn't going to be any book. Not with me.''

''What about our deal? I came straight with you.''

''Screw you. You've gotten enough out of me. And you knew things, all this time, that you didn't tell me. So you can go to hell.''

Bedell followed him to the door and grabbed his arm. His face was flushed red with anger. ''Hold it, Tyler.''

He pushed Bedell away. ''Don't touch me. You make me sick. You can't get enough of the Wyle Group—because you dig it. The book was just an excuse. All that blood gets you excited.'' He spat the words into the broad, sweating face. ''You wish you could've been in there with us, don't you? With me and Slide and Linda, and all the others. But you're not. You'll never be in there. You'll always be on the outside, trying to look in where it's dark. But you'll never know. You'll never know what it's like in there.''

Outside, the sunlight glistened on Bedell's contorted face. From the doorway, he jabbed his finger at Tyler, heading for his car in the driveway. "All right, Tyler!" he shouted. "You go ahead, man. You want your fucking proof, you know how you can get it." His voice hung, high-pitched, in the street's still air.

Tyler yanked the car door open, the other's words beating against his back.

"You're so proud of having been in there, huh? You really know what it's like, don't you?" Bedell's shout scraped hoarse. "Go back in, then—it's easy enough for you. Then you'll know what's true, won't you?"

A glance in the mirror as Tyler drove off showed the trembling figure standing in the doorway, staring after him all the way down the street.

"What do you think he meant by that?"

Tyler looked up from his hand resting on the desk to the therapist's face. "Meant by what?"

Across from him, Goodrich read some notes off his pad. "He said something about it being *easy for you*—some way of finding out if all this about your son was true or not."

He nodded. His twice-weekly appointment with the shrink had followed in a couple of hours after his encounter with Bedell. The time in between had been filled with just driving, a mechanical winding through onramps and streets, the working of wheel and pedal automatic as his thoughts followed their own courses.

Goodrich had listened to the whole account of the words that had passed between Bedell and himself, with no change of expression on the thin, scraggly-bearded face. *Don't even know why I told him*, thought

Tyler. Perhaps it had just been a matter of thinking out loud, running the tape over again in his head to see it clearer. Part of him wondered if he should have told the shrink all of it—admitting that he was entertaining the notion of his son still being alive was, he knew, a sure self-damning confession. *That's the kind of thing you talk about, they know you're nuts.* And he realized he didn't give a shit what the therapist thought of it.

"I suppose," Tyler said slowly, "he meant stop taking my medications."

The therapist nodded, waiting.

"That way—"He pulled the idea out into the light, as much for his own inspection as for the shrink's. "It would come back. From inside me. The shared mind effect of the Host; I'd feel it again."

"That's true," said Goodrich. "As far as we know, the alteration in your brain chemistry is permanent. You had tests, what . . ." He opened a file folder on the desk and paged through it. "About a year ago. The elevated serotonin level is the key index. The CAT scans show no change in that since we started running them on you back at the hospital."

"So if I stopped taking the pills . . ." *Yes,* he heard his own voice say inside his head. *That's the way. Back inside.* "I'd experience the shared mind again."

"You'd experience the *delusion* of the shared mind again." The pencil tapped against the folder. "The Host drug never produced any genuine effects. Those were all hallucinations."

Tell me all about it. Tyler regarded the weedy-looking face, serious with its own wisdom, across from him. *You've never been there. You don't know.*

"It's the same expanded-consciousness line that's

been handed out since the sixties. Leary and all the rest of those drug salesmen. Now he's a stand-up comedian on the lecture circuit, and the streets are full of burnouts mumbling to themselves. That's real enlightenment, all right.''

Tyler kept his voice level. "The Host was different."

"Christ." The therapist looked disgusted, the first emotion Tyler had ever seen in the bland face. "Look what happened with you and your friends. Talk about a sixties rerun. Manson Family all over again.''

"It wasn't like that."

"Tell it to the victims." He looked down at the file again.

Tyler gazed at the pink bald spot on top of the other's head without seeing it. Against the screen inside his own brow, he could see a night street outlined in blue. It stretched on forever, opening at the horizon as he moved slow and effortless down its center. Faces with eyes of the same electric blue turned toward him as he passed, smiling with sharp-pointed teeth. In the distance he saw Slide standing and waiting for him, with the others. A small figure, a child whose face he couldn't make out, stood in front. Waiting.

That's how I could find him, thought Tyler. *That's how Slide found Linda. When they're all in there together, in the dark and the group mind, nobody can hide from anybody else. No secrets, no hiding places. Every street's open when you can see in the dark.*

That was how he could find Bryan, too. Living or buried. The vision became a field of grass, the stones black against the unlit ground and the ragged shadows of the palms.

The grass stirred, as though a hand brushed it softly to let the blue light seep from underneath.

"Tyler—listen to me."

He opened his eyes to the bright office and the therapist's face on the other side of the desk.

"I want to show you something." A thick manila envelope had been added on top of the file. The therapist pushed his bottom desk drawer shut with his knee. "These are photos," he said, "from the original army lab research on the Host drug." He extracted a thin sheaf of 8-by-10 glossies. "Back when it still had the code designation of 83 Blau."

Tyler took the first picture handed over to him. In it, a wire cage framed three white-faced monkeys. One turned his shining black eyes to the camera lens, staring with sharp curiosity.

"Macaques," said the therapist. "They were used for the tests. Cute and furry, huh? That shot's at the start of the series; the animals were given the drug about a week prior to that. A fourth monkey was dissected, and its brain tissues already showed the altered catecholamine levels." He extended another photo across the desk. "This is about three months later; you can see the date in the corner."

The three animals in the photograph were huddled in separate corners of the cage. One bared his teeth and gums at the camera.

"Nothing was given them to alleviate the drug's effects. They wanted to see what the end result would be if left unchecked. This one's six months into it."

He took it and turned it right side up.

Only two monkeys in the wire cage.

Blood leaked around the teeth of the tiny, bright-eyed scream in the photo's gray-toned depth. One monkey, its fur matted into sticky black points, crouched over the other. The small, humanlike hands spread open the wet chest of the fallen one, the delicate spattered rib cage arching over the small knot of the exposed heart. The eyes pressed into the congealing puddle on the cage's floor had already turned gray.

"One more," said the therapist.

Tyler took it from the other's hand. There was no wire cage in the shot, but something that looked like a twisted rag on the table, with a rubber-gloved hand at the side of the frame turning it over. It took a moment for him to make out the thin limbs extending from the ruined trunk; patches of fur had been chewed away on them.

"The last one disemboweled itself. With its little nails." Goodrich took the photos back from Tyler and slid them into the envelope. "I suppose the SPCA would've had something to say about it all, if they had known. They would've asked that the poor things be put out of their misery. But it was still a classified military research project; they could do anything they wanted." He returned the envelope to the desk drawer. "What do you think of those, Tyler?"

He leaned back in his chair. "I remember when I was in high school," he said. "In health class, the teacher made a nicotine extract from some cigarettes and poured it, this yellow stuff, into a goldfish bowl. The fish died and floated to the top. The teacher asked, 'What does this prove? Anyone?' And this smart-aleck voice from the back of the room said, 'Goldfish shouldn't smoke.' "

"It's not a joking matter." The therapist folded his arms on the desk. "I hadn't shown you those before, because I didn't think there was a problem with your attitude about this. I didn't think you needed any more convincing about the Host drug's nature. You have to face the fact that you're *contaminated* with this substance. Those pictures show the kind of risk you'd be running if you let the drug's effects resurface."

"Really." Contempt filtered into Tyler's voice. "But what if my son's alive? What risk is finding him worth?"

"Your son's dead. You know that. It's no justification for indulging in that high the Host gives. Like all that stuff, there's a payback down the line; you know that, too." He drew a different pad in front of himself and started to write. "I realize you've been under a lot of pressure the last couple of days. There have been stressful events stemming from your ex-wife's arrest. But there's ways of dealing with it. Safe ways." He tore off a small square and handed it to Tyler.

"What's this?" He looked at the scribbled-on prescription form.

"It's for Sinequan. Very helpful in anxiety situations, especially in combination with some of the stuff you're already taking. Get it filled and start it with your next scheduled dosage. We'll assess how it's working the next time you come in."

"That's the answer, is it?" Tyler laughed, looking from the paper to the therapist's earnest face. "It's not a question of drugs; it's just that you think yours are better." He crumpled it into a ball in his fist. "You're as fucked up as I am. You and the rest of the whole fucking straight world. This kind of shit is what all of you take. You don't know what it's like in there, because you don't want to know."

The therapist bit his lower lip. "You're forgetting that your cooperation is a condition of your parole.

You don't have a choice in the matter. And frankly, the attitude you're showing is something I'll have to discuss with your parole officer."

"Fuck that." Tyler stood up, pushing his chair away. "You and your monkey pictures, all that shit. What do I care. You don't understand." He pressed his palms against the desk, bringing his face close to the other's. *"Maybe he's alive."*

Goodrich looked up at him. "So what are you going to do?" he said. "Stop taking the medications?"

"I didn't say I'd decided to do that."

"I want your promise." The watery eyes fastened on to his. "You'll think about it. What we've talked about, what I showed you. And you'll call me— anytime, day or night, I'll tell 'em to put you through— and we'll talk about it some more. Before you do anything. All right?"

Tyler returned the gaze for a moment. Even here, at the center of these pale eyes, he saw the dark. "Sure," he said softly. He pushed himself away from the desk and headed for the door.

ELEVEN

"That motherfucker—"

The glass shook in Bedell's white-ridged fist, slopping the brown liquid over his fingers. For a few seconds he stared at the spots seeping into the carpet, then he flung the glass against the living room wall. Shining jagged bits slid down through the wet, drawing lines like fingernails, smelling of alcohol.

A lawn mower sputtered and roared outside the house. Panting, he tilted his head, listening. Down the street somewhere; the noise approached and faded as a gardener guided the machine around one of the manicured stretches of green. He closed his eyes, swaying in the middle of the room, and could see the smug, impassive face underneath the baseball cap, the dark eyes, that calculated and judged without saying a word. "Bastards," he whispered. He could feel the weight of their gaze through the drawn curtains.

The bottle toppled over on the kitchen counter as his hand touched it, sending the last inches of scotch pulsing across the rim of the sink. The smell was even stronger here, welling up from inside of him. Dizzy, he gripped the edge of stainless steel and saw his own face swirling upside down in the circle grate; he didn't know if he was going to be sick or not.

He took a deep breath when he heard the phone

189

ringing. The sound clattered from the other room,
overlapping the noise of the mower from down the
street. He straightened up, pushing himself away
from the sink.

"Yeah—" He switched off the answering machine
and fumbled the handset to his ear, leaning against
the bookshelves. "Who is it?"

His agent's voice came over the line. He recognized it, but couldn't make out the words over the
lawn mower's roar. The noise got louder in time to
the pulse beating at the center of his skull.

"I don't know," mumbled Bedell. The voice went
on drilling into his ear. "Wait. Wait a minute." If he
concentrated; if he leaned into the sound of the voice,
as though it were as solid as the one behind him . . .

The words jumbled together, meaningless. The lawn
mower screamed, metal striking the edge of the concrete sidewalk. Behind his eyelids the sparks arced
and dazzled.

"I don't know, goddammit!" He slammed the
phone down into its cradle. It fell from the bookshelves and hit the floor by his feet. For a moment,
silence at the end of the coiled plastic; then a soft
electronic hum, the dead line, whispering louder than
any other sound.

"Shit." He let out his breath, steadying the room
around him. *That sonofabitch*, he thought. The
alcohol ebbed a fraction in his bloodstream as he
looked down at the buzzing phone. He carefully
squatted down, gathered it together, and replaced it
on the shelves.

The distant lawn mower, softer now, went on its
rhythmic path. Bedell listened to it, as if hearing it
for the first time. And would never hear it again.

"You're really blowing it," he said aloud in the empty house. "You've really screwed it up."

He wandered through the vacant room, back to the kitchen. The glaring sunshine poured through the sliding glass door, a sloping hot slab across the tiles. In the shade remaining by the sink, he looked across the stained and spotted floor. *Ought to take a mop to it,* he told himself dully. He didn't know if he could find one anywhere in the house. The cleaning service, until he'd finally stopped it, used to bring out all the needed equipment. The whole place would have to be cleaned up, he knew. Part of the process of selling a house, squeezing out the little bit of equity he had in it. Though he supposed that was all out of his hands now. That was the virtue in being foreclosed on; you didn't have to think about it anymore. They did it for you—the ultimate service industry.

Maybe there would be enough scraped together for the security deposit and the first and last months' rent on an apartment. He remembered the little one he'd had behind the post office on Fairfax. That had been all right. The book had been written there. *Maybe,* he thought, *that's the only place you can write.* Some little hole like that, with the water stain spreading brown across the ceiling's acoustic tiles as you stared up from the trough of the sagging bed, the sheets smelling of your own sweat. Maybe that was where he should have been all this time.

He looked through the doorway to the front room. Without any furniture, it seemed huge. That old apartment could have just about fit in it. Big house, big lawn, big everything; down the street, he could hear the gardener's air blower pushing the damp green cuttings into the gutter. Too bad to give this up. *And all because of that sonofabitch Tyler,* he thought. He could see his face, hear the smug, infuriating words.

You wish you could've been in there with us, don't you? Tyler's sneering voice unreeled from memory. *But you're not. You'll never be in there. You'll be on the outside, trying to look in where it's dark. But you'll never know. You'll never know what it's like in there.*

On the outside . . . They were all so smug, so smart; all of the Wyle Group, every one he'd met, interviewed, researched so carefully. That was his reward for putting them all into the book: their eyes looking at him with contempt, full of the secrets they hadn't told him, hadn't told anyone . . . Tyler was probably laughing at him right now as he drove down the street.

"Fuck him," Bedell said aloud. His voice echoed hollow in the empty house. *Who needs them . . . any of them.*

A sudden quiet seemed to fill the house, as if the gardener's machines and all the other noises outside had fallen away, the space around the house stretching into distance. He turned his head, listening.

Who needs them . . .

His unspoken words sounded different inside his head, as if in another's voice.

A whisper. . . . *what it's like . . . in there . . .*

Then he remembered. He turned away from the sink and toward the refrigerator. For a moment he looked at it, then stepped closer and laid his hand against the cool metal.

. . . in the dark . . .

His hand trembled as he pulled the door open. A chill breath steamed frost against his face as he stared into the freezer compartment. The thin rectangles of frozen dinners scattered behind him on the floor in a spray of silver crystals. His fingernails scrabbled at the ice built up on the compartment's bottom, finally breaking off a thick layer. Stuck to the underside of the piece melting in his hands was a square of plastic, carefully folded and sealed. He could see the small transparent shapes inside the packet.

Four capsules slid out onto the counter. He crumpled the empty plastic and threw it into the sink. The white powder sifted inside as he held one of the shells to the light.

He didn't need any of them to tell him what it was like. *Easy enough*—his own words to Tyler. Easy enough to find out for himself.

The capsule seemed to weigh nothing between his thumb and forefinger. The substance inside sparkled, catching the light from the sliding glass door.

He wouldn't need Tyler for the new book. *Because*, he thought, examining the tiny object, *I'd be right in there with them*. He'd know—finally—everything they did. There'd be no more secrets.

. . . in the dark . . .

He placed the capsule on his tongue, holding it in his mouth as he filled a glass from the tap. The thin shell had already become slick, dissolving in his saliva, as he tilted the glass and swallowed.

It would take a little while, he knew, to go from his stomach into his blood. The waiting, and then he'd know. Leaning back against the counter, he felt a tiny hard knot in his throat. He turned as his gut contracted, vomiting a wash of sour alcohol into the sink.

The sickness left him panting and dizzy. The blood burned into his face. He swept the other capsules into his fist and brought them to his mouth, tilting his

head back. The powder gritted on his tongue as he
ground them between his teeth. He gripped the edge
of the sink, forcing the thick, bitter wad down his
throat.

He straightened up, brushing his hair from his
damp brow. Now he'd wait. He'd wait and see.

He heard the faint noises of someone working his
way up the dirt slope to the nest. Jimmy knew it
wasn't Slide; Slide didn't make any sound at all
when he came. He was just there, all of a sudden.

Turning around from the sleeping child, he saw a
face peering around the concrete pillar at the nest's
edge. Dirty and all wrinkled—the old woman who
lived in one of the other underpasses close by. He'd
seen her—could smell her, stale piss staining her
tattered clothes yellow—huddled in the middle of her
greasy paper bags, sorting and re-sorting her treasures. *Bunch of old crap*, thought Jimmy. Rags and
wadded-up newspapers. Nothing valuable, like he
had.

The old woman crept closer, into the dim sunlight
angled below the freeway's rim. Her eyes darted
from his face to the little boy beside him.

"Get out of here." He moved between the old
woman and the child. "Go away."

She craned her neck to see, the tendons standing
out like knotted strings. "I heard," she whispered.

"What?" *Crazy old bitch*. Slide would be mad,
when he got back, if he found someone else here.

"About *him*." Her voice curled into a whine. "I
just want to see—"

There were others, down in the shadows at the
base of the slope. He sensed them, watching, muddled awe and fear in their eyes. Out from their little

hiding places, the crevices under the freeway. Too scared to come any closer, but longing to see. The child.

The old woman had come up beside him. One of her dirty hands reached tentatively for the little boy's face. He grabbed her wrist, a bundle of dry twigs, and pulled it away.

"Just to touch—" The rims of her yellow eyes filled with tears. "Just touch—"

"You tell the others," he said, lowering his gaze to hers. "You've seen him. You tell the others. And tell 'em to go away. Okay?"

She nodded, her mouth falling open to show a string of spit between the remnants of her teeth.

He let go of her wrist, and watched as one thin finger touched Bryan's cheek, softly, while the woman's face struggled to comprehend the mystery.

He heard something but didn't know what it was.

Eyes closed, Bedell lay stretched out on the front room carpet, his rolled-up jacket for a pillow. The line of sunlight that came through the opening in the drapes had slid across him until only the back of one hand felt its warmth. He hadn't stirred in that time; hours, he supposed. It wasn't important.

The noise went on, dull rhythmic blows that compressed the edges of the luminous darkness he saw behind his eyelids. Idly, he concentrated on them, bringing the low, distant sounds closer. He recognized them now: someone was knocking on the front door.

He smiled, turning his head on the makeshift pillow. Someone wanted to see him, to talk to him. There was only one person, one thing, that he wanted to see. The sharp-toothed face that the ones who had gone before him had described. (*You want to be in there with them, don't you?*—a voice from long-past memory.) But he could wait. There was all the time in the world in here, in the dark.

The knocking became louder. He opened his eyes and twisted around to look at the door. Somebody wanted to see him badly. The thought made him laugh as he got to his feet and stood up.

"Kinross," said Bedell, smiling. "Come on in." He pulled the door open wider.

The retired policeman looked smaller and grayer than the last time he'd seen him, the brown suit a deflated balloon on his frame. He stood in the middle of the front room, the lined, scowling face looking about; Bedell could see the reel of details scanned and registered passing behind the narrow-eyed gaze. "What brings you around?" he said easily.

"Where's Tyler?" demanded Kinross.

"How should I know?" Standing behind him, he gazed down—as if from a great distance but with an eagle's vision—at the broken blood vessels underneath the strands of hair on the other's scalp.

Kinross turned around and glared at him. "I know you've been talking to him. I want to know what he's told you."

"Really?" He leaned back against the door. "What makes you think he's told me anything? He doesn't have anything to tell me." That was true; he knew that now; Tyler might carry the darkness around inside himself, but he wasn't in it. Not like this.

"Don't screw around with me, Bedell. You could find yourself in some heavy shit. I can promise you that."

The laugh broke out loud. He tilted his head back, letting it escape. It was still ringing in his ears, as though the others had joined in, when he looked back down. Kinross had always frightened him before; the set scowl and small eyes reminded him of some aquatic creature that ate other, smaller ones at a single gulp. But now he was just an old man, shrunken inside a baggy, worn suit.

"You can't do anything to me," he said, returning the other's gaze. The whites of Kinross' eyes were faint yellow, with tiny red networks in the corners. "You can't do anything at all."

The eyes became smaller and sharper. "Maybe not," he said. "Maybe I can't arrest someone and drag them down to the station myself. Not anymore. But my friends can. I've told them everything I've found out."

"And just what have you found out? What great secrets?" It amused him to poke at the old clawless animal.

"I know what Tyler is up to. Him and Slide, and all the others. What they've been planning all along, just waiting for the right time."

Bedell almost felt pity for him. He wouldn't ever know. He'd always be on the outside. He could stare at the darkness for whatever was left of his life, and he'd still never make it across. *Not like I have,* he thought.

"They're going to try and put the Group back together again. That's what they want."

(—*what does he know* . . . A whisper . . . *what* . . .)

He tilted his head, trying to make out the softer voice beneath Kinross' words. Somewhere in the house; he could just hear it. Bitter saliva seeped under his tongue, the same chemical taste that his teeth had ground out of the capsules.

"The Group?" said Bedell softly. He stepped away

from the door, closer to the other. "I don't know
what you mean. Tell me."

Kinross sank into his own bitter musing. The corners of his mouth were wet. "They'll be together
again," he said, his gaze drifting across the room.
"I'll make sure of that. Tyler and all those other
fuckers got off light, but they won't this time. And
nobody will get away, either. I won't let them.
Conspiracy, parole violation . . . they've screwed up
this time. They'll be together again in prison; hard
time, not some cake hospital ward." He turned back
to Bedell. "If you're smart, you'll tell me what
Tyler's been saying to you. A nice little obstruction
charge would do you just fine."

"Together," said Bedell. He nodded, smiling to
himself. The old fool didn't know. He hadn't even
known himself, until now. They had always been
together, in the dark where nobody could see them.

(—yes— Louder this time.)

There was the room around him, filled with the
bright sunlight spilling in from outside. And at the
same time he could see another space, smaller, concrete pressing down onto a hollow scooped out of the
dirt. Slide was waiting for him there. And another;
with Slide's eyes, sharp in the blue-edged darkness,
he could see the child, the small, regular breathing as
it lay huddled up, sleeping.

"You don't know anything," he said, stepping
close enough to touch the other. "We don't have to
put the Group together again. We're all in there now.
All of us."

The small yellowed eyes looked up at his. Bedell
could see the reflection of a face, too small to make
out yet, in the dark centers.

"You're one of them," said Kinross. The sagging

flesh of his face wobbled, as though a gripping hand inside his skull had let go in surprise. "I should have known." The face tightened again, pulled by the heavy jaw clamping into place. "Okay for you, fucker." He jabbed a thick finger at Bedell's chest. "You're going into the can, too. With the rest of your friends. You're all going in—"

(. . . *now* . . .)

He felt himself towering over the old man. He reached down toward the gray, ancient face. "I don't think so," he said softly.

Kinross slashed him across the chest with the back of one arm. Drops of saliva flew from his trembling mouth. "You're not getting off this time! You fuckers . . . you're—"

. . . *now* . . .

His fingers flew, caught and sank into the soft folds of the other's neck. "*We* don't think so."

Now.

Miles beneath him, he saw Kinross' face reddening with blood, the mouth contorted to show the row of dirty yellow teeth under his bottom lip. The brown-suited arms beat against his chest. In slow motion, time freezing, the floor swam up toward him as Kinross fell backward.

The balding head snapped sharp against the floor. The fists opened into trembling claws that reached for Bedell's eyes, then turned soft, boneless as the sagging face beneath him.

His own arms trembled as he pushed himself up from the motionless body. Looking down into the blank eyes, he saw again the face reflected in the dark centers. Standing behind him, he could make out the angled features.

A smile that showed the sharp-pointed teeth.

"Now," came the voice.

Kneeling, he looked away from the slack face under him. The room was darker, smaller, as he turned his gaze over his shoulder.

"Now you're inside," said the Host, smiling.

TWELVE

He sat at the desk in the theatre's office, looking at the small, bright-colored objects scattered in front of him.

Tyler picked up one of the capsules and held it to the light, the rounded ends against the pads of his thumb and forefinger. One half green, the other yellow; the pharmaceutical company's name was spelled out in tiny letters on the side.

What if . . . He no longer heard the other voice, his own words, warning himself. *What if he is alive?*

After Steff left the apartment, taking Eddie to the day-care center and then heading on to her morning classes, Tyler gathered all his medications from the cupboard shelf and dumped them into a paper bag. All the squat cylinders of orange plastic, with the white childproof caps screwed on top, the white sacks from the pharmacy, still unopened and folded over, the receipts stapled on . . . And brought them here. Where he could think.

One by one, he had opened the containers and spilled the contents onto the table. He'd gone through the paper bags after that, wadding them up when empty, throwing them into the can with the cotton stuffing from the new prescriptions.

The surfaces of the capsules glinted in the bright

sunlight. They made a dry, rustling noise as he pushed his hand through them.

Easy enough . . .

All he had to do was nothing. He was already going on two hours late for his first dose of the day, the rattling of the capsules on his tongue and the back of his throat, head thrown back to let the water wash them down into his stomach. If he just waited, the chemicals still in his blood would gradually dissipate, breaking down into nothing, a bitter smell to his sweat and piss, and nothing more.

And then he'd be in there again. He knew that; that was why they gave him the pills in the first place, told him to take them. A few slow hours of waiting, a day's worth, and as the night came on, he'd be able to see again. In the dark.

All he had to do was wait.

He squeezed the capsule between his thumb and forefinger, harder. It broke, snapping along the line between the two colors, spilling a white powder across his knuckles.

That's what they give you, thought Tyler, looking at the smear of dust. *The shrinks, the doctors, all of them. To keep you blind. So fucking self-righteous.* He could see their sober, earnest faces, a line of them.

But what if he's alive . . .

His son didn't mean anything to them. Their job was to keep him from seeing, from finding out. The medicine, the small capsules and pills, was how they did it. And if there was one glimpse, one chance that a child, who he'd been told was dead, was still alive, could be found, brought back from where he'd been taken, back out of the dark . . . Then they gave you more pills. That was how it worked. So you wouldn't ever see that small glimpse again, the sharp edge pressed against your heart would dull and you wouldn't feel it anymore. You'd be like them, blind.

But if he could see, if he could find Slide in whatever dark place he was hiding . . . Then he'd know, one way or another. If his son were alive or dead. *I just want to know.* If the child he'd held only once, the memory of the small weight carved in the flesh of his arms, existed in other than memory.

If Bryan still lived, he'd bring him back out into the light. From wherever he'd been stolen to. And he wouldn't care then what they did to him, what chemicals they poured down his throat, how blind they made him. As long as he could see his son.

And if he found only a dead child . . . then maybe he belonged in the darkness. Not out in the light, pretending the past didn't exist, trying to be a father to another little boy, as if he could replace the one he'd lost. And another woman . . . Steff didn't deserve that. She didn't need to be stained with the dark stuff he had never been able to keep buried behind him. Even to keep up a sham of loving her, he should just go. *Back where I should have stayed. All along.*

He gazed at the capsules and pills for a few minutes longer. Then he reached and gathered them up between his hands, scooping them into a ball. Like the shells of dead insects, they split and crumbled together as he squeezed them harder. He stood up and carried the powdery wad out to the corridor.

In the men's room, the colored fragments dissolved across the top of the toilet bowl's water. They swirled together, a bright whirlpool, as he pushed the chrome handle above.

He pushed open the doors at the end of the corri-

dor and stood gazing at the blank screen. All he had
to do was wait.

He sat with his back against the kitchen doorway,
gazing across the front room. If any sounds came
from outside the house, Bedell no longer heard or
recognized them.

His heart sped up for a moment; he thought he saw
a layer of darkness spreading from beneath the corpse
in the middle of the front room. As he watched,
unable to move from where he had collapsed hours
ago, the dark edge around Kinross' body crept a
fraction of an inch closer to him.

Then his gaze jerked across to the room's drapes,
and he realized that evening was coming on. The
light, dimmer but still strong enough to throw a
shadow, had changed angle. The corpse's outline
was smearing slowly over the carpet, like black blood
seeping from a hidden wound.

Bedell forced himself up on his trembling legs. He
could see Kinross' face now. The yellowed eyes
were open, gazing sightlessly at the ceiling. A line of
saliva had dried from the corner of its mouth.

He reached behind himself and turned on the kitchen
lights. Circling wide around the body, watching it as
it lay unmoving, he reached the bedroom and fumbled the wall switches on. In the bathroom he caught
a quick glimpse of his own white, unshaven face in
the mirror over the sink. There was no overhead light
in the front room, and the table lamps had gone with
the rest of the rental furniture, but enough light spilled
in from the other rooms to see everything. He didn't
want to be alone in the house, in the dark with the
corpse. And the other that he could no longer see,
that he had the one glimpse of as he'd lifted his

hands from Kinross' soft throat. He couldn't see the Host, but he knew it was there still.

The drug's exhilaration had worn off, leaving him weak. He looked down at the body and moistened his dry lips. The memory of his hands upon Kinross' throat inched through his mind, as though watching a slow-motion tape of someone else. The shock when he stood up, realizing what had happened, had driven the chemical's effects away; that and the voice behind him. His tongue curled at the bitter taste still seeping into his mouth.

"Christ," he said aloud, rubbing his sweating face. *Must've been crazy,* he thought. *Even before I took that shit. What the hell was I thinking of?* The blank eyes stared up at him; he looked away, shivering.

His gaze scanned across the empty rooms. Something had to be done with it. The thing on the floor had to vanish, had to be gotten rid of. And soon—he knew that. How many of Kinross' cop friends knew what he'd been poking into? He might even have told some of them exactly where he'd been planning on going today, who he was going to shake down for information. *They'll know.* He wiped his damp hands on his trousers. *They'll come, and they'll find it here.*

Getting rid of it . . . There were places. The desert, a few hours' drive from L.A. Off the main roads; where things were never found. Until maybe years later, when they were just dry leather on splintering bone. If they were found at all.

With the gears of his thoughts slowly meshing, he glanced down again at the corpse. His heart jerked up into his throat. He staggered back, almost falling.

His pulse hammered in his chest as he forced his eyes open and pushed himself away from the wall. Trembling, he stepped close to the body and brought

his gaze down. His pent-up breath rushed out of him
as he saw only Kinross' gray, sagging features.

The other vision was gone. He didn't see any
sharp-pointed teeth smiling up at him.

"Hey, Michael—you all right?"

He heard the voice behind him and twisted around
in the theatre seat. The light from the lobby spilled
down the aisle, silhouetting the figure in the doorway.

"Sure," said Tyler. He'd recognized the projectionist. "What's up?"

"You tell me, man. What're you doing, sitting in
here in the dark?"

Waiting. "Nothing," he said. "Just thinking about
stuff."

"Shit." The projectionist had banged his knee
against one of the wooden armrests as he walked
down the sloping carpet. With the lobby door swung
shut behind him, the only light came from the small fix-
tures at the end of every tenth row, casting hands-
breadth circles on the floor.

Tyler watched as the other sat himself on the
armrest of the seat across the aisle. He could see the
arms folded across the sweatshirt, the stitching on the
denim legs reaching down to a scuffed pair of Adidas
dug against the carpet. *Yes,* he thought, nodding
slowly to himself. A trickle of adrenaline seeped into
his blood. *Easy enough.*

The other's profile, etched in a hairline of electric
blue, turned toward the dark space where the screen
was. "You know," he said, "we're gonna have to
talk to the owners about rehanging that thing. Some
of the customers have started complaining about the
image keystoning."

He smiled, listening to the technical jargon; it

seemed like a transmission from another world, another life. "Those are just wise-ass cinema students," he said idly. "That UCLA bunch. Nothing's too good for them." He shifted, stretching his spine after the hours spent sitting. "Think we're running a museum here or something."

"Naw, they're right, man." The projectionist rubbed the bright microscopic stubble of just-shaved chin. "You can see it even up in the booth—and I've already adjusted the projector angle as far as it'll go. You run a film, and everybody's got foreheads wider than their shoulders." He shook his head. "Just weird, man. Makes Bogart and Bacall look like a love scene between two hydrocephalics."

Tyler laughed, tilting his head back against the top of the seat.

"Just say something to the owners, will ya?" The projectionist sounded sulky. "I get enough abuse from the audience every time one of these crappy old films breaks, without this other shit on top of it."

"Sure." The projectionist was just another poor sucker who didn't know. From where Tyler sat, in the dark, he could see how small these normal concerns were. Black-and-white shadows of dead people cast upon a screen, a world of flat light and nothing more, an illusion. And they complained about how well that illusion was served. *They don't know*, thought Tyler. They sat in the dark, in their silent rows, and saw nothing.

"Don't worry about it," he said, leaning back in the seat. "What time is it?" The other's presence had been the first sign of the hours passing since Tyler's arrival at the empty theatre that morning, to take up his waiting post.

"It was going on six when I let myself in." The

projectionist tilted his head toward the double doors at the top of the aisle. "The rest of the crew are probably standing around outside."

Tyler nodded. The cashier, the refreshments counter girl, the one usher squeezed out of the operating budget—the theatre was no longer going to be empty and quiet. And then the audience; first screening usually started at seven. The theatre would no longer be the silent, empty haven where he'd been sitting through the long daylight hours, waiting while the medications filtered out of his blood.

But the daylight was ending now. It would be dark soon, outside.

"Go let 'em in, will you?" Tyler pointed a thumb at the lobby doors.

Alone again, he gazed up at the blank screen. In the black space he could see a smaller space. It was still indistinct, a dimly lit hollow scooped from loose dust. *Like a cave,* mused Tyler. He could almost sense the sour animal smells of sweat and decaying food. Against his spine he could feel the velvetlike fabric of the seat, and at the same time, faintly, a flat, rough surface weighing down upon him, as if he'd been buried under tons of concrete.

Somewhere—not here in the theatre's high-ceilinged space, but in that other, narrower hollow—a child was breathing.

Not yet. Tyler closed his eyes, but could still see the other darkness behind them. Not yet, but soon. It was coming.

The overhead lights came on; he could see their glow, reddened through the skin of his eyelids. Behind him, he could hear voices on the other side of the doors. He gripped the armrests, pushing himself up from the seat.

The girl behind the refreshments counter said something bright with a smile as he passed through the lobby. He nodded absently at her.

In the men's room, the light bouncing off the white enamel paint and porcelain was bright enough to pain his eyes. He squinted against it, fumbling at his shirt pocket for the sunglasses he used when driving.

As he stood at the urinal, he caught his reflection in the mirror over the sinks. The image, like some hokey hipster routine off an ancient Lenny Bruce record, made him smile. *What's that song?* he thought. *Sunglasses after dark; it's so sharp* . . .

He looked down at the liquid trickling away by his feet. So much for the medications; this was the end result of all that shit they had given him, told him to take. His kidneys had gone about their appointed business of filtering the chemicals out of his blood. They were working now, inside him, cleaning out the rest. Bit by bit; a long job. It was years of blindness to be sent down the drain. He pulled the chrome handle and listened to the water sluice over the porcelain.

The projectionist gestured at him with a paper cup as he headed for the theatre's front doors. "Hey—where you going?" There were already people lined up outside.

"Out," he said. "Enjoy the show."

THIRTEEN

They had left the child sleeping in the nest. Jimmy glanced anxiously over his shoulder as he followed behind Slide. Against the ink blue of the sky a stream of headlights outlined the top of the underpass' black shape.

Slide flexed his shoulders underneath the thin fabric of his jacket, working out the muscles cramped from the nest's narrow confines. Jimmy walked faster to keep up with him.

"Shouldn't we . . . you know—"

Against the sunset reddening the spaces between the distant buildings, Slide's silhouette turned toward him. Jimmy knew he was smiling, his eyes hidden behind mirror shades. The streaming light bled around the face, turning the rows of teeth the same blood color. "What's your problem, jack?" said Slide. "What's troubling you? Huh?"

Jimmy tilted his head back toward the underpass, the nest concealed beyond its dark arch, the child sleeping hidden inside. "Shouldn't we go back?" He looked up at Slide from the corner of his eye. "Nobody's watching him."

"Don't sweat it, for Christ's sake." Slide turned away, gazing into the dying light. "He'll be all right by himself, for a little while. Not going anywhere."

He nodded, as though satisfied with what he saw. "That hole stinks, anyway."

The little boy was important—even more important than what Slide had told him. Jimmy knew that, had felt the realization sink into him during the hours of sitting on his haunches in the nest's scooped hollow, crouching under the freeway's concrete ceiling.

It wasn't that he was worried the little boy—*Bryan*, he reminded himself; *that's his name*—would run away if given the chance. He knew what it was like to wake up, in the dark, too scared to move, able only to huddle warmth and breath into the knot of his own curled-up arms and legs.

The little boy wouldn't run away. He just didn't want the child to be alone when he woke up, with no one around him in the nest's thick silence.

Slide looked toward the city and the elevated curves of the freeways leading to it. "Won't be long now," he said softly.

Jimmy tugged against the invisible leash of the other's presence, straining to return to the nest and its warm safety. The sky was turning darker, the red light bleeding out of the reflections in Slide's glasses. The dots of the traffic's lights on the freeway grew brighter in the lenses.

Slide nodded. "I can feel 'em." He smiled to himself. "They're getting close. Real close."

Jimmy peered at the other's narrow profile. "Huh?" he said. "Who?" The word *close* worried him.

He made out the faint smudge of his own face in the glasses as Slide turned toward him. "Don't worry," he said—soft, almost kindly. "There's nothing to worry about, at all. Come on." He started walking back toward the underpass. Gratefully, Jimmy trotted after him.

                    *   *   *

His shadow stretched out ahead of him on the sidewalk, as he walked away from the theatre and toward his car.

Now it's starting, thought Tyler. He saw, even through the sunglasses' tint, the buildings' red-tinged shadows slide together, filling the street. The windows facing west crawled with the burning reflection of the sun setting through the brown-smudged horizon. Some of the cars already had their headlights switched on, anticipating the dark.

He could feel it inside himself as well. Inside the sleeves of his shirt, the skin of his arms prickled, small needles teasing the flesh. Not unpleasant; exciting, in fact. A sensation he remembered from a long time ago, the body's prelude to the new world that would come into sight. The nerve endings were sloughing off the medications' dull sleep, stripping down to bare wires of signal and action.

In his mouth, the old, familiar chemical taste; he curled his tongue as he walked, pressing the bitter saliva against his teeth. It had been there all along, in every cell of his body. Someone else's words, the official pronouncement: *The alteration is permanent.* That brought his own smile sharper. *Who'd want it any other way?* he thought. *Once you've been inside.*

When the night came, when all the light had bled away, that other city would be revealed. When it was as black as the small, dirt-floored space he sensed, could feel against his shoulders even as he walked in the open air, then he'd be able to see straight through the darkness to it.

As he stood unlocking his car, Tyler looked down the street. At its far end a woman stood, silhouetted by the red sun collapsing behind her. Holding the little purse against her cocked hip, she turned her face toward him.

Too far away to see her features. But he nodded to himself as he shut his eyes behind the dark lenses.

Even if he hadn't been able to see them, he knew the sharp-pointed teeth had been smiling at him.

"Mike?" She closed the front door behind her and called into the apartment. "You here?"

No answer came. Steff bent down and helped Eddie tug his hooded sweatshirt over his head. He lifted his arms for her, the edge of his T-shirt riding up over his pink stomach.

"Where's Mike?" asked Eddie. "I wanna show him something." He dropped the paper bag that had held the rocket ship onto the hallway floor and zoomed the model in a high arc. One of the day-care staff had printed CAPT. EDDIE in small nylon-tip letters under the transparent cockpit.

"Gone to work, I guess." She followed her son into the living room, where the rocket was deposited in its trophylike place on top of the television. "Just you and me, kid."

She hadn't expected him to be there. On Friday evenings she had neither classes nor a shift at the restaurant, so it was her regular turn to pick up Eddie from the day-care center. The way things had been going for Mike, she'd figured he'd take the chance to leave early for the movie theatre and the little office there that he used as a hideaway when one of the deep brooding spells came over him. *Because he doesn't want me to see him like that*, she thought. *Or Eddie*. She was shut out of that world, even though the locked door was always visible beyond his back. Kindness on his part: whatever the darkness inside

there held, the pale outlines of which had been
scratched into the copy of the book he kept hidden in
the hall closet, he wanted to shield them from it. His
memory, she knew, was a weight that she wouldn't
be allowed to put one hand against, even while it was
buckling his knees to the ground.

(As if he could hide the book. When the paperbacks were in every bookstore, always somewhere
among the other bright, shouting covers, and her
hand could pick it up and thumb for just one second
through the slick photos in the middle before trembling
and putting it back. As if he could hide anything.)

In the kitchen, as she maneuvered a knife through
a bell pepper on the chopping board, the smell of
sizzling hamburger around her, she listened to the
television murmuring from the other room. Eddie had
switched on the evening news as if Mike were there
to watch it, slumped in the angle of the couch while
Eddie puttered his cars across the floor.

Maybe that was it. She watched the thin green
strips mount at the knife's edge. Once, from the
kitchen doorway, she had caught a glimpse of (*Linda*)
the face from the newspaper (*his wife*) and the pages
in the middle of the book (*from the room inside his
head, the door always closed*). The angle of his face
that she could see as she stood unnoticed behind him
had shown no change, no emotion; just watching.

Maybe that was it, she thought. The fraction of
memory, the weight on top of all the rest, breaking
his shoulders and spine beneath it. And that was what
he didn't want her and Eddie to see. Until enough
time had passed for him to get the weight back onto
his shoulders, stand up beneath it, go on as if none of
it had ever happened, the door and everything behind
it closed to him as well.

She went on working, making dinner for herself and her son, and enough for Mike when he came back after he shut up the theatre for the night. *Maybe I should call him*, she thought. *Check on him, make sure he's all right.* She shook her head over the chopping board, deciding against it. Some things had to be worked out alone; she had known those times herself.

"Go wash up," she called to Eddie. Her hands went on about their tasks. It was a comfort to watch them, and stop the thoughts clamoring inside her head.

Welcome back, he told himself. *To the new world.*

As Tyler steered the car, driving with no set destination, he felt the muscles of his arms tightening, as if swelling and pumping the blood even harder through his heart. He watched the traffic flowing on either side of the car, the headlights and other beacons of the street carved with fire against his eyes. When the night had come at last, he felt the medications in his blood ebb another stage lower, down to the last dregs filtering out through the fine mesh of his innards.

He recognized, even after all the years it had been damped under, the acceleration seeping into his nervous system. That was the Host, he knew, the drug drawing him up to its own speed. So fast that at times the other cars seemed locked in slow motion, his gaze scanning across them to the shaded faces behind the windshields, the synapses firing into his arms as he one-handed the steering wheel, sliding with a lazy ease through the narrow gaps between them. His teeth ground together—another sign—biting into the bitter chemical taste that welled from under his tongue.

Easy enough. He smiled, remembering Bedell's words. A staggered row of neon flashed multicolored letters in sequence through the car, across the sleeves of his jacket. Glancing up at the mirror, he saw the corner of his own face, garish in the street's beating light, the eyes and one corner of his mouth smiling at himself. *Easy.* Bedell had been right; the stupid sonofabitch had got it down for once. *Like they say*—the smile grew at the thought—*the answer lies within.*

This was the way it had felt before. Every hour, every minute that passed brought him closer to the Host and the group mind. Then he'd be able to see where Slide had hidden Bryan.

But he had to be careful. It would be easy to just go with it, to let the drug carry you along until you were drunk on your own blood. Easy to forget what he had come back into this world for, and to let the black streets unroll in front of him, stretching into the night and all the mysteries the Host would show him, one by one.

Bryan, he thought. He had to remember that. Once he had found his son, and brought him back out to the light, then he could let the Host do what it wanted. It wouldn't matter then. They would all be together again, inside, and he wouldn't care what happened. It might even be—an echo of Slide's coaxing voice—*nice*. Nice and dark.

He brought the car to a stop, watching the flow of traffic ahead. Turning his head to the side window, he saw a rose burning across the street, the colored light from it streaming across the empty sidewalk. *Right*, he thought, nodding. That's how it worked. Just letting the car head where it wanted, something in his arms turning the wheel, had brought him here, a station on his way.

She might have been lying before, he thought as he gazed at the bookstore. *When I asked if she knew anything. They might have all lied to me. Because I wasn't back inside yet, with them. So they couldn't trust me.*

The girl at the counter said something to him as he walked past. He ignored her, heading straight for Bonnie's office.

She looked up at him as he pulled the door open. He could tell, without a word being spoken.

Like a rabbit, he thought. Her lip trembled as she pushed her chair back from the desk, farther away from him.

"Michael—"

She didn't know anything about Slide, about Bryan, about anything. Except for what she saw in his face, the fragment of the past confronting her. That had scared her so much that she had come to hide in this safe little hole, away from the dark outside.

His laughter broke out of him as he turned in the door. The shelves behind him were lined with the I Ching and dewy-eyed mystics bending their sympathetic gazes at him. "Look at this shit." He could feel Bonnie watching him as he reached up and swept a row tumbling to the floor.

The noise of the books falling brought the startled eyes of the few browsing customers around to him. He could look right through them to the backs of their skulls, the hollow spaces stuffed with the same rags of milky Buddhism and bean sprouts.

They were all afraid of the dark. But he wasn't. Not anymore.

He strode toward the door and the outside, the girl behind the counter shrinking back as he passed.

She snapped her head back, blinking at the late-night news on the television. The anatomy text had slid off her lap, landing in a pile of her class notes scattered across the carpet.

Jeez, thought Steff, rubbing the corner of her eye. *Out like a light*. She had no idea of how long she had been asleep. No memory of the news starting, and now the weatherman was pointing at numbers on a map of Southern California—that always came toward the end.

So much for getting ready for her midterms; she could still barely keep her head up. As on so many nights, the threat of the next morning's early classes, or the combined fatigue from work, studies, a five-year-old boy, knocked her back exhausted into the bed hours before Mike came home from locking up the theatre. Or before he had finished working through his long thoughts as he sat in front of the television, the bright colors and laughing voices washing against him unnoticed, like waves against a stone shore.

She leaned forward and gathered the papers together. Her mouth tasted dry and soiled, as if she had been breathing through it while slumped in the corner of the sofa. An odd fragment of memory ran through her mind, like a tape loop an inch long: in a car, driving through the city night. The lights had slid over her face and hands as she had turned toward the driver. It hadn't been Mike; she hadn't been able to see who it was, the face behind the wheel had been all dark . . .

Some cop show, she decided. Whatever had been on TV, sliding underneath her eyelids as she slept, mixing in with the slow working of her own jumbled-up thoughts. She glanced over her shoulder at the kitchen doorway and decided again not to call him at the theatre.

In the hallway, she looked into Eddie's bedroom. The thin wedge of light showed the small figure curled up, clenched hands close to his face. (*Another fragment, further back: Mike sitting on the edge of the bed.*) She leaned her forehead against the doorframe, even more weary. (*Not far enough to forget; silently watching the sleeping child.*)

Gently, she closed the door and headed toward the other bedroom. The street in her dream went on unrolling, the lights glittering holes in the darkness.

He heard Slide laughing. Jimmy looked up from the sleeping child. His legs had gone numb a long time ago, the blood pressed out of them by his crouch underneath the concrete ceiling, but he hadn't moved from the small bed of rags.

Slide was smiling at him. "You're the little mother, aren't you?" The long legs stretched out across the scooped-out hollow as Slide lay back against the side, his arms wrapped around himself as if to ward off the night air. The bright eyes caught the yellow glow of the flashlight pushed into the dirt. Gray bones shining with grease were scattered around the red and white stripes of a Kentucky Fried Chicken bucket.

Jimmy said nothing as he looked back to the little boy. The round baby cheeks were all white, no longer pink, like when Slide had brought him to the nest. A glistening rim around the tiny nostrils bubbled in time to the breath rasping from the open mouth. He had gotten the little boy (*Bryan; his name's Bryan; don't forget, it's important; Bryan*) to eat some of the cold mashed potatoes that came with the chicken. Then he had shaken his head, the dirty little hand pushing away the plastic spoon, and said he wasn't hungry. He had been sleeping since then, with Jimmy hovering over him.

"I think he's sick," said Jimmy softly. He didn't even know if he wanted Slide to hear him.

"Fuck that." From the corner of his eye he could see Slide shaking his head disgustedly. "He's a tough little shit."

He brushed the child's brow. "What if something happens to him?"

The laugh barked louder behind him. "I was right," said Slide. "I knew you'd take care of him. He's brought out your maternal instinct."

Little Bryan. The hair was so fine and silky against his fingers. Even through the constant rumble of the traffic filtering from above, he could hear the shallow breathing.

He knew Slide was laughing at him again, watching and laughing. He didn't care.

Fuckin' waste of time, he thought. Tyler ground his teeth together, scanning the street's light and motion as he drove. And there was no time to waste. Not now.

The memory of Bonnie's scared-rabbit face heated the blood ticking at the corner of his brow. His hands tightened on the steering wheel; he knew he could easily have wrapped them around the woman's throat. Easy to imagine how her pulse would have felt beating against his palms, the round eyes growing wider as the gasping face fell backward . . .

Everything was easy now. That was why he had to be careful. He smiled to himself, willing his hands to loosen on the wheel, easing up on the accelerator. Letting the night around him become soft and fluid again. He tilted his wrist to check his watch. Another piece of time (*closer*) had been swallowed up: close to midnight now. That was how the Host liked to play it. Teasing you; slowing time to a crawl and then eating it up in a flash of adrenaline through your veins. The prickling skin tightened across his arms again. *Just wait*, he told himself. *Soon enough*. He swung the car to the left, toward the stream of brighter lights. *He'll come when He wants to*.

The traffic was thicker here. He didn't care what street it was. On either side, across the other cars tracking through their ceaseless courses, the neon looped and burned over the heads of the pedestrians, tinting the faces with colors like masks. He worked his way through the crawling street, patiently watching.

First, he spotted the two bright snake eyes. The colored stones winked at Tyler from the rearview mirror, catching the overhead streetlight and flashing sharp points of it in time to the motion of the woman's thighs underneath the fabric as she walked. From the belt's knot, the silver ornament dangled an inch above the teasing hem of her skirt, swaying as the tiny knives of her heels stabbed a purposeful line along the crowded sidewalk.

The same one—Tyler studied the image in the mirror. The traffic signal and the taillights of the car ahead washed red over his hands on the steering wheel. He recognized, and remembered her from the late-night driving home—*What?* he asked himself. *A week ago*. Even though the top edge of the mirror cut off her head, showing only the sheer, tight dress, the standard small purse on a thin strap over her shoulder, and the metal snake belt; that was enough. He reached up and tilted the mirror to see her better.

The blue of the streetlamps darkened her lips to black. Her face—her own, not the overlaid skull mask the drug's effects had raised before—was sharpened by the hard-edged makeup carving out the cheekbones from her pallid skin. The eyes were soft, still human, at this close distance, not the lightless scanning devices that he remembered sweeping across the horizon when he'd seen them before.

As she came within a few yards, the signal changed and the car ahead pulled away. Tyler eased on the gas, not losing sight of her in the mirror, and swung the car into the first open space at the curb. The traffic closed and flowed past as he waited.

"Hey—come here a second." He leaned over to the window on the passenger side. "I want to talk to you." The adrenaline high triggered in his blood gave him a loose, easy grace. He could do what he wanted.

The eyes, fringed with mascara-thick lashes, tracked around at the sound of his voice, narrowing into hard points when they spotted him.

"Bug off, jack," she said, still walking. Other faces along the street turned, sized up the situation, looked away without interest. "I ain't working. I'm getting something to eat."

He edged the car forward, keeping up with her. "Well, maybe I'm hungry, too, sweetheart."

She sneered at his smile. "Yeah, I bet."

"Tell you what." He stopped the car.

The hooker turned and waited, hands on hips, feet spread apart, the glare of the store window behind her outlining her hard, efficient thighs in a sheen of neon. "What?" she said, patience stripped from her voice.

He felt his own smile loop wider as his half-lidded eyes connected with hers. He could see, magnified, the street's moving lights reflected in the dark circles at their centers. The electric blue crept through the snaking tendrils of her hair.

Closer, he thought. The needle pricked at his arms again. *Almost there*.

"My treat," he said.

He had waited until the street was dark outside.

Bedell parted the drapes a fraction and pressed his face close to the cool glass. He peered down the street in either direction. Now that it was past midnight, the lights in most of the houses had finally gone off. On a Friday night, the houses stayed lit up longer, the traffic around the block steady until much later. After two A.M., when the bars had closed, there'd be another few cars pulling up into the driveways, and then dead quiet after that. That'd be the best time, the time with the least chance of being seen, but he couldn't wait any longer. Not in this house.

He turned around and studied the object in the middle of the floor. A sheet pulled off his bed covered it now; the big, thick-soled cop shoes protruded from one end. The outline of the arms and legs could be seen through the fabric.

Preparations—he rubbed his lip, tasting his own sweat on the back of his hand. He had already pulled the car up as close as he could to the front door. And unlocked the trunk, bringing the lid down so that the catch rested on the lock without snapping shut, so it could be pulled open with one hand and the corpse tumbled in on top of the spare and the jack. At least the car's own shadow in the nearest streetlight covered the two or three yards to the house.

What else? What else, what else? He paced alongside the stretched-out body. If he could just grab and slow down the thoughts racing through his head, the memory of Kinross' face filling with blood above the hands at the ends of his own arms, that image fluttering against the confines of his skull like the end of a film run through a projector and the take-up reel not stopping . . . If he could just *think* for a moment without seeing that other face, the long teeth bared in a smile . . .

That was why he had covered up the corpse with the sheet. He didn't want another flash of Kinross' gray face changing to something else, something that wasn't dead. Or at least in the same way.

What else, what else? He had to hurry, get it into the car's trunk and start driving, get out of here before it was too late, already too late—

He tasted warm salt on the tip of his tongue. Stopping his pacing, he pulled his hand away from his face and saw that his teeth had gnawed through the skin of his knuckle. A bright red dot seeped through the abrasion.

In his mouth, another taste uncoiled as the blood dissolved into his own saliva. A bitter, chemical savor, the same he had tasted grinding against his own teeth, leaking out through the splintering capsules. The drug's contamination; it had reached every cell by now.

"Shit." He clenched the hand into a trembling fist. There wasn't any more time, to try and think.

He had to get going now. Before anyone came.
Before—

Before *he* came back. With his sharp-pointed teeth.

A quick, panting run through the house and he had
all the lights switched off. He opened the front door
an inch; he'd be able to catch the edge with his elbow
when he had the body up in his arms. Another glance
through the narrow gap showed no traffic on the
street.

He took a deep breath and squatted down at the
corpse's shoulders. The sheet slid down its face and
chest as he slid his arms under it and lifted it up. The
head lolled back against his chest, the mouth gaping
wider. In the dark he could see the gray strands
brushed across the mottled scalp, the smell of the
old-fashioned rose-water glycerine holding the hair in
place mingling with the sour odor of Kinross' last
lunch decomposing in the corpse's stomach.

His arms circled the unbreathing chest, grabbing
his own wrists to lock the bear hug solid. He lifted
the body higher against himself and stood up from
his squat.

The body's slack weight pulled him off his balance. The dead limbs sprawled across the carpet as
Bedell landed heavily on his knees, barely catching
himself from falling across the other form.

He crawled backward, away from the splayed-out
corpse. The palm of one hand set down in something
wet and sticky. In the dark, the stain on his hand
looked black as he turned it toward his face. A small
cut on the back of Kinross' head, from when he had
toppled backward with Bedell's hands at his throat,
had leaked blood into the carpet. He could see it now,
an irregular, inklike stain a few inches across.

Convulsively, he wiped his hands across his chest. The wetness smeared black on his shirt.

Go. He heard his own voice screaming at him. *Get it out of here, go, hurry—*

He stood up and bent over the corpse. This time, he managed to lift it up into a sitting position. Its heels dug through the carpet as he dragged it to the door.

His heart took a few moments to slow down before he could start to pull the corpse outside. The thing was so heavy and awkward, a loose, disjointed mass that flopped and rolled against him, the gray face lolling to one side. His own breath wheezed in his throat as he tried to gather his strength.

Carefully, he checked outside once more, then pushed the door open wide with his foot. Hunched over to keep his grip under the corpse's arms, he staggered backward. The corpse dropped and slid to the concrete path leading to the driveway.

"Come on. Come *on*," he whispered. The legs spread into a V, the toes of the cop shoes turning inward, as he tugged at the weight. The tightness in his chest become a rhythmic stabbing pain. He bit his lip to keep the hot blood flushing his face from squeezing out tears.

When he had finally dragged the weight into the driveway, alongside the car's rear wheels, he lifted his head over the fender. He saw nothing moving in the street. The corpse slid at an angle against his shin as he let go one side. His fingers scrabbled at the trunk lid. As it started to rise, he saw the beams of headlights swing around the distant corner of the block.

He let the lid drop and crouched down beside the rear wheel. From underneath the car he could see the headlights at the end of the street. They slowed to a crawl, inching toward him.

Raising his head, he saw the light from a streetlamp shining through the car as it slowly approached. The silhouettes of two heads were framed against a metal grille above their seats. A police car on a routine patrol; one of the advantages of living in a posh neighborhood. As Bedell watched, the cop on the passenger side tilted the spotlight mounted on the door. The beam painted a wide circle of flat, shadow-dissolving light over the front of each house they passed, scooping out the darkness from under every parked car.

He could feel the blood pulsing in his face now. He looked back up the driveway. There wasn't time—not with the corpse's weight straining through his grasp—to get it back into the house.

The car—he reached up and scrabbled at the door handle. Locked; he let the corpse fall against the concrete as he crouched and tore at his pants pocket. He fumbled the jangling bits of metal, stabbing at the tiny slot for the key. The police car was close enough that he could hear the murmur of its engine.

He pulled the door open, the edge swinging a fraction of an inch from his face.

His heart hammered against his breastbone as he lifted the corpse on the point of his shoulder. The back of one cold hand fell against his face, the curved ridge of fingernail catching at the corner of his eye.

The corpse flopped down into the space between the dashboard and the front of the passenger seat. The slack, sightless face gazed at him as he bent the legs double, jamming them against the chest.

The beam of the spotlight washed over him just as he stood up and slammed the door.

He stood frozen in the glare. Squinting, he could see the outlines of the two cops regarding him.

The words barely squeezed out of his throat. "Forgot my car keys," he called. He held up one hand, the metal bits dangling in it. "Stupid, huh?"

Wordlessly, they watched him as he went back up to the house's front door and fumbled with the keys. "Hey!"

He heard the cop's shout just as the door swung open. He looked over his shoulder at them.

One cop gestured out the side window. "Did you lock it?"

His face managed to split into a smile. "Shit." He shook his head as he stepped down into the driveway again. "Don't know what I'm thinking of."

"That's how cars get stolen. Especially nice ones."

"Yeah, right." Under their gaze, he turned the key in the door. Through the window he could see something that looked like dirty laundry tumbled in a heap. "Thanks."

From inside the house, he watched them drive off. After their taillights were no longer visible at the other end of the block, he forced himself to close his eyes and count to a hundred twice over.

Outside again, he walked quickly down the driveway and let himself in on the driver's side. He slid into the seat, and felt his heart twist inside his chest as he reached for the ignition.

One of Kinross' hands had fallen across the steering wheel when he'd dumped the body inside. It rested there, caught by the crook of the wrist in the wheel's bottom curve.

Carefully, he lifted the hand by the shirt cuff and folded the loose arm away from himself.

Get the sheet, cover him up—

But he couldn't wait any longer. He started up the car and let it shoot backward onto the street.

As he drove, he looked down and saw the streetlights, one by one, slide over the empty seat and the crouching body on the car's floor.

What she had wanted was a hamburger, from the old Tommy's down on Beverly. Tyler glanced over at the hooker as he pulled out of the L-shaped parking lot. The wrappings were a grease-stained orange flower in her hands as her teeth sank into the meat and tore away a mouthful.

"God, I love that place." She swallowed and looked out the side window. This close to downtown, the office towers were a light-studded black wall against the night sky. "I used to get this one freak who'd bring me here in a rental limo, have me go down on him in the back seat. He just dug all the people walking around the big car, eating and stuff, and watching. Made him feel rich, I guess."

She had become more talkative after a twenty had slid from between his outstretched fingers and vanished into her little purse. "Okay, if you just want to talk," she had said, shrugging. "Cheaper to use the phone. I could give you some numbers."

(What did she used to get? he wondered. Even for just talk, and her precious, metered time—the thought tapped inside his head, slid away. A lot more, at least five times as much; maybe just a year ago, or less. That was how fast the street cut away the flesh beneath the skin.)

Tyler leaned back, arms straight to the wheel. The

traffic was lighter along here than back at the edge of
Hollywood where he had picked her up. He could let
the car glide by itself, synchronized with the timing
of the traffic lights, so that they rolled through the
night without stopping.

Grace, thought Tyler. *That passeth understanding*.
He felt his own face tightening, the corners of his
mouth drawing back into a thin smile. In this world,
in the night, things moved and worked a certain way,
the gears meshing along their razor edges, just the
way *He* wanted . . .

Close. He gazed out through the windshield, across
the streets flowing like slow black liquid toward him.
The dark glasses had been stowed on top of the
dashboard, but he still kept his eyes half-lidded against
the streets' stabbing pinpoints of light. *Real close*.
He could make out the squares of the deserted sidewalks, the segments dully translucent as a shed snake-
skin, the blue radiance from underneath leaking around
each edge. *Won't be long now*.

That was why he'd picked her up. Hoping that
he'd see the other face again, behind hers, smiling
and whispering. *Not yet*. But now he could smell her,
the scent masking the other underneath. He knew
how the hard points of her shoulders would press into
his hands as he bent her backward, pulling her laughter into his face until it broke and the sharp edges cut
the skin and let their blood mingle . . .

No. He had other things to do first.

The blaring light of the hamburger stand receded
in the mirror. "They say you used to be able to see
Frank Sinatra there," he said. "At Tommy's. Order-
ing chiliburgers."

She took another bite. Her teeth shredded the wet
red center of the meat. "Who's that?"

"Come on, sweetheart." He swung his smile toward her. "You're not that young."

The hooker glanced at him, her eyes narrowing to hard gun slits. Then she tilted her head back and laughed. A dribble of the meat's watery blood appeared at the corner of her mouth; the long, tapered nail broke when she dabbed the spot away with her finger. She peeled off the red shell like the dry carapace of an insect and flicked it out the window.

Her laughter died into silence as he turned his gaze back to the street. He heard her whisper beside him.

"I like it when it's dark."

He looked around at her. "What did you say?"

Her cool gaze examined him. "I didn't say anything, jack. You want me to say something, tell me what you want to hear." Her coy smile appeared, tugged into place by the machinery behind. Softer: "You're the boss."

Ahead of him, the street opened, the space between the curbs slowly widening as the car cut through the darkness. The street lengthened, the distance between every light growing, empty of everything except the dark. Soon enough, he knew, the street would go on forever, to a horizon of absolute vacuum.

Closer, he thought. He had heard the other voice whispering. *Closer and closer*.

He drove, the headlights of the cars across the divider slashing over his face.

As soon as he'd gotten the car out of the driveway, Bedell had found himself lost, on streets that he no longer recognized in the dark. He'd headed straight for the bright lights and noise of the all-night traffic streaming on Ventura Boulevard, and had dead-ended in a cul-de-sac, the streetlamps of the main road he

wanted teasingly visible somewhere on the other side
of the dark houses. Cursing and sweating, he had
turned in and backed out of one drive after another,
the car dropping heavily to the street as he'd steered
over a curb. The jolt had flopped the corpse's arm
against his leg. He had shoved it away with one hand
as he'd leaned close to the windshield, scanning the
lawns and parked cars sliding alongside for the exit
out of the tract.

Once he'd thought he'd seen the police cruiser
crossing his path from a side street ahead, its headlights sweeping out through the darkness. Bedell had
swerved around the nearest corner, away from the
distant arching lamps, tangling himself farther into
the maze of unfamiliar streets and houses.

When he'd recognized his own house out the side
window, the drawn curtains hiding the unlit interior,
a wave of nausea clenched his stomach. He had no
idea of how long he'd been driving, circling and
winding through the few blocks around the house; it
had felt like hours, with the folded weight in front of
the empty seat beside him. He had beat against the
steering wheel with his fists, his panting breath squeezing through his clenched teeth, his foot jabbing the
accelerator flat, just missing sideswiping a parked
car.

And had finally found himself, with no memory of
the route, as though it had been snipped from a tape
inside his head, on some bright-lit street surrounded
by moving cars. The white letters on green signaling
a freeway onramp had come up on his right, so fast
that he almost passed it. He had swung onto it, tires
squealing, not caring where it went to.

Go. Just go. Get away from here.

A sign with arrows and words flashed overhead.

He looked up too late to read it. The freeway was dividing, branching in two directions. He didn't see any of the city's lights, the downtown buildings piled up together and glittering, anywhere ahead of him. *Must be going north*, he thought. *Through the Valley*. He didn't recognize anything on the streets alongside the freeway. The tires suddenly chattered underneath the car, drifting over the raised dots dividing the lanes as he scanned over the rail for any landmark. He jerked the wheel, swerving the car away from the other traffic. The red taillights ahead dazzled him; they receded from him or came swooping back as his foot slid on the accelerator, trying to match speed with the other drivers, the dark silhouettes turning to look at him through their side windows.

From the corner of his eye, he saw something white from the well of the passenger seat beside him, every time one of the freeway's lights flashed overhead. He looked down and saw Kinross' face turned up toward him, the blank eyes clouded with a gray film. The motion of the car and the body's own stiffening, the blood settling into the lowest parts, must have shifted it. He couldn't remember if the head had been twisted about on the thick neck like that when he managed to get it into the car. A blaring horn jerked his gaze back up in time to swing away from the side of a truck in the next lane. The wheel went too far, slipping out of his sweating hands; the road dividers chattered as a blurred shape of metal passed within inches of the side window.

Another sign swooped overhead, too late for him to do more than see the white letters on floodlit green vanish upside down, unreadable. "Shit—" He squeezed the word through his teeth, biting his lip. He recognized nothing beyond the traffic streaming on his right. All he could tell was that the freeway went on unreeling into the dark ahead. Something warm stung his eyes. He rubbed the back of his hand against them, not knowing if it was sweat or his own tears. Then, underneath the roar of the traffic, he heard the whisper.

Soft: *I like it when it's dark.*

No— The bitter taste suddenly seeping from under his tongue nauseated him. He could feel, without glancing down, the clouded eyes looking at him. The mouth would be open, he knew, Kinross' yellow teeth showing, a clot of blood darkening the pool of saliva at the back of the throat.

It's dead. The skin over his arms tightened; for a moment he imagined his own blood being squeezed out in little droplets through the pores. *It's dead*, he told himself, *just drive, you didn't hear anything, you're fucked up, just drive, it's dead, it's dead.*

Under the spinning noise of tires on concrete, the battering of wind, the muffled screaming of the engine; just breathing at the margin of his ear.

Nice and dark.

The other cars' lights were brighter. He had to squint through the narrow slit of his eyelids to keep the blurring red and white streaks from gouging to the back of his skull. His shaking hand managed to find the radio knob on the dash—anything to fill up the car, drown out the whisper when it came again.

He saw the glow of the radio dial, but heard nothing. It remained silent as he twisted the knob, punched the buttons, his hand scrabbling at the chrome and plastic. "Come on—" He balled his hand into a fist and beat at the dial, the stabbing lights ahead rolling in his tearing eyes. "Fucking sonofabitch," he sobbed aloud.

That's when you can see the most.

The whisper pulled his gaze down, away from the bright, pounding windshield. The corpse's mouth gaped wide, the tongue a red-spotted gray wad lolling to one side.

A thin wire twined through the blunt fingers of one of Kinross' hands.

It got pulled loose, thought Bedell. He looked back up at the traffic. When he had loaded the body into the car, the hand must have caught the wire under the dash, jerked it free; that was why the radio was silent. *That's all it is.*

The lights swam over his face, dizzying. His own hands clutched weakly at the steering wheel, barely able to hold on. He let the car fall of its own accord, toward the bottom of the darkness ahead. He knew he'd have to wait until he was spoken to again.

He took her back to where he had picked her up.

"Thanks, jack," said the hooker. Standing on the curb, she leaned in the side window, hitching the strap of her purse higher on her bare shoulder. Behind her, the bright neon painted the faces passing on the sidewalk into masks. "Sure there's nothing else I can do for you?"

Tyler laid his wrists on the top curve of the wheel and looked into the smile of hard-edged red. "Like what?"

Her voice crooned into a whisper. He closed his eyes as he listened to it.

"I could show you things." Softer, as if the glossy lips were right at his ear: "Things you want to know."

He opened his eyes a fraction, as if the dark street carved up by the pulsing lights were a dream from

which he was waking. Through the haze of his lashes
he could see the pallid face of a high-mileage prostitute, skin the color of the nicotine edge on a cigarette
butt floating in cold water, the hair dangling in crescents over the hollow cheeks a chemical extruded
from a factory press. He could see, could know
without seeing, that the greasy hamburger and the
twenty for just talk had left her still hungry. Hungry
and working.

But just under that face, he could see another one.
Another smile, other teeth lengthening. Waiting for
him.

He shook his head, sliding the wheel into his grip.
"I'll see you later."

She was already standing straight, the little purse
dangling on the angle of her hip, her gaze scanning
down the street. "Sure, jack," she said, not looking
at him. "You do that."

For a moment, as he drove, he watched her in the
mirror. Then the traffic walled her away behind its
shifting lights.

A dream; the car, like before, when she had been
nodding in front of the television. Steff rolled the
back of her head against the pillow, one hand brushing her face, as if the dream were a spiderweb drifted
there in the bedroom's dark.

She still couldn't see who the driver was. The
black face turned toward her, silhouetted against lights
that were all blurred and wavery, an underwater city.
Driving and driving, in the slow motion of her sleep.

Somehow, without seeing it, she knew the face
was smiling at her.

FOURTEEN

The lights were so bright now; his face felt numb with them. Bedell let them beat in waves against him, holding on to the wheel with the last of his strength so he wouldn't be torn free, a tattered balloon, and jammed against the car's back window until he burst. All the hollow, thought-drained air inside his skull would leak away then, and he'd be dead. He didn't want to die; not while the car was still sliding through a night so dark outside.

The thing down on the floor moved, as if shifting into a more comfortable position in the narrow space.

It had been whispering to him all the time he had been driving. There was a trick to driving, and he had found it. He just had to let go, let the car go along by itself, part of the river flowing down the freeway, wherever it went, pressed on either side by the other cars and their dark-faced drivers.

He couldn't make out what it said. It talked so soft, just under the murmuring noise of the traffic. But now, if he listened, if he tried . . .

Soft, inviting: *I could show you things.*

It knew. It had always known.

He looked down at it. The eyes in the white face were no longer clouded. The dark at their centers fastened on to his gaze.

Things you want to know.

The face swung slowly in and out of shadow as the freeway's lights wheeled overhead.

He didn't know how long he had been driving. The drug uncoiling in Tyler's blood made it easy to pick up the night and the street's rhythm, locking into the motion of the traffic. *Easy enough*, he thought, tilting his head against the back of the seat. It was like being in a theatre, the windshield a screen that the other cars and faces floated against. He turned his wrist to see what time it was. Three in the morning; hours since he had dropped off the hooker. A thread of unease tugged at him through the drug's slow-motion grace.

Time was running out. He knew that; even on this street that seemed to have no end, the darkness was bleeding away. It would end with the sun coming up, the light churning like reddened smoke between the office towers, and all of the night's cool, thin-aired life would seep back into the shadows at the edges of the buildings.

He hasn't come yet, thought Tyler. *Not yet.* There had just been those little glimpses of the Host, the long-toothed smile peeping out for a fraction of a second from behind the hooker's glistening lips, a blank face turning slowly toward him from behind the wheel of the car next to him at the light, a reflection in a bright store window of a dark-jacketed stick figure on the sidewalk, the mask pulled aside for a quick, teasing glimpse . . . That was how He liked to play. Tyler remembered.

And He might not ever come. There was that possibility, too. *Capricious* . . . Tyler looked across the street's moving field, leaning over the wheel,

searching for the next trace. *When you want Him,
you can't find Him. That's the deal. You have to wait
until He wants you.* If He did; the Host could always
leave you outside. Fucked up and alone, in the cold
light of day. No matter how much you wanted to get
inside. Into the dark where you could see. That was
how it worked.

The street sped up as he pressed the accelerator,
pushing through the gaps between the other cars. If
the night ended, if the Host didn't come—Bryan
would still be inside. Where Slide was laughing at
him, where he couldn't get to him, couldn't find out
if his son were alive or dead . . . He'd be on the
outside, with the little silent grave, the hard-edged
shadows of the palms arcing over it. And not knowing what, if anything, was buried there.

Come on— He bit his lip as he drove, knowing
that any prayer was useless. The Host came in its
own time, if at all.

Then the next wave hit him, welling up from his
gut. He almost let go of the wheel, tilting his head
back as the pinpricks dug deeper than ever before,
toward the bones at the center of his arms. The blood
sang, purer, as though the last of the medications had
finally filtered out. *Yes* . . . His mouth filled with
the molten taste of the drug.

He opened his eyes to see the lights of the street
brighter, pouring like charged glass into the luminous
darkness at the end of the street. A death's-head
angel swiveled her gaze toward him; every face on
the sidewalk followed, and he could read what their
unmoving lips were saying.

*Of course, of course—*How could he have forgotten? That's where He'd be. Of all places; there. Tyler
nodded, feeling the weight of the bitter saliva collect

on his tongue. He brought his swaying head upright,
his tingling arms anchored by the wheel, and swung
the car into one of the dark side streets. He'd have to
work his way back to the other side of Hollywood.
But now he knew where he was going. Now there
was plenty of time.

The studio's parking lot was empty when he got
there. Tyler let himself in through the chain link gate
and walked to the glass door. No one was visible
inside, the chair behind the receptionist's desk empty.
Only the overhead lights in the corridor beyond were
switched on. It didn't matter; he pushed the button
underneath the speaker grille.

A moment's silence, then Ken's voice crackled out
of the speaker. "That you, Mike?"

He leaned close to the grille. "Yeah. It is. Let me
in, Ken."

"Sure." He could hear the smile in the other's
voice, tracing down the wires from the editing room
in the back. "I knew you'd come." As Tyler listened, the thin voice changed, shifted lower and
more knowing. "I've been waiting for you."

The buzzer sounded and the glass door yielded
under his palm. It closed behind him as he crossed
the empty lobby, under the whisper of the air-
conditioning, the murmur of the street traffic sealed
away.

He couldn't go on driving any longer. Bedell let
the Mercedes coast to the edge of the freeway, scraping along the curving guardrail, and come to a stop.
The engine coughed and died. Open-mouthed, he
gulped air into his fluttering lungs, feeling himself
sink into the sweat-drenched seat.

No longer in motion around him, the night hung

leaden beyond the windshield. He knew it was much later now, the traffic coursing beside him reduced to a thin stream of headlights.

He looked over at the thing crouching in front of the other seat. All the way here it had been talking to him, whispering, the soft words sliding from the mouth, as though the red wad in Kinross' throat were being bit into drops by his yellowed teeth. A stain had seeped into the fibers, the wet edge of it creeping up to the hump of the gearshift.

His own throat was raw, the bitter taste changed to an acid cutting the flesh from inside. Or maybe the salt from his own exhausted weeping, his eyes watering from the jabbing knife edges of the lights that had kept sweeping toward him in pairs, had filled his mouth, a drowning ocean.

I'm sorry, Bedell heard his own voice saying inside. *I'm sorry. I'm sorry—*

He couldn't remember what the thing had been saying to him. There was just the memory of the words tapping at his skull as he drove, the white face pulsing at the corner of his eye every time a light swung overhead. Somehow it had gotten onto its knees, the stain soaking into the faded brown trousers. He had dreaded the moment he knew would come, when he would feel the soft touch of its hand upon his knee, the thing straightening, rising to bring its face closer to his, his own scream beating against the windshield as the last strip of skin tore out of his throat and unrolled blood across his tongue . . .

The touch hadn't come. He pressed his hot forehead against the wheel. The bright eyes were still fastened on him, he knew, from the thing's hunkered crouch under the dash.

Now, the car dead and still around them, it was quiet enough to make out its whisper.

The smile, drawing back from the teeth.

I've been waiting for you.

Part of her knew she was dreaming and wanted to wake up. But Steff couldn't; she was still in the car, even as she felt the warm pillow, damp with her sweat, pressing against her face. Still there, the slow, submerged lights of the street outside the windshield washing over her.

Behind the wheel, the black face's smile grew wider. She couldn't even see it, but knew it was there, like a hole that her hand had fallen through, feeling what was inside. The teeth drew apart, and it spoke to her softly.

We're nearly there.

Its laughter licked at her ear as she turned her face away, toward the dark glass, against the pillow.

He stepped from the corridor into the editing room. In the dark, Tyler could make out the backs of the empty seats, the velvet nap outlined in a fringe of blue. The blank screen gaped back at him.

"Hello, Mike."

At the top of the carpeted aisle, he turned and saw Ken sitting behind the wall of the editing desk. The glow of one of the small curved-neck lamps carved his face into shadows, the corner of his mouth lifted in satisfaction.

Tyler breathed in the cool filtered air, listening for the whisper behind the sigh of the hidden machinery. *Close*—he could feel it, his arms tightening around the chemical blood inside the muscles. *Almost there*.

He brought his own smile up at the sight of his old

comrade (*right, right*, he heard his own voice cautioning, *make him believe it*), as though this pocket of the darkness had fallen through memory into the old red past they shared. *You've got to find out, got to know*.

"What's up?" he said easily.

Ken laughed, tossing his head back from the circle of light. "Don't you know?" he said, leaning forward again.

He stayed silent, watching the other. The Host would tell him.

The words came, filtering through Ken's voice, quietly: "Now we can have some fun."

Tyler nodded, eyes closed as he stood. Sparks of the blue light burned in that darkness as well. Now they were all inside, he knew. At last. They were all inside again.

For a moment she didn't know if she was still dreaming or not. Steff lay in the bed, eyes closed in darkness, her cheek pressed against the pillow warmed to her skin. She remembered being in a car, riding, but she couldn't remember where; it had been all dark, and her throat had gone raw from shouting someone's name. *Must've been*, she decided. *Dreaming*.

She let the confused, fragmentary images fade, already passing from memory. She felt the weight of her head on her hand underneath the pillow, the threads of the sheet against her palm. Grateful to be in bed, and not in that dark street that had flowed around the car as she frantically searched the horizon, a thin edge of blue that receded from her as the car headed toward it, as though it were somehow above her and she was falling . . .

More than half asleep, suspended right at the edge

of slipping under again, purged of dreams this time,
she listened to the twice-distant night sounds outside
the apartment. Dark enough—she knew there'd be no
change if her heavy eyelids managed to open—and
quiet enough, so that she knew it was still a long way
until morning. Now that the dream's racing pulse and
the swelling stone of breath in her throat had faded,
this was better than her usual waking to the clatter of
the alarm clock set a quarter hour fast, rolling over to
gather in those luxurious semiconscious minutes before she absolutely had to get up. This was like a
little piece outside of time, a warm segment expanded from between the marks around the face of a
clock with no hands.

Plus Mike was home. That was nice—through the
blurring weight of sleep she could hear the soft,
familiar sounds, a breath above the room's quiet, of
him moving in the dark beyond the bed. He always
undressed with the light off, so as not to wake her.
His feet, already bare, on the carpet, the whisper of
the buttons sliding through the stitched fabric of the
holes as he took off his shirt, the rustle of the stiffer
denim as he folded his jeans onto the chair by the
closet door. Sounds she had heard so many times
before—

Worry had made this night's sleep slow in coming,
despite her inability to keep her head from nodding
over her textbooks. Maybe that was where the dream
had come from—she tugged at the small thread of it
left dangling, trying to remember if it had been her
son's or Mike's name she had been calling on the
dark field. *Doesn't matter*, she thought, letting it and
herself drift further apart. He had come back here,
out of the night. That was what had fastened on to
her, unshakable behind the commonplace motions of

dinner and putting Eddie, and finally herself, to bed. That he wouldn't come back; that, when she woke, he would never have been there beside her at all—at least for another night that fear was gone. A knot of tension that had clamped on the joint between her spine and neck let go; the bed felt softer and warmer around her.

She realized she had fallen all the way asleep, a few moments snipped painlessly from semiconsciousness, when she felt Mike slipping into the bed, the sheet lifting from her shoulder and the mattress bending with his weight. The angle of the shallow well (*bed's shot*, she thought sleepily, *need a new one*) made it easy for her to roll her back against his chest, drawing up her legs to fit, spoon-wise, into the angle of his lap. She nestled the back of her head against him. That was nice. She drifted deeper toward sleep.

Must've turned cold outside—part of her, the last fragment following the rest into the dark, puzzled for a moment as Mike's palm brushed her thigh, lifting the hem of the thin cotton nightgown to rest on her bare hip. His hand was ice-cold.

She let the thought fade away. At the last, just before complete sleep, she had a glimpse of the dream from which she had woken. The same horizon was etched in blue in the darkness, and she was falling toward it again.

But something blocked the horizon in the middle: a figure, the silhouette of a man, featureless and black as the surrounding dark, unmoving as she fell closer, unable to stop.

She pressed herself closer to Mike, a shiver between her spine and his chest, as though the bed's warmth had bled away.

*   *   *

"Come on up here, Mike. You'll dig it."

He had been standing in the aisle with his eyes closed, still listening for the other voice he had heard behind Ken's words. Tyler opened his eyes and saw Ken, his hands moving across the editing desk.

Past the rows of empty seats, he walked into the control area bounded by its walls of equipment and blank video monitors. He stood behind Ken, resting his hands on the top edge of his chair. "It's you and Slide," said Tyler quietly. "Isn't it? You're the ones."

Ken finished threading a tape into one of the decks and looked back around at him. "It's all of us, Mike. The whole group." The light cast by the small lamp caught the edge of his smile. "They tried to kill us. They tried to, but they couldn't." He pushed a button on the deck and the tape started its crawl through the device.

One of the screens on the wall flickered into life, the black-and-white movement fluttering at the corner of Tyler's eye. "Now you're going to try and bring it back."

The other's expression grew even happier. "Don't even have to try. It's always been there." He pointed to the screen.

It took Tyler a few seconds to make out what it was. For a moment, as he looked at the screen, the phosphor dots added up to nothing, ragged shapes moving under crude amateur lighting. Then he recognized the faces. He wondered if he would eventually see his own among them.

Ken was leaning forward, reaching into a leather satchel by his feet and taking out more of the flat square boxes. "So you kept them," said Tyler, watching him. "All of the old Wyle tapes."

"Historical documents, man." He looked up, grinning. "Relics. I had to hide 'em—for a *long* time. But I wouldn't ever have destroyed them." A different light came into his face, fervent. "They were all I had. Until now."

"Until Slide came back," said Tyler.

Ken nodded. "And you. And the little boy. He's the key—we can make it the way it was before. With him." His gaze moved past Tyler to the video screen. "Look."

He turned and saw the face of a girl filling the screen. He recognized her from one of the photos in Bedell's book; one of the victims. There were hands around her face, as though the people around her, outside the screen's frame, were trying to soothe away her fright, stroking her brow and her long hair.

Another hand, gray, with the darker gray of a knife in its grip, came up from the bottom of the screen and drew a black line across the girl's throat.

The black flowed, shiny, spattering the hands around her as the girl's mouth opened in its unrecorded scream.

Ken's gaze was transfixed, watching. The black-and-white shapes covered and moved across his face.

"Just like it was," he whispered.

He looked at the thing crouching beside him. It still had Kinross' face, but the other, the thing that laughed, was moving behind the avidly watching eyes, pulling the mouth into words around the blunt yellow teeth.

Bedell's head lolled weakly on his neck, unable to tear his gaze away from the pale bag of flesh that opened and closed a slit that revealed the wet red inside it. He could smell the decay of its breath, filling the Mercedes, the intestines rotting around the cud of cheap food in its gut. His own sweat, beaded on his face, had absorbed the sour odor; he could taste it as it trickled into the corners of his mouth.

Its hands, folded in broken angles against the pit of its groin, pressed down into the stained flooring. Kinross' spotted skull washed blue under the freeway light slanting through the windshield, as the thing inside lifted the hollow face to Bedell. It stopped when the string between its eyes and his tautened a few inches apart.

He had to listen to what it said. There was no getting away from it.

The mouth parted in its distorted smile. This close, Bedell could see the tongue move, pulling a strand of pink saliva with it.

The whisper. *Now we can have some fun.*

"No . . ." He shuddered, his spine contracting up between his shoulder blades as he pressed himself into the angle of the seat and the door, straining away from it. His cheek smeared against the cool glass of the side window, his hands thrusting blindly at the face to keep it away. "I don't want to, I'm sorry, I'm sorry—"

His palms sank into the soft, loose flesh, his fingertips trembling at the crevices around the eyes. The coldness of the skin brought a shock like ice up through his arms. A flash of his own thoughts, unpoisoned by the drug, sparked inside his head.

"It's dead," he whispered to himself. "You're fucked up, it's not really, it's dead, it can't—"

Against his palms the lips parted, drawing a line of cold saliva against his flesh.

He jerked his hands away, scrabbling at the handle across from him as the thing's face fell against his thigh. The door slammed against the steel guardrail outside, jarring him back into the seat. There was just enough space, an opening of a few inches, for him to squeeze through, sobbing as the door edge tore his shirt across his stomach.

The cold air in his face, and the oncoming headlights dazing his eyes; he found himself running, staggering, his feet scraping through loose gravel at the side of the freeway. He stopped, doubled over, gasping for breath as he held on to the guardrail to keep from falling. When his lungs stopped burning, he looked over his shoulder and saw the Mercedes, door ajar, yards behind him. Nothing was visible through the rear window, as if the car were empty, abandoned.

He shook his head, trying to clear it. The swooping noise of each car passing in the sparse traffic brushed against his ear. The drug's effects seemed to have subsided again, leaving him trembling but able to force his thoughts into motion. No idea of where he was, where the car had gotten to in its hazed progress. He could just remember the freeways unrolling in front of him, the lights tearing at his eyes, the whispering he heard from the corpse folded in front of the empty seat beside him.

With the freeway lanes at his back, he gripped the rail with both hands and leaned over it. A slope of gravel and dry weeds tilted down to a riverbed of dry concrete, faint silver in the dark. A black line of muddy water trickled through the ditch at the center.

He had seen this place before. The memory teased him. Lots of times . . .

It came to him, the same scene in daylight, seen wheeling beyond the car's windshield. Now he knew. He turned and saw across the freeway the black shapes of hills, their edges ragged with brush. And beyond the curving lanes, past the red smears of the receding taillights and the empty Mercedes at the side, in the distance a carpet of lights shimmered.

He had been heading back into L.A. He had gone in a circle, gone nowhere, the signs all blurred too fast for him to read, the lanes ahead tangling and twisting, the thing beside him whispering and smiling.

And now there wasn't time. There wasn't time to get to the desert, get rid of the body, drag it out of the car in the dark where no one could see, leave it where no one would ever find it. It was too late now; even this night, he knew, would end sometime.

He wanted to run, to fill his lungs with the night air, each breath a stride away from the car and the thing inside, and go on running.

But then they'll find it, he told himself, gripping the rail. In the morning, the Highway Patrol would pull up alongside the empty car, they'd get out and look inside. They'd find nothing that moved or whispered, just a dead body, with the imprint of Bedell's hands still around its throat. *That's what they'll find*.

He looked back at the car, the headlights in the near lane pulling it in and out of darkness as they swung past. Slowly, he pushed himself away from the guardrail and walked back toward it.

The empty tape boxes scattered about the floor as Ken fitted the reels onto the decks. Gray light flooded the control room as each screen filled with the shapes and movements of the past.

In the middle of the space, he turned about, his hands lifting into the overlapping wash of images. "It's always been there," he said, voice filled with fervor. "Always . . ."

Tyler backed against the desk. The hiss of the

tapes running over the video machines' heads combined into a breath of metal consuming the air. Beyond Ken's slow pirouette he could see knives, the wet blackness that was blood shining on the blades. *Just like it was*. The words went on sounding in his head, looping in sync with the tapes until he was dizzy. He reached behind himself to hold on to the desk and keep from falling.

The other stepped close to one of the screens on the wall, marveling at the things it held. The gray light superimposed the image of another face on top of his. It was distorted into an open-mouthed scream even as his smile showed underneath, his hand spreading to gently touch the curved glass.

"It's stronger," he cooed. His gaze darted toward Tyler. "*He's* stronger. All this time . . . He's been growing. Waiting for us to come back to Him. They won't be able to stop us now."

Tyler felt the bitter taste welling up on his tongue again. The screens' light grew brighter, dazzling him, blurring into one scene, one image. The knives darkened and jabbed around the other's figure, as though they had sliced through the glass like cellophane and found the waiting flesh in real time.

It's true, thought Tyler. He knew it inside himself. This was what the medications had hid, kept buried where he couldn't see it. It had never ended—the other world, the dark one, the shared mind that the drug had created inside them. It had gone on, seeping through their bloodstreams, gathering its power, waiting for its moment. *His* moment.

"Slide told me . . ." Ken's voice went on at its high, ardent pitch. "He came, and he told me. He told me how we could do it, bring it back the way it was. Because of the little boy—that's how. The little boy is the way . . .''

Tyler closed his eyes against the flood of burning lights. *Just like it was . . . Or worse.* Now the Host was even stronger. He had been waiting a long time.

Now the night would be even deeper, the dark street going on and on, without end. The whisper: *I could show you some things.*

His tongue curled in his mouth, the chemical strong upon it.

Things you want to know.

Bryan.

Around him, the tapes went on reeling through the machines, Ken turning from each screen to the next, his face and hands raised to bathe in their cold glow.

Inside the Mercedes, Kinross' corpse lay tucked in the position he'd managed to squeeze it into back at the house. Nothing moved behind the clouded eyes, the mouth lolled open in slack silence. Bedell's breath eased out of him as he held on to the door for support.

It's over, he thought, eyes closed. *It's just dead, that's all, it's dead.*

He knew he couldn't get back in the car and drive back to the house with it. Even if he managed to get it back into the house without anyone seeing, before morning came, there was still tomorrow night, and all the nights after that, to wait for. The thing that had whispered from inside the corpse would be waiting as well.

If he dumped it here, into the thick brush at the side of the dry river, there'd be a little time, at least. From when it would be found to the moment, the day, the hour, when the police car came inevitably to

the house's door with the few questions they wanted
to ask . . . A little time. Driving time. That was all he
needed.

The car shielded him from the lights and eyes
passing on the freeway. He squeezed through the
door's narrow gap and reached for the corpse's arms.
They lifted above its head as he tugged, straining to
get it up onto the flat of the seats. One elbow caught
on the edge of the dashboard, then came free. The
corpse flopped facedown, the back of its head under
the rim of the steering wheel, the feet tangled together where it had squatted. Bedell panted, dizzy
with the effort of pulling the awkward weight with no
leverage.

He stepped back against the car's side and tugged
again. The head and arms slid through the opening,
but the thick shoulder and chest jammed solid against
the frame. "Shit—come *on*." The blank face gaped
up at him as he twisted the body on its side to no
avail.

Its mouth came close to his ear as he knelt down in
the gravel and squeezed his arm past its chest, grop-
ing for the window handle. He flinched when the
cold lips touched the side of his face. (*The whisper,
the red thing in its throat, the soft words*.) His ragged
breathing had almost broken into sobs when his fingers finally caught hold.

When the window was rolled all the way down, he
pulled his arm out and got his hands and one shoulder underneath the corpse. One of its arms dangled
along his back as he pushed it up onto the sill. It
hung there, half inside the car, the mouth gaping
wider in the upside-down face. Hands digging into
the brown folds of its armpits, he tugged again,
dragging it over the top of the door. His feet slipped

out from under him in the loose gravel as the corpse's waist cleared; it came tumbling on top of him as he fell backward.

She came up from sleep—partway, to that easy, floating state—and found she was still in Mike's arms. The same position in which she had drifted off, her back against his chest. He had slipped one arm between her side and the bed so that with the other he could completely encircle her. The nightgown was now hiked up under her arms; his hands cupped her breasts, drawing her against him.

Nice, she thought, half smiling to herself. *That's nice.* Catlike, she curled her spine, tucking herself into a ball in the warm zone held by the covers. The soft, curling hair of his legs traced across the backs of her thighs as she pressed herself closer.

(*A small flash of memory, like light squeezed under your eyelids: the first time they had gone to bed together; he was so much sweeter than Eddie's father, the last one until then; kinder; and afterward, the relief in being in that place again, after so long, all warm squeezed against his chest; she had reached down and run her hand across his leg, the damp hair twining around her fingers.*)

And now they were in that same place again. She could tell; Mike's hand moved over her breasts, the nipples stiffening against his fingers. She tilted her head back, letting her loose hair tangle across his throat, signaling with her shoulders against his chest and a soft, drowsy sigh. He made no reply, but one hand moved down across her trembling stomach.

This was the first time since that picture had shown up in the newspaper—*her* picture.

(*Another flash of memory, but she couldn't tell from*

*when; as if she were facing Mike's ex-wife, older than
in the photo, sitting on the other side of a table in a
small room, someone watching them as they spoke—
she brushed her cheek against the pillow to get rid
of the image.)*

Maybe now that was all over. That's what this
meant, his hands attentive to her again, moving between her thighs to open her. All of the rest could
fade back into the past where it belonged.

She arched her spine, tasting a strand of her own
hair as it made a web across the side of her face,
letting him lift her higher against him. His hand
found the warmth dissolving into liquid at her center
as she drew her knees up, taking him inside.

Her small movements and breath fell into rhythm
with his. She loved it (*nice: yes*) when she was half
asleep like this and it all seemed like a dream going
on in slow waves forever. The hand reaching from
behind to cradle her breast squeezed her tighter.

(*Another flash, not memory, she knew she had
never seen this before: a dark space of hollowed
earth. She felt underneath her, not the soft warm bed,
but loose dust and the edges of small stones cutting
into her bare skin.*)

"Mike . . ." she whispered, twisting against him.
She could barely breathe, both from his crushing
hold around her and the feeling that, in the room's
darkness, a ceiling of rough concrete was pressing
down on her, vibrating with a muted roar that filtered
down from even farther above. A sour smell of decay
filled her nostrils.

The back of his head struck the ground, the edges
of the stones stabbing into his scalp. Above him, the
corpse's weight pressed against his chest. Something

wet was against his face. When he opened his eyes, he saw its face, the slack mouth close to his.

His pinned hands strained against it, the arms flopping on either side as if to embrace him. In his mouth, something bitter welled and cut the salt taste of his own sweat.

The sagging, damp skin of Kinross' face started to slide across his. He could see its eyes.

They were clear again, the dark centers staring into his.

Before he could hear the whisper, before the mouth could open and let out the soft words, he was screaming, beating against the corpse's chest with his fists. He scrabbled backward from underneath, his elbows digging into the gravel, but it held on, the arms tangling with his.

Under the guardrail, the gravel gave way to their weight, the edge of the slope crumbling beneath them. The part of him that could still sense anything other than the shrill tearing in his throat felt the falling backward through the brush, the freeway's lights blocked by the shape clasping itself to him.

He was hurting her. The motions suddenly became a jabbing pain deep inside her. "Mike . . . please . . ." She couldn't pull away from him; his hands gripped her tighter, pinning her against him. "Stop . . ."

Then they were in the dark place, not a quick glimpse of it like before, but there in it, bodies pressed together and clawing at the dirt floor of the hollow, the smell of rotting food and unwashed sweat choking in her small gasps for breath.

The concrete above pressed down on her, inches above her face, as each thrust snapped the back of her head against his chest.

She could feel them watching, the bright eyes and the others.

Somewhere close, a child was crying, its thin voice mingling with her pleas, echoing under the rumbling noise of the concrete.

"Mike . . . stop—" She twisted her head about to see his face.

In the darkness, the long, sharp teeth were visible, becoming long as knives as the smile drew wider over her shoulder.

The images on the video screens beat against his face. In Tyler's mouth, the bitter taste was so strong it nauseated him. Holding on to the desk, he turned away from them and Ken swaying in the middle of the floor.

Beyond the empty seats, the big screen was no longer blank. He could see things moving on it as well.

The Host's sharp-toothed smile glinted through a loose tangle of dark hair. A woman's face, a fragment dimly seen; he could almost remember it, not from the tapes, not from the past. The echo of her scream came from beyond the studio walls.

The screen faded, changed as he watched. He saw Kinross' face, but the wide, dark-stubbled jowls were slack and mottled with blood. The old cop was dead, he knew. The face tilted, dry brush tearing at it, and the pair of hands, someone else's, still alive, pushing at the face to keep it away. Now he could hear a man's hoarse-throated cry.

It faded, replaced with the silence that he recognized as from the crawling skin along his arms. He bent his head down to hear the soft words.

Now we're all together again.

The whisper was so close. He could almost tell . . .

Lower, just for him: *Aren't we?*

He looked up at the screen and saw the dark silhouettes of palm trees, swaying against the night sky. The blue fire outlined each frond, and their shadows on the black grass stretching away before him.

There. He should have known. Always there.

The chair fell over to the floor as he pushed it aside. Heading to the door, his feet breaking into a run, he saw Ken down on his hands and knees, his face uplifted to the burning screens.

He felt the corpse's hand pull across his face, one of the blunt fingers catching at the fold of his eye. The dry weeds crackled under Bedell as the corpse rolled with him down the slope.

The face blotted out the stars above him, and the cold hand covered his nose and mouth, the weight pressing the air from his lungs.

For a moment, the sharp-pointed teeth grew larger, filling the wheeling sky. Then they darkened, and disappeared with everything else.

As the last of her breath went out in a scream, light flooded across her. She rolled onto her back, pushing herself up from the bed with her hands. The covers were pushed down into a pile at the foot; there was no one beside her. Eddie stood in his pajamas at the bedroom doorway, his hand coming down from the light switch.

"You woke me up," he said accusingly. His other hand knuckled the corner of his eye. "You were shouting."

She quickly pulled down her nightgown to cover herself, a damp spot at the top of her thighs. Her

breath slowly came back to her as she ran her trembling
hand through the sweat-damp tangle of her hair. She
looked down at the empty half of the bed next to her.
Not even the imprint of another body was visible in
the sheet.

Leading Eddie by the hand, she took him back to
his own bedroom. "What were you shouting for?"
he sleepily demanded, frowning as she pulled the
covers up to his chin.

"Shh. Nothing. Nothing at all." The tremor was
still in her hand as she brushed his hair from his
forehead. "Just a bad dream. Mommies get them,
too." The frown relaxed only a fraction as she watched
him fall asleep.

She didn't go back to her bedroom. In the kitchen,
she checked the time from the clock on the stove.
Hours after midnight; Mike hadn't come back after
locking up the theatre. She filled the kettle and waited
for it to boil, sitting at the table and tucking the
nightgown close with her folded arms. There would
be no point in trying to sleep again. She could still
see the dream image of the long teeth, smiling where
Mike's face should have been.

(*And the space of dirt and concrete, with the eyes
watching—where was that? Somewhere else, somewhere she had never been, as though someone else's
vision had bled into hers, like one photo transparency
laid over another . . .*)

No sleep. Instead, the vigil of staying up the rest of
the night, waiting for him. When the light came,
she'd decide what to do next.

As she stood up to pour the steaming water over
the tea bag in the cup, she felt the thin pain below
her stomach. She sat back down and lifted the hem of
the nightgown over her knees. A ragged scratch arced
across the soft skin inside one thigh. As she looked,

a bright red dot welled from the deep point closest to
the top.

The gates were locked when he reached the cemetery. But it was easy for Tyler to find toeholds in the
elaborate curves of the ironwork and climb over.

He had seen the cemetery like this already, on the
screen in the studio. The dark grass was alive, charged
with the blue current separating the blades, seeping
up from below. Over him as he ran, the black shapes
of the palms swayed in the warm night air, the dry
fronds rustling.

At the small metal rectangle that marked his son's
grave, he stopped, panting to catch his breath. The
traffic noise was left with his own car beyond the
cemetery's walls. He stood and listened to the small
noises filtering through the silence.

Bryan . . .

He knelt down, his knees sinking into the grass.
His hands spread through the blades, cool and damp
on top, warmer toward the soil, as he pressed the
side of his face down below the edge of the marker.

For a moment, nothing but the night's silence and
the crumpling of the grass against his ear. Then he
heard it, faint, then closer.

From below, a child's crying. The sobs grew louder,
as though the child's ribs would burst with them. No
words, no name called, only being alone and frightened in a dark place, until Tyler's skull ached with
the noise and his fingers dug into the grass, the dirt
balling inside his fists.

"Bryan . . . No, don't—"

The crying stopped when he spoke. Then another
voice.

"*Come on, Mike,*" whispered Slide. The mocking

laugh behind the words pulled the image of the narrow, bright-eyed face into Tyler's mind. "*You know what you want, don't you? Don't you, Mike? It can be like it was before.*" The words teased, coaxed. "*Better than before. That's what you want. Isn't it, Mike? Isn't it?*"

"Shut up—" The earth came loose in his hands, the grass and soil tearing apart as his fists squeezed tighter. "Shut up."

Silence. He heard nothing below him. There was nothing but the yards of dirt and the small box buried in it, silent as the others around it, beneath the grass.

Another shadow, broader than the thin palms fell across the marker with his son's name on it. The grass darkened beneath the silhouette of a standing figure.

He heard the voice behind him. The whisper.
Now.

Raising himself on his knees, he turned and looked up into the face. Only a few feet away from his, watching and smiling. The points of the teeth were like stars, cutting through cold air.

Now you're inside. All the way in.

As Tyler got to his feet and stood up, he realized he was alone again. The Host had gone, back into his blood. But it didn't matter. Turning toward the cemetery's gate, he realized there was plenty of time now. *All the time I need.*

He could see out across the street to the hills beyond the city. The sun rising was as dark as the center of the eyes into which he had gazed.

Through the curtains in the front room, she saw the light coming, the darkness ebbing as the night finally ended. First gray, then the traces of red would smear above the buildings and the traffic.

He's out there, she thought. The cup with the long-cold tea dregs in it sat by her elbow on the kitchen table. The silent, wordless prayer that had run through her mind during the waiting hours hadn't been answered.

Even before the light started to filter through the window, she had been able to see what was left for her to do. She could go on waiting. Or start the long process of forgetting.

Or find him.

She clasped her arms across her breasts. *Now you're scared*, she told herself. The dream had left her with the residue of her own crying voice in her mouth. And all the other things that had come bubbling back to the surface, up from where Mike had hid them, since the photo of his ex-wife in the paper . . .

You don't know, she thought, rocking herself, *what you'll find, when you find him*.

The light grew brighter in the window. She watched it, still feeling the night's chill around her.

He opened his eyes in the first thin light of morning. The corpse's face was next to his.

Kinross' face was slack, empty, gray in the dim light. Bedell jerked away from it, pulling free his arm that had been trapped beneath its weight. He slid the last few inches through the loose gravel to the dry concrete of the riverbed. On his hands and knees, he looked up at the freeway. The slope's angle hid the traffic lanes. He could see only the Mercedes at the edge of the guardrail, its door ajar.

There's still time. The thought broke inside his head. Nobody had seen yet. He could still get away from the thing sprawled in the weeds beside him. Back to the house, get his stuff, the little bit of money he had stashed there, and out onto the bright morning freeway, away from here.

Panting, he started scrabbling up the slope toward the car, his fingers digging into the sharp gravel.

He watched Slide stretch himself like a cat, his spine arching against the curved side of the nest, arms thrust out to release the muscles. Jimmy knew he hadn't been sleeping. *Just lying there*, he thought as he crouched by the bundled rags with the child in them. The bright eyes had stayed closed, but the thin smile had passed across the narrow face as the night hours crept by.

The eyes opened and looked straight at him. The edge of the gray light touched one side of Slide's face. He looked pleased.

"Now we're there," said Slide, nodding to himself. "Finally there."

Jimmy turned away, back to watching the little boy. His face had gone paler, Jimmy could see now, the breathing even shallower.

He stroked the soft hair. He knew better than to wonder what Slide's words meant.

The night hadn't ended. *Not for me*, thought Tyler. *Not for any of us*. It would go without end, like the street. Now that they were all inside again.

He walked over the dark grass, under the palm's shadows, black against a black sky. The graves were silent again.

Beyond the cemetery gates, the sun rising above the distant hills gave no light. That didn't matter. he knew, not anymore. In the dark, he could see everything. Straight through all the shadows and gray shapes of the other world where he had lived for a while. Now he knew where his son was.

He walked, heading for the gate and the car beyond, with the black sun streaming around it.

Tyler left the graveyard behind. Now he knew. His son was waiting for him to come.

FIFTEEN

"**W**here we going?" said Eddie. The rocket ship model sat on his lap, carefully held.

Steff glanced over at her son as she drove. The novelty of being out riding around in the car on a Saturday morning seemed to have compensated for his regular bout of TV cartoons. This was the one morning of the week she ordinarily allowed herself the luxury of sleeping in—ten o'clock the latest, eleven a guilt-provoking indulgence—while Mike supervised Eddie's cold cereal and mopped up any spilled milk afterward. She usually came out in her bathrobe to find the two of them watching *Scooby-Doo*, Mike halfway through the *L.A. Times* and his second cup of coffee. *Not today*, she thought. Maybe it would never be that way again.

"We're going to the theatre," she said. "The movies—where Mike works. Okay?"

He nodded. "Mike going to be there?" Without looking at her, he worked the rocket's hinged plastic cockpit.

"Yes. I mean, I think so." *I hope so*, she thought. There was no point in making the promise to Eddie, which she had no way of knowing would come true. Or even if there were a chance of finding Mike there; she had dialed the theatre's office number before they left the apartment, and the phone had rung at least twenty times, the tone drilling at her ear, with no answer. *But he might still be there*, she told herself again. The black mood's silence might have wrapped around him so tightly that he wouldn't want to answer the phone, preferring the company of his own brooding thoughts to any voice from outside his head.

It would be better, she knew, to leave him alone—if that was all that was going on with him. Just let the past work out of him, like toxins from a long-festering wound, until he emerged, as he had always done before, into the light again. *If that's all it is*—the one thought crept under all the others. And if this time it didn't work out of him, the past reclaimed him, the brooding went on and on without end—*better not to find him. Better to lose him, you've already lost him.*

She gripped the steering wheel tighter, pushing down the urge to swing the car around, a U-turn at the next light, and head back to the apartment. There to put Eddie in front of the bright-colored, racketing cartoons, and to make another pot of coffee and stare at her textbooks without seeing them. And wait.

But that was already impossible. There was no more waiting in her. The dream last night had scared her. It went on unreeling in her mind; the slow movements in the warmth of the bed, the arms clasping across her breasts and pressing her harder against the cold flesh at her back, the barely seen smile, all knife points, that had brought her scream out of her throat. She squeezed her eyes shut for a moment, as though the image of the face were somehow in the morning light glaring in the windshield.

That part had been bad enough. It was the other, the dream of riding through the night-filled street, the face she couldn't make out turning its dark formlessness toward her.

She didn't know, couldn't remember, if she had cried Mike's name. And if it had been a cry for help or of recognition.

Beside her, Eddie had gotten bored with the rocket ship and its imagined flight against the backdrop of the side window. He pressed his face close to the glass, studying the traffic. A report on any exotic cars spotted was being prepared—for Mike's benefit. *Because that's where we're going*, thought Steff. *To see Mike. That's what I told him.*

Instead of bringing Eddie along, she would rather have dropped him off someplace. (—*someplace safe*, a little biting thought among the rest, *but what's not safe, it's all right, no danger, everything's all right*—) But the only one she knew, Pauline from her chem class last semester, with the four kids and the huge Labrador bounding around the Culver City tract house, hadn't answered the phone this morning, either. *Bad luck with phones today*, Steff had thought, before remembering the postcard three days ago from Zion National Park, describing the midpoint chaos of having the whole lot stuffed into a rental RV for two weeks. Too bad—Eddie would have happily agreed to a morning spent with Quincy the Lab and Pauline's oldest boy, who—it had been excitedly recounted after the last baby-sitting session—could make a basketball spin on the point of his finger.

That would've been all right. Instead of being dragged along by his freaked-out mother—who was doing a good job of smiling and talking light and keeping the fear (*what's to be afraid of? what's wrong?*) bottled up inside—to check up on the guy who didn't have to be in the loony bin anymore because he carries it around in his own head, doesn't he? *Shut up, shut up*, she told herself. *There's nothing wrong, nothing wrong—just drive and stop thinking.*

So no Pauline and her hectic household. And shuttling back and forth, all of Steff's time cut close, between classes and the restaurant had kept the rest of the students at one end and the waitresses at the other on no more than a hello-and-good-bye basis. *That's the breaks. But no problem, nothing to worry about.* Mike would be there and he'd be all right, or close to it. *Nothing wrong at all—*

"Hey!"

Eddie's shout startled her, jerking her shoulders back against the seat. "What?" She knew what to expect, some Italian car name most likely.

He swiveled his face against the glass, looking at the traffic behind them. "Wow," he breathed. "A Studebaker." He turned back around, having lost it. "I think. Mike would know," he said definitely.

The light outside the house burned his eyes. He'd had to squint into the fire all the way, the squeezed-out tears cutting muddy tracks through the dirt on his face as he leaned over the Mercedes' steering wheel.

Bedell had scuttled out of the car with its banged-up door and across the driveway, knowing everybody on the street was watching him. *They saw, they saw everything.* Looking over his shoulder as he jabbed the key at the front door, he spotted a kid on a skateboard studying him with smirking insolence as the little wheels clattered over the sidewalk. He slammed the door and fell back against it, panting, shutting out the watching eyes.

Nice and dark inside, the light all filtered by the curtains into a shaded cavern. As he caught his breath,

he scanned across the empty rooms. The stain that
had leaked out of Kinross' broken scalp colored the
center of the living room carpet. He wondered if it
was possible to scrub it out, eradicate the damning
evidence before he got back into the car and started
driving again. *No point*, he decided. *No fucking point
anymore*. All he could do now was go, get away from
here, as far as he could. Time equaled distance now.

Go. Just go.

He kept the stash of money in one of the books on
the shelves. For an emergency—the thought brought
a rasping laugh up into his throat. The book fell to
the floor as he pulled out the thin wad of bills.

Fucking shit. He counted them again, his hands
shaking. Two thousand exact—*that's all?* There
had been more than that, he knew it. He couldn't
have dipped into it that much. He jerked the rest of
the books off the shelf, shaking each one in turn and
then throwing it down.

The money in his fist was sweaty and crumpled
when he stopped, the books scattered around him.
Trembling, he thrust the wad into his pocket. That
was it. After all this time, that was all that was left.
He was too tired to feel anything more than the
weariness in his limbs.

Go.

Tired, his aching muscles weighing sacklike on
his bones, drawing him through his trembling knees
to the floor. He wished he could just curl up into a
ball on the carpet, far enough away from the dark
stain in the middle, and sleep. But there wasn't time.
Soon the corpse out in the dry riverbed would be
found, and the machinery of the police would grind
into motion, catching what it wanted in the teeth of
its gears. Even that wasn't what he was afraid of,

what kept him in motion, his eyes stinging with the effort of keeping them open.

In the bedroom, he stuffed what clean clothes he could find into a brown supermarket bag. He knew he had to hurry, had to get a long way from here.

Before the night came again.

If he fell asleep, he knew he wouldn't wake until the light would be draining away again from the world outside the house. And then he'd be screwed.

Because it's still inside me, he thought, shoving a handful of socks into the bag. *That shit.* Maybe this respite from the drug, the soft words and face of sharp, smiling teeth having ebbed out of his brain, would last all through the daylight hours. There might be enough time to get far from here, where the drug's effects seemed to have seeped right into the fabric of the house, like the stain in the carpet, and into some-place safe, a motel room or just the car pulled over to the side of a deserted road. Where he could hunker down and ride out the next wave of it in his blood. He could drink himself blind, unconscious, cheat it that way. Every night, until he was so far away that nobody could find him, and he could start scoring tranquilizers and all the rest, telling sob stories to some hick-town GP, buying downers from high school kids, whatever it took to put together the kind of dosage that kept the Host bottled up inside, where it couldn't get out, no matter how dark the night got. *There's ways*, he told himself. He looked around the bedroom, trying to think of anything else he could take. *I just need time, that's all I need—*

He heard the phone ringing in the other room. The noise turned him slowly toward the bedroom door. It stopped, switched off by the answering machine.

At the doorway, he listened to his own voice

droning off the tape. He stepped closer to the shelf that the machine and the phone sat on, as the go-ahead beep sounded.

"Bedell?" The voice barked out of the answering machine's speaker. "You there?"

His throat tightened as he recognized the voice. It was Tyler. Something tightened the skin along his arms, so that he couldn't pick up the phone, only let the words curl out of the machine's speaker.

"All right." Tyler's voice came again after a couple seconds' wait. It sounded harsh, stripped and flattened by more than the wires between the phones. "When you get back and listen to this, there's something I want you to do. It's important, so listen."

A bitter taste, like the last crystal of the drug dissolving on his tongue, seeped into his mouth.

"I know," said Tyler.

He seemed to be whispering right into Bedell's ear. He could barely see the two flashing red dots on the answering machine through the shadow that filled the house, as if clouds had covered the sun outside, dimming the windows behind the curtains.

"I know all about it," came Tyler's soft words. They didn't sound angry or rushed any longer, but smiling, filled with secrets that could only be told in whispers.

He had to brace himself against the wall as he listened, the bitter taste welling up from his throat, nauseating him.

"I know because I was there. With you. We're all together now. I saw what you did. And you're scared now. Aren't you? I know."

His hand trembled toward the machine, reaching for the cords between it and the phone, anything that he could pull loose, and stop the voice trickling into the darkened room.

"You're scared because you're all shit inside. Aren't you?" The voice sneered at him. He had never heard Tyler speak like this, with the words blurring and twisting into sharp-edged things. "Aren't you? You wanted to go inside, in the dark, and know things, too. Only you didn't deserve it. You got scared. You're just shit, aren't you?"

Stop it. He raised his fist to hammer against the machine, but couldn't. The soft words went on, tapping at his ear.

"You're not going anywhere." At any moment, the voice would break into laughter, sharp and tearing. "You're going to wait for me."

No—please . . . He tried to force the cry out, but his throat was blocked with his thick breath. His knees gave way, sliding him against the wall until he was kneeling as he heard the last words trickling out of the answering machine.

"You'll be seeing me."

He closed his eyes, the click of the phone disconnecting swallowed in the room's distance. His fingers clutched at the carpet fibers, digging into them. The voice hadn't been Tyler's, not by the time it finished. He knew where he had heard it before, seen the mouth moving and smiling over Kinross' yellow teeth.

His legs curled up toward his chest as he laid his head against the floor. He could barely see the outline of the window behind the curtains, the light had drained away so much. In the dark, he listened to the voice whispering and smiling, locked in memory.

At the theatre, she found the glass front doors chained shut, the dull metal links wrapped around the chrome loops of the handles and padlocked. *Well, that shoots that,* thought Steff. Eddie stood beside her under the marquee and watched as she shaded her eyes and peered into the dark lobby behind the doors. He must have locked up after the last show and went—*who knows. Anywhere.*

"Mike's here?" said Eddie, looking up at her after he had gazed inside as well. The rocket ship had been left in the car parked at the curb.

"Guess not—" *Wait, wait. The back door.* Every place had a back door. The alley that ran behind the theatre; probably there. *Or what's his name—the projectionist kid—Mike had him lock these doors before he went home. So he'd be undisturbed.*

It was worth checking. From her pocket, she fished out the ring of spare keys that Mike kept in one of the kitchen drawers. The third one she tried worked, the padlock snapping open in her hand. She unwound the chain and pushed open one of the doors.

"Mike?" The door closed behind her and Eddie, sealing them into the lobby's dim quiet. The fluorescent tube in the candy counter was the only light, leaving the corridors branching to either side deep in shadow. "Hey, Mike . . ." she called again.

She heard nothing, her own footsteps swallowed up by the carpeting. Eddie let go of her hand and skipped ahead into the semidarkness. The water fountain gurgled as he stood on tiptoe at it. He knew where the little steps on the side were that enabled someone his size to get a drink; Mike had brought him to the theatre enough times, up to the projection room and down to the mop closet under the ladies' room, for Eddie to have memorized the place.

He came back, wiping his mouth on the back of his hand. "I was thirsty."

"Yeah, well, don't go running off. I don't want to have to go looking for you." The mild claustrophobia that she supposed everybody got in dark, empty buildings tightened her spine. You never knew—sometimes bums got into places like this when no one else was around, scuttling like rats through secret holes in ventilation grilles to catch a quick sheltered sleep before the real people came back. She saw them on the campus all the time, figures huddled underneath outside stairwells, shopping carts full of rags and cardboard, their ratlike treasures, parked nearby.

Should've brought a flashlight, she thought, looking down the corridor to where, she knew, the office door was, behind the ticket booth. *Come on, come on. Get it together. There's no one here, it's all right, nothing to worry about. Quit scaring yourself, for Christ's sake.*

"You stay here," she told Eddie, positioning him in front of the candy counter. "Right here, okay?" He nodded, intrigued by the bright cartons and wrappers inside the case. "I'll be right back."

The cold around her spine scooped under her stomach as she walked down the corridor. *Stop it. Just stop it.* She could just make out the doorknob and the NO ADMITTANCE sign at eye level. "Mike?" She knocked, and heard nothing from inside.

She turned the knob. It was locked. "Shit." She pulled out the key ring and fumbled through the keys, trying each one in turn. The door finally swung open, and she reached in—her stomach, for a second, contracted around ice—and switched on the light.

Nothing but the desk, scattered with papers, employee schedules, rolled-up promo posters. Just the way she had seen it anytime before, an accumulation of the candy counter's waxy cups stained with brown coffee rings inside sitting on top of the filing cabinet, the bottom corner of a *2001: A Space Odyssey* poster curling up where the thumbtack had been taken out in order to stick a bra on the opposite wall, the latest one that the clean-up crew claimed to have found under the back row of seats.

But no Mike. He might never have been there at all last night, or come in and taken off—whenever. *Who knows*, thought Steff. The coldness at the pit of her stomach had changed to a hollow space. As worried (*scared?*) as she had been, she had also hoped. One way or another; at least to know. But nothing—she didn't know where to look, to even begin looking, after this.

Maybe the projectionist. She remembered the kid, a gangly blond with the dirtiest Adidases she had ever seen, from one of the times she had come down to the theatre with Mike. Or the ticket seller, or the girl who worked the candy counter—any of them might remember if he had come in, when he left, if he said where he was going. Anything. She went behind the desk, pushing the chair out of the way, to look through the mess of papers. *Must be a phone list or something*, she thought. *Some way he gets hold of them*.

She pushed aside the rolled-up posters. A spot of color—two colors, bright green and yellow—leaped to her eye.

Between her thumb and forefinger she picked it up and slowly turned it around. She recognized it, had seen it dozens of times before. For a moment, she could see Mike's fingers, rolling it and the other ones, the other bright-colored cylinders, into a little square of aluminum foil.

One of the capsules of Mike's medication.

The hollow in her stomach wasn't big enough to hold the chill, to keep it from spreading up to her heart.

He dropped it. That's all. It meant nothing. There were so many of them, filling the center of his cupped palm, all washed down with a mouthful of water the way he did, the way she had seen him do it, standing at the kitchen sink back at the apartment. She had never seen him drop one. He was so careful. Still, so many of them—how many times a day? He was bound to drop one sometime. *An accident. That's all*, she told herself as she rolled the capsule's smooth skin against her finger.

She spotted another one, blue and white, tucked into the edges of a loose stack of papers. When she picked it up, the white powder inside leaked onto her fingers. One side of the capsule was pushed in, as if it had been squeezed until it split.

Backing away from the desk, she saw a white tablet on the floor.

"Mom—"

She looked around and saw Eddie at the office door. She didn't know how long she had been there, how long he had been waiting for her to come back to the candy counter.

Her hand closed around the capsules, hiding them. "Almost ready to go," she said, bending toward him. "You go back out to the lobby, okay? And I'll be there in a couple of minutes, and then we'll go."

When he had reluctantly pulled himself from the door and gone down the corridor, she turned back to the desk, her mind spinning too fast for the thoughts to be more than fragments. *Something happened—he did something—*

The wastebasket. She saw it beside the chair, picked it up, and tilted it out across the desk.

The orange prescription bottles clicked against each other as they rolled against the papers, the white plastic caps scattering about. Crumpled into balls, the pharmacy's paper bags still bore the shape of Mike's fist.

"Jesus." She poked through the debris with her finger. *He's done it*. The whole business, everything that had happened since the picture in the paper, his loony ex-wife, all that raving about his dead kid—it had pushed him this far. He had probably flushed the whole lot, all of his medications. The time-honored traditional way of getting rid of drugs. And why?

Because, thought Steff, staring at the orange bottles, *because that stuff kept him sane*. And what he wanted was what Linda, his ex-wife, had.

Their son. Bryan.

He could be a sane man, and have a child who was nothing more than a marker with a name on it in the middle of carefully mown grass, under the nodding palms around the cemetery. (*Flash of memory, waking up to find him sitting on the corner of Eddie's bed, watching the sleeping child*.) Or he could throw away the meds and go where *she* was, that place in her mind, half the past and half delusions, where that other little boy was still alive. (*Soft words. Now you're inside—where had she heard them? The dream, that was it*.) And just needed to be found.

Now was the time. She knew it; that was what the scattered empty containers spelled out. Now it was time to start forgetting him. He had gone where she couldn't follow.

Her arm jerked around in a convulsive arc, flinging the capsules against the wall, as her vision blurred

with sudden tears. "That fucking bitch," she said
aloud. She needed a face to pour her fury against; the
one from the picture in the newspaper would do.
Linda would have him, all nice and cozy, together
again in their mutual hallucinations even if locked up
in separate bins. That was the way it worked, the
way it always worked: you could only love somebody for as long as his past left him alone, as long as
it let you have him. Because it was stronger, stronger
than anything.

(*Strong because you're scared; strong because
there's scary things in there; those pictures, those
shiny black-and white corpses in the middle of the
book, they're in there; and you're scared.*)

No.

She leaned on her balled-up fists against the desk,
pulling her breath in until her lungs ached, shaking
the stinging salt out of her eyes. *No.* She didn't care
how scared she was. *I'll find him.*

(*Angry because she was scared; it wasn't right,
it's not right.*)

She stood upright, rubbing a damp smear from her
cheek, and looked around the office. The projectionist wouldn't know anything. None of the people who
worked at the theatre would. He had been here and
gone. It was the ones from that other world, the past,
that would know where.

A small white rectangle poked out from under the
papers on the desk. A business card, with scribbling
on the back. She turned it over and saw the neatly
printed name and address. *Bedell*, she thought. *That
writer. He'd know.* Mike had told her how Bedell
kept file cabinets full of stuff about the Wyle Group;
his life's work. *And he's been calling Mike. Bugging
him about Linda and all that shit.*

And here was his address, right in her hand.

"Come on." She slowed her run to grab Eddie's hand and pull him with her. The card with Bedell's address was in her hand with her car keys. She didn't take time to relock the theatre's doors.

He could hear it outside. Moving around—sniffing at the doors and windows of the house like a dog, a big black Doberman, only with eyes that were sometimes blank and clouded gray, sometimes so clear that the dark at their centers was deep enough to fall into. The lips would be pulled back from the sharp-pointed teeth—he could see them as he rocked back and forth, clutching his knees to his face—and laughing, laughing at the thing that wept and rocked itself inside the house.

Bedell didn't know how long he'd been waiting, unable to leave, unable to get away. As long as it was out there—the dark that filled the windows made it impossible to tell if time moved at all. *Maybe it's night already.* He rubbed his face against the tear-wet cloth of his trousers. *Maybe it'll always be night.*

For a while he had thought he wasn't alone inside the house. In the dark, the stain on the carpet had grown, as if seeping from a wound, until it was a man-shaped outline. He had been afraid to lift his eyes and look at it hard enough to bring it into focus. Because, right at the edge of his eyelids, it had looked like Kinross lying there in the middle of the floor, as if all of last night hadn't happened, the corpse hadn't ridden with him on the looping free-ways, smiling and whispering. He had buried his face tighter against his knees when he had seen it pushing itself up on its hands, raising its head to gaze across the room at him. He couldn't bear to see its face, whatever face it had, even as he had felt its hand reaching to touch him . . .

That had passed. He had managed to bring his eyes up and see, dimly, just the stain on the carpet. Then he had heard the thing outside. Just at the edge of silence, moving around, peering in at the corners of the covered windows. He crouched, spine bent, and listened. The red dot on the answering machine went on blinking above his head, signaling the message recorded on the tape, the words that had started in Tyler's voice and ended in the other's.

The air stirred, echoing through the empty house. Bedell lifted his head, wondering. Then he realized what the noise was.

Something had knocked at the door.

"You stay here," she told Eddie. She had spotted the house number and pulled over to the curb in front of it.

"Where you going?"

Steff took the keys out of the ignition and pointed to the house. "Right there. And I'll just be a couple of minutes, okay? So don't you move."

She hurried up the driveway, past a brown Mercedes with an ugly, recent-looking scrape across its front fender and door. In her jeans pocket she tucked the card she had taken out of the book.

It looked like nobody was home. Behind the precisely trimmed bushes, the curtains were drawn across the wide front windows. She heard nothing from inside when she pushed the button underneath the brass number plate.

"Mr. Bedell?" She leaned her head close to the door, then raised her fist and knocked. "Hello?"

Silence. She knocked again, louder. "Bedell?" she shouted. "Are you there?"

Shit. She chewed her lip, looking back across the lawn to where Eddie was watching her from the car. *Wait for him?* she wondered. There wasn't anything else she could think of, anyplace that might lead to Mike. And how long could she afford to hang around and wait? There wasn't time.

Maybe Bedell was in there; maybe he was asleep or something. It was still early in the morning, especially for somebody who wasn't tied in to a regular nine-to-five schedule, like a writer. *And it's Saturday, for Christ's sake*, she thought. She wouldn't ordinarily have been up at this hour.

She stepped off the porch and walked behind the bushes. A small gap was visible in the center of the curtains. There might be some sign of life inside.

He crawled on his hands and knees across to the window. Twitching the curtain apart a fraction of an inch, Bedell peered out at the doorstep.

It looked like a woman standing there. From this angle he could only see the backs of her legs and the fall of dark hair across her shoulders. *Who?* His thoughts spun furiously as he heard his name being called. *What does she want?*

The point of one shoulder swung about as he watched, as though she were about to turn around. He pressed his face closer to the glass, straining to see her face.

Then he saw, and knew.

She turned and looked at him, her gaze penetrating the glass and sinking into his like wires. He couldn't draw his breath around the thick wad swelling in his throat. The dark centers in her eyes opened and the night swam out.

It laughed as it stepped off the porch and headed for him. The lips pulled back from the sharp-pointed teeth and he saw the face that had moved behind the corpse's face, that had whispered and smiled at him all through the night. Now it was uncovered, the teeth longer than ever before and glistening wet as the laugh grew louder, echoing in the street and the house and tearing at his ears as he scurried back away from the window.

Too late. The dead-white face, the only thing visible in the darkness outside, had spotted him. White like bone, but soft. When it touched him he knew it would be like something decaying over the blackness that showed in the eyes. It would reach through the window, laughing, and the night would pour in. And he'd be alone with it, in the dark.

Go—

He managed to stand upright and run to the door, tearing at its edge until his hands found the knob and it swung open. There was a quick flash in the corner of his eye, the thing in the woman's body turning around at the window, the dead face gazing at him as he scrambled into the Mercedes.

The key—he dug into his pockets, fingers raking through a few coins. It was moving toward the car, in its easy, unhurried motion.

He found the key and jammed it into the ignition. The roar of the motor mingled with the laughter.

The Mercedes swerved back in the driveway, dropping off the edge of the curb and narrowly missing the car parked there. He dropped it into gear and felt himself pressed into the seat as the car jerked forward.

*   *   *

She turned when she heard the door flung open. A man's face, drained pale underneath the smeared dirt, gaped at her; she recognized him from the picture on the back of the book.

He was in the Mercedes before she could reach the driveway. Through the windshield she saw the filthy hands gripping the steering wheel; the engine gunned, sending the car in a wide curve out into the street, an inch clear of the front of her own.

"Hey!" She ran to the sidewalk, waving her arms. The Mercedes was already to the end of the block. In a moment it would be out of the tract and onto the boulevard beyond.

Eddie bounced in his seat, eyes wide, as Steff scrambled behind the steering wheel. "Fwoosh!" One hand sailed above his head in ecstatic imitation of the other car's taking off.

Just like TV, she thought. "Sit down, honey, okay?" She could see the Mercedes at the end of the street, turning right, as she twisted the key in the ignition. "Don't jump around like that."

For a moment she thought she had lost him, swallowed up in the traffic outside the tract of houses. She craned her neck, stretching to see over the other cars for a sign of the Mercedes ahead. *Shit*. He could tell her something, she knew; his face, when she had seen him come running out of the house, had been contorted with fear. There was only one scary thing going on now. Anything that had touched Bedell like that had at least a thread leading to Mike.

She tried to speed up, but both lanes were blocked by cars slowing down for a light turning red. The high-pitched squeal of tires in a skid sounded from in front. Pushing open the car door, she stepped out onto the empty space on the other side of the line. A station wagon from the cross street swerved to a halt in the intersection, its horn blaring. The Mercedes went on without stopping.

"Come on—" Back in the car, she urged the others into motion. They slowly moved ahead when the light went green.

"Mom . . ." Eddie no longer looked so excited. A bit of the fear had crept into his face.

"It's okay, sweetheart." She took a hand off the wheel to squeeze one of his. "You just hang on and be quiet, all right?"

He nodded gravely.

A gap opened in the lane on the right as one of the other cars pulled into a parking space. She swung into it and pressed the accelerator.

He had to get where there were other people. Lots of them. Then he'd be safe. Somewhere it was all lit up, with no dark corners for things to come out of, even though the sunlight lancing off the cars around him sank splinters into his eyes.

The street blurred around him as Bedell drove. A shape of glass and metal filled the windshield, then spun around, screaming at him. He didn't care, there wasn't time to try and see what it had been, there was no longer any time at all. The steering wheel was a sweating rod in his hands, unconnected to the blaring motion sweeping by him.

The mistake, he knew now, had been in trying to hide. *Where nobody could see me. In the dark.* Because that was where *it* was. The thing with the white face and the dark at the center of its eyes, it lived in the darkness, ate it, the sharp-pointed teeth tearing the darkness, vomiting it out, pressing its soft face to his until his throat was filled with the bitter, sick clogging—

Other people. He nodded, chewing his lip and tasting the salt leaking from it. *All around.* Then he'd be safe.

Even out here, on the street, it felt better. He could pull breath into his lungs, even though he was alone in the car and it smelled of Kinross, stale cigarette smoke and the rotting food inside the corpse. There were people, living people, around him, in the other cars.

One of them was looking at him. He felt the gaze at the side of his face, from the car beside him. He turned to the window and looked.

The white face in the other car smiled at him.

He screamed, tearing the hoarse wound of his throat open again. The other car fell away as he twisted the wheel blindly, away, no matter where.

His forehead cracked against the wheel as the Mercedes jolted to a stop. The single broad line of a streetlight post showed beyond the hood.

He pulled himself across the seats and out the passenger side, away from the metal shapes filling the street. Across the sidewalk, a black asphalt sea crossed with herringbone white lines surrounded a glass-walled building.

There were people in there. And light. He knew it. *Safe there*—the one thought left; the rest had been battered out.

The ivy tangled at his feet, sprawling him backward, as he stumbled down the slope surrounding the parking lot. He got to his feet and ran toward the shopping mall.

* * *

She spotted the Mercedes, empty, at the side of the street. A pool of water leaked out from the radiator behind the crumpled front grille.

When she pulled up behind it and got out, running around to the open passenger door, she spotted the trail of crushed green slanting down from the sidewalk. Bedell was halfway across the mall's lot, his own run more of a stagger, bracing himself from falling against the fenders of the parked cars.

Back behind the wheel, she put the car into gear and swung out around the Mercedes, heading for the entrance ahead. Beside her, Eddie hugged himself in the corner of his seat, staring at her.

If he gets in there—he'd be lost to her, she knew, and whatever he knew about where Mike was. He was so freaked out, all dirty and wild-eyed, and running into the mall like that. *They'll throw a blanket over him. And call the police. And that'll do it.* The mall's sign, letters on a concrete obelisk, flashed by as she rounded the corner into the lot.

She saw him across the roofs of a line of cars, still running. The stone overhang framing the entrance into the mall was only a few yards away. His hands were already reaching for the glass doors.

At the curb surrounding the mall, she snapped the car to a halt, in time to see Bedell disappear into the mall.

"Stay here!" she shouted, jabbing her finger at Eddie.

"No!" Terrified, he grabbed hold of her arm and clung to it.

No time to calm him, to tell him that everything was okay, that she'd be right back—she took his hand and pulled him from the car, and ran with him to the entrance.

*   *   *

The cool air inside the mall streamed across his sweating face. Light, and bright, shouting colors—there were no shadows, no dark, only the brilliant, eye-battering glare streaming down from the echoing high roof. He staggered forward, raising his arms to gather it in.

And people. There were people in here, all around him. Through his tears, he could see their blurred shapes. His breath sobbed from him in relief. Now he was safe. The darkness outside couldn't get in here, where it was so bright, so bright it jabbed and tore at his eyes.

Until he could see.

The faces, all along the wide corridor, turned toward him, as if in welcome.

And smiled.

Just past opening hour; some of the shop fronts still had their metal security grilles pulled down, while inside others, the salespeople were adjusting the clothes and shoes on display, switching on the rows of televisions, sorting change into the cash registers. She ran past them, tugging Eddie behind her.

She heard his scream ahead of her. High, wailing, until it choked around the words it tried to cry out.

He stood, backed against a railing where the mall's other corridors branched under the central dome. From the opposite side a crowd of teenagers gaped across the open space that dropped down to the mall's lower level. A blue-uniformed security guard, unfastening a set of handcuffs from his belt, hurried toward Bedell.

She dropped Eddie's hand and ran. There was still

time, time to find out where Mike was, before the guard took him away, just a few words, that was all—

He saw her. The eyes in the contorted face fastened onto hers. He screamed again, flattening himself against the rail.

The faces were all white, staring at him with their dark eyes. And smiling, the sharp-pointed teeth curving into their cruel laughter.

Then he saw it coming, the one, the one who had always been there, behind all the other faces, moving behind the dead eyes, whispering behind the yellow teeth.

It ran toward him, reaching for him. Behind it, the darkness, the perfect night, burst through the glass doors, a flood that mingled with the black curling like fire from the white face. Until there was just the white face, the teeth opening wider to reveal the dark inside, that smelled of decay and his own vomit welling in his throat.

For a moment he could see his own face in the center of the eyes, his own mouth open to let out a cry too large, tearing his throat.

Then the white, the soft, rotting stuff, peeled away, just as the hand reached to touch him.

The face was all darkness.

It swallowed everything, even his scream as he scrabbled to get away.

She was still yards from him when his gaze broke from hers, and he turned, his hands pulling himself up over the railing.

The security guard shouted as Bedell fell forward into the open space under the dome.

She saw him hit the nearest of the interwoven steel cables. He jackknifed around it, the web vibrating as the cable dug into his stomach.

Someone else was screaming in the distance, others running past her as she stood, staring.

It looked as if he were holding on to the cable, his hands tucked at the base of his abdomen. Then he lifted his face, and something red bubbled up into his mouth.

He slipped free and fell, as she looked away, jamming the knuckles of one hand against her lip.

Quick—the thought moved, racing. *They saw you, they saw you running after him*—

She pushed her way past the others. Eddie was a tiny figure huddling against a planter.

"Come on." She saw the tremble in her hand as she reached for his. "Shh. It's okay, it's okay." She walked quickly toward the mall's doors. She held herself from turning around to see if anybody had spotted them. Eddie pressed close to her, running to keep up with her.

/IXTEEN

It had taken a long time. But now he knew.

Tyler hung up the pay phone and stepped out of the booth. Above him, the black sun, like a hole torn in the sky, swallowed the light, leaving the unending night. The street was wide and empty, deserted except for the last few forms crouched against the cold, scurrying to their hiding places. He could see through the dark, past the buildings' silhouettes, to the end of the city.

Now, he thought as he slipped behind the steering wheel. *After all this time.*

The call to Bedell had been the last piece of business to take care of. He supposed the writer had been there listening all the while he had been reciting the message into the machine. After that last reaming out he had given Bedell, a certain amount of caution had probably set in. It didn't matter; he knew Bedell would go where he told him to.

Where he was heading now. The engine's surge traveled up his arm from the key in the ignition, as though he had reached through and squeezed the pulsing metal in his fist. He closed his eyes, savoring the moment, then brought his hand to the wheel. He turned the car out to the street and toward the freeway.

* * *

She had managed to get the car away from the curb in front of the mall's entrance and to a distant corner of the parking lot before she broke down.

The wail of an ambulance siren sounded beyond the bank of ivy as she pressed her forehead against the steering wheel and burst into tears.

"Mommy—" She felt Eddie pressing against her shoulder.

Biting her lip to hold back the sob lodged in her throat, she lifted her face and palmed the wetness from her cheeks. "It's okay," she said, gathering him against her side and rocking. "It's all right, honey, it's all right. Everything's fine." She held him tighter, trying to press her own fright down into a ball small enough to swallow, so she could get her breath again.

The siren on the street grew louder, approaching, then cut to silence as it rounded the corner of the lot's entrance. Too late for that, she knew—if she closed her eyes, went into the dark of memory, she could see the red breaking over Bedell's lips as he hung from the cable. If the fall hadn't killed him, the fear she had seen in his eyes, the trembling gaze locked on to her as he clawed at the rail behind him, would have done it. Whatever he had seen coming toward him, whatever vision, had already eaten him from inside, left only the sweating pale flesh and the scream, raw from its own terror. The cable cutting through his gut, and the shiny tiled floor of the mall waiting to embrace him into a pile of bleeding rags, had been a release. Better that than whatever it was he had been running from.

And it had scared her, too, even unseen. *Something to do with Mike*—that knowledge lodged stonelike in her stomach. All the little pieces came together there: the broken capsules scattered on the desk in the theatre office, Mike's back to her as he sat watching Eddie sleep, the silences, all the way to the picture in the paper and all the past that had come seeping out of it.

Now's the time, she told herself, holding her son. *To give up.* She should call the police, or Mike's parole officer, tell them he was off his medication, running around all screwed up. That was their job, to round him up, take him where he belonged, where they could help him. Or at least where they would say they could. If they couldn't get rid of the past, they could wrap heavier chains around it, stick enough needles into him so that it was buried way far behind his blurred, unfocused eyes.

And maybe—her own voice twisted inside. *Maybe if you got special permission—because you were never married to him, you just loved him—they'll let you in to see him. Once in a while. And you can sit there during visiting hours and let the silence fold around the two of you, too thick for speaking, until you can't stand to go there again and he won't even know the difference.*

Who could blame her—she was a mother with a child. Scared child, scared mother. That came first.

All she had to do was admit that everybody else in the world was right, that she knew at last what everybody else had known all along. That the past was stronger than you, than anything. There was no point in loving anybody. Then you just had to go on living like that, in that world.

That was why she wept, why the tears wouldn't stop. Why she was scared. Of that, more than anything.

Another siren swallowed the first. She lifted her face from where her cheek had rested against Eddie's

soft hair, and looked in the mirror. A police car cut
through the parking lot toward the mall's entrance.

There's no time, she thought. *Not for sitting here,
crying like a jerk.* She took Eddie by the shoulders
and put him back in the other seat. He watched as
she dug a pack of Kleenex out of the glove compartment
and wiped her face.

"Where we going?" he said, subdued and wary,
as she turned the key in the ignition.

No time for finding a place to drop him off for
safekeeping, even if she could think of one. *Just have to
watch out for him*, she thought, putting the car into
reverse. *First priority.* "Back where we were," she
told him.

"That house? Where that man was running?"

She swung the car into the lane behind and headed
for the street. "That's right." She hoped he wouldn't
ask *why*—a child's constant inquiry—because she
wouldn't be able to tell him. What she hoped—or
feared—she'd find there. Bedell had come running
out of there, afraid of something. All she knew was
that she had to hurry, to get back there before the
police identified the crumpled form on the floor of
the shopping mall and went there themselves, before
she had the chance to see what was inside. Whatever
little thread would lead to Mike, wherever he was.
There was nowhere else to look. At the lot's exit, she
pulled the car into the first gap in the traffic.

She parked in the house's empty driveway. Bright
morning sunshine washed over the street, burning off
the dew from the groomed lawns. The rocket ship
had fallen to the floor under Eddie's feet a long time
back. She picked it up and handed it to him, keeping
her voice as level as she could. "I won't be a min-

ute, sweetheart. I promise. So you stay right here, okay?''

He nodded, still quiet but no longer filled with his mother's contagious emotions. One of the model's fins had come loose; he waggled it experimentally while she got out of the car.

The front door was open, revealing a foot-wide slice of the dim interior behind the drawn curtains.

What do you think you'll find? A dead body. Mike with his eyes swirling around in two different directions, a carving knife between his teeth. Or worst of all, nothing. She pushed the door open wider and slipped inside.

Nothing. She looked across the front room. An empty house, with hardly any furniture in it. A row of file cabinets against one wall, an unvacuumed carpet with a dark stain in the middle of it. In the kitchen, the counters were stacked with crusted dishes and flat frozen-dinner cartons. When she pulled aside the curtain covering a sliding glass door, she saw dry weeds poking up through the plastic webbing of an aluminum chair. The smell of unwashed sheets filled one of the back rooms, with clothes scattered across the bed.

She hurried out to the front room, trying to spot anything she might have missed. The file cabinets filled her with dismay. Mike had told her about them, about Bedell's research—obsession—on the Wyle Group. If there were any clue in there, among all the pieces of paper stuffed in the metal drawers, she didn't have time to find it. There was no telling how soon the police would show up. All it would take was Bedell's driver's license in his wallet.

Anything— She turned about in the middle of the room, trying to piece the debris and clutter, and the stale sweat odor of the cooped-up air, into something she could read, something that would tell her where to go next.

The books had been tumbled onto the floor, thrown about, some lying broken-spined against the carpet. The only thing left on the shelves was the phone. Beside it, a steady pulse in the dim room, a red dot of light blinked.

An answering machine. *Of course*. Everybody's got one. She ran to the shelves and looked at the machine and the two cassettes visible through the plastic lid.

One button was marked PLAY. She punched it down with one finger. All she heard was the hiss of the tape running through. *Shit*. Turning up the volume knob only made the hiss louder. *No, stupid*. She found the REWIND button and held it down, the tape whirring until it clicked to a stop.

PLAY again. And, after a second, Mike's voice. It came out harsh through the machine's tiny speaker.

"Bedell? You there?"

She leaned over it, straining to make out the words.

"—there's something I want you to do," said Mike's voice on the tape. "It's important, so listen."

He sounded different, as though the muscles of his jaw had gone tight, biting each word off hard. But she knew it was him.

"I know where Slide is. I know he's got my son with him. Bryan's alive; I know he is, now."

Bryan. His son. Her thoughts raced parallel to the uncoiling voice. *Alive. It was true.*

"You were right. I stopped taking the medications, and then I could see. Everything."

The image of the crushed capsules on the desk

swam up from her memory, blotting out the turning wheels of the cassette inside the machine.

The voice went on: "I'm going where Slide is. I'm going to take my son from him. There's a city maintenance yard on East Seventh, near the freeway. You meet me there, and I'll give you Bryan. Then you take him to Linda's father—he'll take care of him. And then you'll be able to write all the books you want. You'll just have to wait, and I'll get hold of you. I'll tell you everything you want to know. Because I'm back inside now. All the way inside, with the others. And I won't be coming out again."

She closed her eyes, holding on to the empty top shelf for balance. Now she knew why he had left, where he had gone. For his son.

"You got that, Bedell? Maintenance yard, East Seventh. You'll see me there."

The answering machine clicked as the message came to its end.

How long ago had the message been left on the machine? No way of knowing. *Maybe he's there now*, she thought. *Where he said. Waiting.* Or maybe not—there had been a cold determination in the voice, the promise of violence. *Because of Slide.* A name. He had Mike's son, for whatever reason. And Mike was going there to take him away from Slide. She felt the clenching under her stomach grow colder.

Slide was scary. And something else; something that had driven Bedell screaming out of the house and falling to a welcome death. Maybe that was waiting there, too. Waiting for Mike to come to it.

No time. It had all run out. Either she went to find him now, with the fear lodged tight in her gut, or she didn't. Maybe the fear would become memory, like everything else.

She pulled the front door shut behind her and ran
to the car. Unmindful of Eddie's wide-eyed gaze, she
reversed out of the drive and headed for the freeway.

There was a carton of milk left from the stuff Slide
had brought to the nest the day before. Warm and
sour, but the little boy drank it anyway, tilting it up
to his face so that a white trickle ran from the corner
of his mouth.

Jimmy knelt beside him and watched. The child's
face was still flushed red, shiny with sweat beneath
the dirt. He stroked the child's forehead as he gulped
the milk; the skin still felt hot.

At the other side of the nest, Slide raised himself
up on one elbow. Without looking around, Jimmy
could feel the gaze fixed on his back, the half-lidded
eyes mirroring the thin smile.

"Hey, kid."

Jimmy looked over his shoulder. Slide's hands flattened against the concrete overhead, the muscles in
his arms flexing and drawing blood into themselves.
The little boy didn't seem to have heard; Jimmy
crouched lower, as if to shield him.

"Hey—" Slide's smile grew wider. "You want
your daddy, kid? Huh? You want your daddy?"

He shook his head slowly, tucked down against his
chest. "Don't . . ."

"Shut up." Slide dropped his hands to the nest's
loose dirt and stretched forward, catlike, to peer at
the child. "Wouldn't you like your daddy to come
and see you? A little visit?"

Bryan looked up at him, then to Slide. "I want my
mommy."

"Fuck your mommy." The smile contorted Slide's
face into a rigid clown's mask. "Your mommy's not

coming. No, she's not. But your daddy is. Won't
that be nice? Huh?''

The child, frightened, backed against the nest's
sloping wall. Jimmy wanted to push between him
and Slide, but couldn't move.

Slide snorted and rolled onto his back in the center
of the shallow space, gazing up at the concrete. The
traffic's vibration seeping from above drifted parti-
cles of dust, catching the morning light angling between the pillars, onto his face.

"Won't be long now," he murmured.

Bit by bit, it had come to him, in the darkness
behind his eyelids. Where his son was; Tyler leaned
back from the steering wheel, letting the car glide
across the night-wrapped freeway, past the shadows
of the other cars with their blurred, indistinct figures
crouched inside. For him, the margin of the sky was
etched in blue hairline against the black. He knew
where he was going.

Fragments of the darkness seen through someone
else's eyes; through Slide's, and someone close enough
to see Slide's face. It had taken Tyler a long time, an
hour or more parked on a side street near the cemetery, his eyes closed as if asleep and dreaming, to
piece together the glimpses of the downtown skyline,
the edges of freeway overpasses, the silent hulks of
machinery lined up in rows. And then the odors and
sounds—rotting food and stale sweat in a zone of
rumbling, growling air—and the confines of the narrow space against the flesh of those who shared this
night with him, that the Host had accepted as part of
its shared darkness. Even as he drove, he felt both
the smooth curve of the wheel and loose dust under
his palm, the fabric of the seat and, at the same time,

rough concrete against his shoulder blades. More
pieces of the puzzle sliding together, until at last he
had known.

Somewhere under the freeway. Close to where the
road equipment was kept; that narrowed it down,
reduced it to a small section of the grid overlaying
the city. *That's where Slide is. And my son.*

He spotted the offramp he wanted, a narrower
thread splitting off from the freeway's coursing black
ribbon. As the car curved to the street below, he
could see the city's towers in the distance, from a
different angle than the glimpse of them that the
other's eyes had seen.

Silent below the freeway, the streets deserted even
of the shades that moved along the lanes above. *Not
too near*, thought Tyler. *He knows you're coming.* It
would be hard to surprise Slide.

A chain link fence topped with sagging barbed
wire surrounded the maintenance yard. He cruised
slowly along the street running parallel to the fence,
looking across the ranks of bulldozers and trucks to
the elevated freeway. The yard was large enough to
stretch through half a dozen or more underpasses,
filling the network formed by the street grid in the
freeway's shadow. *Close*—what he saw almost over-
lapped the vision in his head. *Real close.*

He stopped the car and got out. Watching the
freeway as he ran, he came to one of the streets
cutting through the yard, the equipment fenced off on
either side of the asphalt. In a few seconds he was
under the freeway, its shade a deeper black in the
night through which he moved.

Beyond the fence a dirt slope—loose dirt, which
he had already felt in his hands without ever touching
it—went up to the freeway's concrete underside. He

knew how that felt, too, a spine scraping along the gritty surface.

Something was up there. He could see it in the dark, as though the warmth of bodies huddled in the crevice at the top of the dirt were visible to him. The fence sagged in the middle here, a single strand of barbed wire rusted through and broken so that it dangled down either side. Tyler gripped the mesh and climbed over, dropping onto the soft slope beyond.

Crouching where he had landed, he looked up at the crevice formed where the dirt and the freeway met. Whatever was up there had made no sound. Digging in with his hands, he scrambled up.

Behind the ridge of a scooped-out hollow, a pair of rheumy yellow eyes widened and blinked at him. He looked quickly around. There was no one but the woman, age unguessable beneath the layered dirt. In the small space, her breath smelled of sour alcohol as she shrank back from him, burrowing into a nest of rags. She clasped a plastic bag full of flattened aluminum cans to her, protecting her treasure.

Tyler leaned across the hollow. "Where is he?" he said softly.

The mouth in the wizened face opened to reveal a few broken teeth as she gaped uncomprehendingly at him.

"The little boy." He brought his face closer to hers, into the stench of the tattered sweaters bundled around her. "There's a little boy here. You know where he is, don't you?"

She shook her head, wisps of gray hair straggling across her cheeks.

"Yes, you do." He kept his voice soft, coaxing. "The little boy. You know. Where is he?"

The fear that silenced her broke under the weight

of his approach, his even, level words. "That way."
Her bony hand pointed, trembling, as she pressed
herself tighter against the mounded rags and away
from him.

He looked around, then back to the woman. "The
next underpass? That's where the little boy is?"

"No—" A low shake of her head, eyes held by
his gaze. "Farther."

"The one after that?"

She nodded.

His heels dug into the loose dirt as he turned away
from the nest and slipped down toward the fence.

"Mommy—"

She glanced over at Eddie. He was drawn back
into the seat, watching her. *The speed*, she realized.
*Driving like a maniac—you'd be scared, too, if you
knew what you were doing.* She eased off the accelerator,
slowing to the pace of the other traffic on the
freeway. Now wasn't the time to have a cop stop her
for speeding.

"It's okay, honey." She took one hand from the
wheel to pat his knee. *Christ*, she thought, how
many times can you say it? And have him believe it?

All he had to do was look at her, read the fright in
his mother's face, and know she was lying.

Past the guardrail, she could see down to the edge
of the city maintenance yard. The offramp zoomed
up before she was ready for it. The tires squealed
underneath the car as she cut the wheel hard, clipping
the edge of the ramp before she could straighten out
and slow to the street below.

Another fence, this one topped with three strands
of barbed wire, all whole. Panting from his run, Tyler

looked along the length of chain link, trying to spot an opening.

There—at the bottom. A clearance of a foot or so, the edge of the fence hanging over a shallows gap scooped out of the dirt. Parallel ridges showed in the dust, as though something heavy had been dragged through.

He wormed himself under, holding the fence up from his face and chest. On the other side, he pulled his legs clear and rolled onto his hands and knees. Above him, the freeway blocked out the sky. The dirt sloped up to the concrete and the niche at the top.

Easy. He knows you're coming. He pressed himself flat against the slope, looking up for any sign, any motion. Silently, he crawled at an angle to the first pillar, holding himself back for a few breaths before he looked around.

Something up there—he could hear breathing other than his own. The angle of the slope hid whoever it was from his sight, although he could make out every grain of dust in the air, the coarse texture of the concrete above. *Like where the old woman was*, he thought as he strained to see. *A hollowed-out place at the top*.

A slow crawl to the next pillar brought him closer. Now he could see it. The lip of the hollow, and a space where the dirt butted right into the overhead concrete. If he stood up, he could touch the ceiling and feel the vibration of the traffic filtering down.

Now. Easy.

His stomach against the dirt, he pushed himself the rest of the way up. He held his breath when his head was just below the hollow's edge. Then reared up above it, almost touching the concrete, and gathering his weight up onto his knees and one hand for balance.

A few feet away, two pairs of eyes looked back at him. A man he had never seen before, frightened dumb.

And, held against his side, a little boy.

Slide's voice came at his ear, in the darkness beside him.

"Hello, Mike." The laugh just beneath the whisper. "I knew you'd come."

The smile, out of the dark. Jimmy watched Slide's bright gaze appear beside the stranger's face, turning sidelong to look at him.

His daddy, thought Jimmy, holding the child to him. *Bryan's daddy—that's who it is.* The boy made no move, clinging to his shirt as he stared at the others.

Before the strange man could move, Slide had vaulted across the nest, his hand touching once at the bottom, and spun around beside Jimmy. Crouching, coiled to spring again, he pulled the child out of the arms holding him and to his own chest. Something shiny in one of his hands caught the thin light slanting through the pillars as he held it up under the little boy's throat.

"That's right," said Slide to the other man. "You just stay right there." The edge of the shiny thing lifted Bryan's chin. "I'm not sure how friendly you are."

The other balanced himself against the side of the nest, his head lowering between his hunched shoulders as his eyes locked on to Slide's. His face was all hard, like Slide's, but unsmiling. Jimmy shrank back against the sloping dirt, unnoticed by them. The centers of their eyes were dark, as though the same night had broken through in holes around the rest.

"I want my son."

Slide's smile widened. "Sure you do. That's why you came."

The shiny thing pressed a line into the soft flesh. Bryan started to whimper, his hands pushing against Slide's arm. The small sound contracted Jimmy's spine, turning his own breath into a stone against his heart.

He could reach out and grab Slide's arm. He was close enough. Grab it and pull the knife away from the little boy, topple Slide off balance, down into the center of the nest. And then Bryan's daddy could gather up the child, grab him, and run away from here, and it wouldn't matter what Slide did with the knife then. When he got his knees onto Jimmy's chest and one hand shoving the back of his head against the dirt—it wouldn't matter at all.

Jimmy's hand clenched in the dust, squeezing it in his fists. He wanted his hand to reach out and grab Slide's arm, but it wouldn't move. *Because you're scared*.

He couldn't move at all, except to press his back even harder against the slope. Anywhere, away from Slide.

Because it wasn't Slide. Not anymore.

In the dark, inches from him, the smile grew, pulling back from the sharp-pointed teeth.

The knife at the throat of the child struggling in Slide's arms flashed blue, catching the radiance crawling around the outlined figures. Shiny enough to be a mirror, throwing Tyler's own gaze back at him. His arms tensed as he crouched on the other rim of the hollow.

Slide's voice curled around its suppressed laughter. "You can have more than your son, Mike. You know that, don't you? Much more. It can be like it was before. Even better than it was. Stronger. It can be that way, Mike. You know that."

Underneath the freeway, the world shrank down to this little space, a circle bound by the curving dirt and the concrete pressing down on them. His fingers curled, drawing lines in the dust, already feeling the other's neck between his hands. He felt as if he could spring straight across the space, reaching and gathering in Slide's throat and tearing it open, the laughing words coming out in a wash of blood—

But the knife was at the child's throat. He knew how fast Slide could move.

Keep him talking, thought Tyler. *Keep him talking, and smiling, and laughing so he doesn't see you coming just a little bit closer. And closer.*

"I don't know, Slide." His voice level, held tight as his tensed arms. "I don't know what you're talking about. Tell me about it, Slide. Tell me."

Slide laid his face close to the child's, watching Tyler from the corners of his eyes. "Yes, you do. I know you do, Mike." Soft, coy. "Because you're inside again. Aren't you? With all of us. I can tell. Just the way it used to be."

He nodded slowly as he leaned toward the hollow's center and slid his knees a few inches through the dust. "Yes," he said, holding Slide's gaze with his own. "You're right. That's what you wanted, isn't it? For all of us to be together again. All of us inside."

"Yes . . . it's nice, isn't it?" Slide's eyes drew closed with pleasure. "Just the way it was."

Another inch forward, hands pulling at the dirt. "Why don't you let the little boy go?" said Tyler.

"You don't need him anymore, Slide. You got me here. And it's nice, you're right, it's nice. I forgot, but now I remember. We're all together again, Slide." The dirt grated under his knees as he brought them under himself. "Let him go."

Slide's eyes opened. He drew himself back, shaking his head. "No—don't you see?" He rubbed his face against the child's, smothering the sobs against his own cheek. "He's the key, Mike. He's the way we can do it. Make it stronger. He's inside with us, Mike. You know that. You know that, Mike." His voice lowered, pleading. "You got to know that."

"I don't know, Slide." An inch, reach and pull. "I don't know. Tell me."

The words squeezed out, fervent. "*He was born inside*. You and Linda—you were both inside when you had him. When you got her pregnant, when she gave birth." The other hand, without the knife, ran through the child's hair, gathering it into the fist that he pressed against his mouth. "Don't you see? We had to come inside, we're nothing without it. Without Him. But the child—he was born inside. The dark was always inside him, from the beginning. And now he's grown. It's strong." In ecstasy, he twisted his face against the child, tasting the tear-streaked skin. "Now we'll always be together. They can't stop us now."

"Yes . . . I see it now," soothed Tyler. He leaned ahead, balancing on one hand, slowly reaching up with the other.

Slide's tears mixed with the child's. He rocked back and forth, cradling him. "Just like it was . . . always . . ."

The knife, inches away. "Yes . . . always . . ."

He drew his legs under him, coiled, and leaped forward, reaching for Slide's wrist.

His hand closed around it for a moment, before he flew back into the center of the hollow, thrown by Slide's arm flung wide. The knife spun and glittered, falling down the slope. A scream drowned out the traffic above, filled the space, washing over him and pressing him into the dust.

Above him he no longer saw Slide's face, but the other, contorted with its exultant shout, the sharppointed teeth a gate over darkness that swallowed light, swallowed the world bound by dirt and concrete.

Slide scrambled down the slope, one hand reaching back against the dirt, the other holding Bryan to his chest. The child's small hands tore at his shoulder, trying to get free. The cry echoing against the freeway's underside came from that terrified face.

Tyler sucked in the aching breath that had been knocked out of him, and rolled onto his hands and knees. Slide had already reached the bottom and had pushed the child under the fence. He crawled through and scooped up Bryan, as Tyler shoved the edge of the hollow away and fell down the slope.

She spotted the car first, empty on the empty street. On either side, beyond the fences, the silent trucks and bulldozers filled row after row. She slowed the car and craned her neck, trying to spot any other sign of him.

Where— The wheel sweated in her hands. Mike could be anywhere here; the maintenance yard seemed to stretch ahead for miles. The shadow of the freeway, streaming out from the sun, pulled the street into darkness. *Come on*. A prayer, restraining her tears of frustration. *Please*—

Then, where the fence ended, she saw the running figure. Running away from her, small in the distance. And another, yards beyond the first, running, stumbling with the weight of the burden cradled in his arms.

Mike. The one nearest; she knew it. Eddie fell back into the seat from his knees, where he had knelt to see where she was looking, as she pushed against the accelerator.

He had torn open his shirt and gouged the skin on the bottom edge of the fence as he had crawled under it. Tyler felt the blood welling out and stinging as he ran after Slide.

Past the maintenance yard, the fence bounding the freeway was no longer topped with barbed wire. Slide looked over his shoulder, Bryan clasped tight to his chest. His face was white, chin spattered with the saliva of his panting breath. He stumbled once, falling before he caught hold of the chain link beside him. With one hand and his feet digging at the mesh, he climbed, still weighted with the struggling child. At the top, he threw Bryan over, the small body sprawling in the thick ice plant slanting up to the freeway. His own hands crushed their imprint into the plants as he jumped clear of the fence.

Tyler shouted at him as Slide got to his feet, scooping up the child. Bryan's mouth gaped open, soundless with pain and shock. The fence rattled in Tyler's hands as he climbed it, watching through the wire diamonds as Slide struggled up through the foliage toward the freeway's edge.

A vertical flank of concrete separated the slope from the bottom of the guardrail. Slide's free hand

tore at the wall, inches from reaching the rail, as
Tyler jumped down into the broken plants.

Slide saw Tyler coming, hands and feet digging at
the green slope. He coiled himself and leaped, fingers straining for the metal above.

They caught, pressed white against the rail's cutting edge. Cradling the child one-armed, he pulled
himself up, feet digging at the concrete. The traffic
above streamed past, no eyes seeing the arm, tendons
straining, clawing a foot away from their wheels.

Too high to pull himself over; Tyler only a yard
away. The child whipped his head back and forth,
screaming against Slide's chest.

Tyler felt his heart battering in his chest, his blood
singing in his ears. Above Slide, the perfect night
sky wheeled, the lightless stars gouging out spirals of
cold fire. For a moment he saw his own face, stark
and etched into a mask of clenched teeth and pulse
hammering at his throat, laid over Slide's panting
features. The two visions blurred and swam, his own
sweat stinging his eyes, until there was just one face,
one breath roaring in their chests until it burst.

He saw his hand reaching, away from him to grab
his son, toward him to pull the child, the precious
child, out of the grip that crushed him to his chest,
Slide's chest, his heart pounding in sync with the
other's—

Slide's foot caught him in the throat, lifting him
off balance and sending him sprawling on his back in
the damp foliage.

Scrambling onto his hands and knees, he saw Slide
push against the concrete with his feet, slipping his
bloodless hand along the guardrail's bottom edge.
The metal sliced into the crook of his fingers, blood
trickling down his wrist. He worked himself, inch by

inch, past the ice plant and the fence below, and out over the maintenance yard.

Tyler reached the top of the slope and flattened himself against the wall, stretching to grab hold of Slide's leg. He caught a handful of cloth and squeezed it into his fist.

Slide froze, pinned against the concrete arch of the underpass, one hand raised straight over his head to the guardrail, the other crushed with Bryan against the wall.

"Give him to me." Tyler squeezed the words past the thick salt in his mouth. He pressed his face against the concrete, straining to keep his feet from slipping out from under him on the angle of crushed plants. If he tugged on the pants leg trapped in his hand, Slide would fall to the yard below. With his son.

"No—" Slide twisted his head about, the rough surface scraping the skin away. "You can't—you don't know . . ."

"Come on." He felt the cloth turning wet in his grip. "He's mine." The traffic sang louder inside his head. "Please—"

For a second, Slide's eyes locked on his. The reflection of his face, a tiny spot in the black center of the other's gaze, fell away, swallowed by the darkness behind. Then another face came.

Reflected twice, in the lightless center of each of Slide's eyes, sharp-pointed teeth gaped wide.

Slide screamed, arms flung wide, clawing at the air behind him to get away.

He fell, and the child hung motionless, turning as Tyler jumped, his hands tearing open the distance between them.

He gathered the child into his chest, rolling with him

down the slope, until his spine slammed into the fence.

The child, his son, gasped and sobbed in his arms, trying to pull breath into the small body. He could feel the rapid heartbeat against his own.

From the car, she had been able to see the two figures, Mike and the other, pinned against the side of the freeway underpass. She was running toward the fence as they fell. Her own shout mingled with the cry of the one arcing down to the maintenance yard.

Cradling the child, comforting him against his chest, he pulled himself upright, his hand gripping the fence for support.

He could see across the yard to where Slide's body lay broken against the blade of a bulldozer. The head lolled against one shoulder, the arms dangling on either side of the curved metal.

Something moved inside the dead face. He could see that, too. Everything in the night sweeping across the empty streets to the distant hills was visible to him.

It called to him. Soft words, smiling behind the bloodless, blank-eyed face.

You were the one I wanted. The one I really wanted. The face turned toward him, smiling in triumph. *Slide didn't matter. None of them do. Not even the little boy.* The eyes cleared, then darkened. *They're all weak. But not you. You're strong.*

Tyler lifted the child higher, muffling its sobs against his shoulder. The voice went on, touching his ear, each word gentle.

Now you've come back to me. We're all together

again. Aren't we? The way you wanted. Together inside here.

Softer, crooning.

Now I'll show you everything.

The face went slack, became a dead thing again. He heard someone calling his name. Turning with his son in his arms, he saw Steff on the other side of the fence. As he watched, Eddie came running up behind her, grabbing his mother around the leg and holding her fiercely to himself.

He could barely lift his feet above the thick foliage. Steff's fingers reached through the mesh to touch him.

Stroking Bryan's hair, he looked at her. "You'll have to take him," he said quietly. "Take him to Linda's parents. They'll look after him."

Her gaze darted from the child to him. "What do you mean?" She searched his face. "Where are you going?"

He shook his head. Already the darkness was folding around him, pulling him away, into its promised depths. "I can't. I'm too fucked up. It's inside me now, and I can't get out. Not anymore." He pressed his forehead against the cold wire. The other world, of night and streets that unwound forever, into the dark and the hard empty eyes that turned and watched, meeting his own gaze and nodding in recognition— that world had claimed him. There was no leaving it now. Even if he wanted to.

He lifted the child above his head, above the top of the fence. "You take him," he said. "He can't go where I'm going."

Steff stood on tiptoe, Eddie looking up alongside her as she lifted her hands to take the other child from him. She held Bryan against herself, looking down into his face.

There was no more time. *Not for me*, thought Tyler. It was all there on the other side of the fence.

She looked up at him. Without warning, her face set emotionless, her hands circled around the child's neck. Bryan's legs dangled against her, kicking as his small hands flailed helplessly. She squeezed harder, looking straight into Tyler's eyes.

His wordless shout tore out of his throat as he wrenched at the chain link mesh. The wire cut into his hands as he strained to reach her, to pull his son out of her grasp.

She stepped backward, still looking at him, her hands twisting the child's throat.

As if with strength out of a nightmare, her clenched hands moved apart, the child's head separating from the body with a noise of snapping cartilage and tendon. A gush of blood spilled across her.

He sagged against the fence, only the hooks of his fingers holding him upright. "Why—"

The headless corpse, a tiny thing of arms and legs flopping loose, dropped to the ground in front of her. He looked down at it, his own vision swimming and breath gasping.

His son's head fell from Steff's hands. His eyes swept dizzyingly across it. He felt the world drop away.

A doll's blank, idiot face looked up at him. Clear plastic eyes gazed from under the stiff bristle of the artificial lashes.

He dropped to his knees, his fingers trembling through the fence as he reached to touch the stiff-jointed doll. The limbs were flat pink, mocking a baby's chubby flesh. Parodies of infant fingers curled at the ends of the arms.

Steff was crying when he looked up at her. She pressed Eddie against herself. "Don't you see—" The words choked her.

He's dead. His son was dead. All this time. Years going by, while the little box underneath the silent grass had held the small body, the real one. Holding the dead.

And all this time Linda had been insane. The little boy, her son, had gone on living inside her. And outside, too, in the props of the delusion. A little boy, a child no one else saw, because he stayed inside the little house, where she could love him and mother him. And bring him toys, all the supports for the fantasy that was nothing but the drug seeping through her blood, the child's words as she rocked him in front of the TV nothing but the drug murmuring at her ear. Keeping her crazy.

Crazy even after the doll was stolen away, stolen by someone else just as crazy, who listened and could hear when the drug, the unwinding darkness, put a child's voice into the dead plastic thing.

And then I heard it. I saw it. That was how it spread, from one to the other. Until they were all crazy together. Because that was how it worked. That was how it made you do things.

If it could give you the past, the thing from the past you thought you'd lost, the dead child, then it could give you anything. And you'd do anything it wanted.

(*A vision, the last one, the world they had shared seeping out of his blood; somewhere in a little room, the one she'd always be in, she was weeping for her lost child, whom no one would go and look for and bring back to her. She'd weep there forever.*)

He raised his face, his own tears trickling salt into the corner of his mouth. Eddie, clutching his mother's leg, looked at him, eyes wide with fright.

"It's okay . . ." He pressed his hand flat against the fence. "Don't be scared, it's all right. I promise. It's all right."

His legs trembled under him as he got to his feet. With his strength ebbing from his arms, he pulled himself up the fence, scraping his chest over the top, then his stomach. Steff reached up to steady him as he caught himself from falling.

She gathered him to her, his face resting against her shoulder. Eddie squeezed in between them, looking up at him. He reached down, pulling the child against himself.

"Let's go," said Steff softly. Her arm across his back drew him away from the fence.

At the edge of the shadow cast by the freeway, a sharp dividing line between the dark shade and the morning light, the doll's head stared up at him. The bright sun glittered in the plastic eyes.

He stopped to look down at the thing. There was a small black circle at the center of each of the lifeless eyes. Steff's tug at his shoulder came from farther and farther away, as the doll's gaze connected with his.

The pouting baby mouth carved into the plastic seemed about to smile, to grow wider, open, and whisper his name. Softly—he could hear it at the edge of his ear.

Together. At his back he felt the shade lengthening from under the freeway, reaching toward him. *Just like you wanted.*

He raised his foot and held it over the doll's head. *I'll show you everything.*

He brought his foot down into the doll's smile, pressing his weight into the ground until the plastic split open. One round eye popped from the hollow face and rolled away in the dust.

"Come on."

Eddie ran ahead as he walked with Steff to the car, and the streets that would lead back home.

He saw everything. Jimmy crouched in the loose dirt below the freeway, in an underpass a long way from where his warm nest was. He had scrambled after the others, Slide and the other man who had wanted the little boy, keeping to the dark under the freeway so they wouldn't see him.

Slide was dead. He could look into the yard, past the rows of trucks, and see the body, snapped in two against the bulldozer blade. Somebody would find him, soon enough. For now, the blank face gaped up at the sky, its mouth open.

And then along the fence, past where the yard ended, they had killed the little boy. Jimmy crept along the chain link toward the spot. The scream, the man's shout as the little neck had snapped in the woman's hands, went on inside his head without stopping.

Only it hadn't been a little boy. Not a real one. He looked down at the plastic torso and the two halves of its head, the baby face—not the face he had seen in the nest, that he had fed and watched sleep—split down the middle. He couldn't understand that.

He stooped to pick up something round from the dust. A plastic eye. The doll's eyes.

He could see himself in the shiny dark at its center.

For a moment he looked back along the freeway, toward the overpass where the nest was scooped out of the dirt, with the bed of rags, and the quiet warmth, the murmur of the traffic above lulling him, wrapping itself around him. He held the eye in his hand, a little treasure to take back there, a comfort.

He looked down at it in his palm, then jerked his arm around, throwing the plastic eye into the shadows under the freeway. He turned and started to run across the empty streets and toward the downtown buildings.

K. W. Jeter
Soul Eater £3.99

*'She woke up and felt for the knife under the pillow. Ghost light
from the city's blue streetlamps flowed into the room. Her heart and
breathing began to slow as the shapes of the room formed and
became solid. Now she knew where she was'*

Braemer knew something was wrong with his daughter. She still had
that bright childhood light in her eyes. But then the light would
disappear and some sinister power take it's place – a dark, brooding
force far beyond his own comprehension.

From where the power emanated it was impossible to say. One thing
Braemer was sure about – it didn't come from inside *his* Dee. It came
from something both dead and alive. Something that was eating the
soul of his daughter – and trying to kill him.

'An exhilarating writer' THE NEW YORK TIMES

'Oppressively intense and hallucinatorily vivid, deeply felt and
unflinchingly honest. His tenaciousness deserves not only our
admiration but our gratitude' RAMSEY CAMPBELL

'Scary as hell . . . a wonderful and chilling read'
T. M. WRIGHT, author of *The Waiting Room*

K. W. Jeter
The Night Man £3.99

Poor little Steven. The weird kid nobody wanted around. The kid the others liked to pick on, bully and hurt. Only in his dreams did Steven have what he wanted . . .

A good friend to look out for him. A real friend to put things right. A friend who'll kill for every wrong that he's ever been done . . .

'Dark, intense, unflinchingly honest' RAMSEY CAMPBELL

'Scary as hell' T. M. WRIGHT

'K. W. Jeter just keeps getting better' SCIENCE FICTION REVIEW

'Brain-burning intensity' VILLAGE VOICE

'Exhilarating' THE NEW YORK TIMES

'Stunning' PHILIP K. DICK

All Pan books are available at your local bookshop or newsagent, or can be ordered direct from the publisher. Indicate the number of copies required and fill in the form below.

Send to: **CS Department, Pan Books Ltd., P.O. Box 40, Basingstoke, Hants. RG21 2YT.**

or phone: 0256 469551 (Ansaphone), quoting title, author and Credit Card number.

Please enclose a remittance* to the value of the cover price plus: 60p for the first book plus 30p per copy for each additional book ordered to a maximum charge of £2.40 to cover postage and packing.

*Payment may be made in sterling by UK personal cheque, postal order, sterling draft or international money order, made payable to Pan Books Ltd.

Alternatively by Barclaycard/Access:

Card No. | | | | | | | | | | | | | | | | |

Signature:

Applicable only in the UK and Republic of Ireland.

While every effort is made to keep prices low, it is sometimes necessary to increase prices at short notice. Pan Books reserve the right to show on covers and charge new retail prices which may differ from those advertised in the text or elsewhere.

NAME AND ADDRESS IN BLOCK LETTERS PLEASE:

....

Name ⎯⎯⎯⎯⎯⎯⎯⎯⎯⎯⎯⎯⎯⎯⎯⎯⎯⎯⎯⎯

Address ⎯⎯⎯⎯⎯⎯⎯⎯⎯⎯⎯⎯⎯⎯⎯⎯⎯⎯⎯

⎯⎯⎯⎯⎯⎯⎯⎯⎯⎯⎯⎯⎯⎯⎯⎯⎯⎯⎯⎯⎯⎯

⎯⎯⎯⎯⎯⎯⎯⎯⎯⎯⎯⎯⎯⎯⎯⎯⎯⎯⎯⎯⎯⎯

⎯⎯⎯⎯⎯⎯⎯⎯⎯⎯⎯⎯⎯⎯⎯⎯⎯⎯⎯⎯⎯⎯

3/87